Royce O'Rourke - Realtor!

Robert H. Eltzholtz

Royce O'Rourke Realtor!

1

Royce O'Rourke, Realtor. That's me, was me, still is me, really. Welcome to my open house. It's a beauty, right smack in the Catalina Foothills, among the best Tucson has to offer. The best. That's what I'm all about. Me, Royce O'Rourke, soon to be a member of the Billion Dollar Brotherhood.

I'm not some middle-aged housewife. Decides she wants a career. Gets a real estate license, joins the NAR, and starts selling houses. Says stuff like "You snooze, you lose." Brandishes her cell phone like a mobile twat. I'm not that. I started first thing. My mom taught me. She was a realtor too, but came to it after my father died. Not like me. I was born to it.

I've done really well. I have a great house in the best location, and I have a wife and a son and a daughter. They love me.

They do! Oops. No exclamation marks here.

You. You know why you are reading this. Don't you? I'll make it clear. I promise. And I keep my promises. A promise is like a contract to me – a covenant – no. I won't use dashes either.

I also promise to be honest here, as I take you through all the rooms, all the nooks and crannies of this house, just as I was taken, that strange, zombie-filled night by.... No. I'm getting way ahead of myself, and I allow ellipses.

I want to start at that open house that Sunday afternoon in mid-May because, looking back on it all, now, that's where it starts making sense to me. That house was mine, my sale, not Fitzroy's. Fitzroy was my business partner. We both ran FitzRoyce Realty. We were both among the most influential, highest grossing realtors not just in Tucson, not just in Arizona, not just in the States, but in the whole fucking universe.

Right. That may sound hard to believe, I mean, coming from Tucson, not Manhattan. But it's true.

"My reelater told me the association fees are high here," a woman, one with several face lifts under her brow, came up and said to me.

"Your realtor," I said, emphasizing the pronunciation of the noun, "is right. And it's realtor, not reelater, ma'am."

If anything pissed me off, other than the ants, it was people who couldn't take the trouble to pronounce correctly the word that was so tightly intertwined in the biggest financial, personal, and familial decision of their lives. You'd think, wouldn't you, they would bother. But most people, truth be told, and I'm telling the truth, are stupid, antlike idiots.

Speak of the devil, there they were, those pesky ants, each wearing a yellow fanny pack, instead of holding a professional briefcase. They were sisters, so the story went. Crystal and Chrissy Diamond. Realtors. Fitzroy told all sorts of dirty stories about how they were really lesbians who frequented truck stops and whored themselves out on the Internet. Oh, how I wanted to believe those stories, but the ants were too boring and ordinary to be so colorful. And they looked just like each other. Like twin sisters. Short. Petite. Short bobbed dirty blond hair. They could have been knockouts, but even by thirty their angular faces and almost buck teeth, and big bug eyes, on which they wore black plastic glasses, made them look like giant insects. Like human ants. Their pixie pointed upturned noses didn't help. Neither did their ultra-high pipsqueak voices. Plus, they liked to punch guys, really hard.

I couldn't explain it, never could, still can't, but I hated them, had a visceral hatred for them. I think it was because they had a degree of confidence and an air of assured power wholly inconsistent with their antlike bodies, personalities, and, well, I was going to say souls, but ants don't have souls, do they? That is very, very important.

What was also important was that the ants seemed to be with none other than Father Flannery O. Flannigan, president of the Billion Dollar Brotherhood.

Damn. I had to go out and explain solar powered pool heating to some rubes from Chicago who had no business being here. I humored them, to avert the ants from approaching me. Those rubes clearly couldn't afford this house, and it was going to be a big sale for me, a crucial component for me to qualify for the Billion Dollar Brotherhood this year. My year.

Oh, listen to me. Listen close. My story, my history, my tale, my defense, my justification is for you. Even if you don't understand why some things were so important to me, you must know that my dream is your dream, is everyone's dream. The American dream. Not some over-the-hill European capital where people live all crammed together in tight spaces with no yards, no pools, no landscaping, and no sprinkler systems. No. I, you, we are all Americans and our birthright is our own detached house with a lawn, a pool, and a double or triple garage, our integrated security systems, our home-owners insurance, and most important of all, our covenants, those special contracts that are so pertinent to the specific block, something that supersedes city, county, state, and national ordinances and laws. Yes, our very identity and self-worth is tied to our homes, our block. A good realtor gets that, ensures that he is not just selling a house, but is in fact ensuring the integrity of a neighborhood, guaranteeing a way of life, that is, block by block, the American dream.

There is no higher calling. Yeah. I sometimes thought, think even now, that Father Flannigan was more divinely inspired by real estate than he was with the teachings and the ways of the Catholic Church.

That, in a nutshell, is what the ants didn't get. To them, they were just selling houses, like selling cars, like selling fucking shitty toilet paper. That alone earned my dislike, and almost physical aversion to them.

"What's the buzz on this one, Royce?" Chrissy asked me, inappropriately grabbing my arm.

The buzz that concerned me was not her, but Fitzroy, who had just now invaded my open house and had button-holed Father Flannigan.

"We've got not two, but three potential buyers, Royce," Crystal said. "You're going to have to be very shrewd to get the best deal on this one."

She, like her sister, took my arm, the other one. Clearly they were infatuated with me. They didn't just take my arm; they dug into it, wetting themselves over their rare chance to feel a man at his physical and professional peak.

"Cash offers to the front of the line," I said.

"We don't represent drug dealers, Royce," Crystal said.

"Unlike some realtors we know," Chrissy sneered, glancing toward Fitzroy.

"Just between us," Crystal whispered, "he looks so wrong standing next to Father Flannigan. How he ever got into the Billion Dollar Brotherhood is beyond me."

"It's 'among' us, since there's three of us, not two," I said, diverting them away from talk about Fitzroy.

"We went to college, Royce. We don't need our grammar corrected," Chrissy said. "What's more important is a rumor is out that you are going to try to get into," and she whispered the next part, "the Brotherhood this year."

"How do you even know about the Brotherhood, and about Fitzroy getting in?" I asked, for the Billion Dollar Brotherhood is a secret organization.

"You'd be surprised what we know, Royce," Crystal said.

"Good luck," Chrissy said, releasing my arm. "On the house and on that other secret thing."

Crystal released my other arm and the pair of them found their client and went off to look at the pool. I wished both ants would fall in it and drown.

Then, as if I'd said a prayer for deliverance, a total contrast to the ants created a wake in my direction. It was he, my priest, president of the Billion Dollar Brotherhood, the august Father Flannery O. Flannigan. O. Not O with an apostrophe. An O with a period. And since I've taken a moment to provide some instructive information, I guess, since I'm sure the secret is safe with you, I guess it's time to clue you in on what the Billion Dollar Brotherhood is all about.

The Brotherhood is not known to the average realtor, you know, the silly ones who play by the, I mean the housewives who chuck it all to get their license. Fuck them. The Brotherhood is for the big boys. The powerful. The movers and shapers. Yes, I said shapers, not shakers. These are the cats who shape the market and end up shaping where you live and where those not in your socioeconomic historical racial ethnic tax bracket do not live. They make the deals possible. They grease the wheels. They shape the whole fucking world. Shit. The top echelons of the Brotherhood are tapped into some of the biggest multinational banks and investment firms. The very top hail from Yale and Princeton, and Oxford and Harvard. Most are born to it. Some, some rise to it.

Father Flannery O. Flannigan is up there, not born, well, kind of born, but he took a different path. It didn't hurt that he had several billion dollars of unused church assets to sell in the downturn that brought some much needed cash to his parish and lined his pockets with silk. He does real estate "on the side," but the man is a prodigious talent, very lucky, and very well positioned. He's also charming as hell, and a born politician, which rose him to great heights in the Brotherhood.

He became President last year and helped Fitzroy get in. That's how I know about it. I didn't even know the Brotherhood existed until Fitzroy started slacking off. It wasn't like him, as he was usually buzzed and buzzing on coke. So I sat him down one day and put my concerns to him. He trusted me implicitly and told me all about it and how he was spending all his time on the application and qualification documents. He gave me the whole scoop. It went on so long that we adjourned to a bar where his lips loosened with each successive drink until he finally told me something really impressive.

You see, the Brotherhood is heavily insinuated in government, business, the church, the school boards, the university regents, hell, even the media and entertainment industries. And the goal was, is, not just to affect policy and business conditions through the traditional channels. Oh no. The Brotherhood is aligned with fundamentalist religious groups to route out the liberal, permissive, irresponsible, degenerate influences in all spheres of Western culture and commerce. It has no philosophical bent against all that. As Fitzroy explained it, the ability of industry leaders and politicians to garner massive support by appealing to moral authority and stoking fear in the public at large played to their real goal of securing influence and control they couldn't buy or legislate outright. That's why the Brotherhood's reach and scope is so broad, Fitzroy explained. That part scared me a bit, I will admit. On the other hand, it mightily impressed me with its ambitious goals, deft organization, and successful secrecy. It is an extremely powerful group, in spite of and because of all that, and it cares for its members like brothers.

You can see where this was going for me, me, Royce O'Rourke. It's not the money, per se. It's the network. Yes. The Brotherhood. They open doors, they cover your back, they lead you on the right path. Get in the Brotherhood, and you are set for life. Of course, some would argue that you have to be set for life to get in the Brotherhood, but what they miss is that once in the Brotherhood, you are assured, insured, guaranteed that you will stay set for life.

It's an international organization. Now, you ask why they were headquartered in Tucson? Location, location, location: Flannigan's parish was in Tucson.

He was something of a contradiction. After talking to Fitzroy about the goals of the Brotherhood, I had a hard time reconciling Father Flannigan the priest, head of a small, wealthy, but moderately liberal congregation, with

Flannery O. Flannigan, champion of the global corrective goals of the Brotherhood. Indeed, Flannigan always had struck me as solidly Tucson. After I got the scoop from Fitzroy, Flannigan seemed more Phoenix to me. But isn't that the essence of a great man, the harmony of contradictions? So as I watched him approach me, not as Father Flannigan, but as Flannigan the real estate mogul, the contradictions crystallized into a beautiful paradox. He walked with an assured, confident stride that bordered safely just this side of a swagger. As he walked, he slowed without fully stopping to say hello to a realtor, or a member of his congregation, spending just enough time to be cordial, but not enough time to be sucked into a vapid conversation. He was a man who knew the value of his time, and as he progressed elegantly from one supplicant to another, greeting everyone by name, he masterfully apportioned that time according to the recipient's current value to him, keeping his eye, his intention, his entire bearing and being on the prize, like a master politician. And the prize was me, Royce O'Rourke.

"Excellent showing, Royce," he said, stopping his walk and showing to the entire room where the real value was.

"Thank you, Father. It is a great property," I replied.

"And so well staged." He looked around, then in a low voice said "I can always distinguish between your stagings and Fitzroy's. This is almost a work of art here today, Royce."

Score.

"Thank you, Father. Even in this economy, there is a lot of interest, qualified interest."

"Indeed. This is the place to be in Tucson today."

This was going so well for me, a one-eighty from the ants crawling about my feet.

"Royce, I wanted to talk to you. Do I hear right? Are you aiming for the Brotherhood?"

Score. Double Score. Triple Score. For the president of a secret society to say those words to me, to me, Royce O'Rourke, in this stunning setting, well, it was almost a sign from above that my destiny was assured.

"I've been thinking about it, sir," I said. "I think I may qualify this year, this quarter even."

"Ah, a quarter qualifier already," he said.

At the time, that struck me as an odd, almost mocking remark. It would make more sense later, on that night in June, at the haunted house.

"But Royce," he continued, "I want to be clear. It is important to qualify, to be sure, but there are other factors."

"Oh, I know," I bullshitted. "I'm not being presumptuous."

"Let's not go too far in the other direction, Royce. My advice is to be open to all possibilities."

"Thank you, sir, Father."

"Now Royce, you don't need to address me that way. Here, today, I am Flannigan, like you are O'Rourke, realtors."

"Yes."

"And my counsel now is to be on your best game today. This is the biggest property and of the greatest interest in the last two quarters. I want an impressive deal. I gather the Diamond sisters have three ideal buyers, who all more than have the resources. I think we may have a record setter here."

"I'll do my best," I said.

He moved in close, almost uncomfortably close, so close, I could tell, for sure, as I had long suspected, that the fountain pen in the breast pocket of his suit was a Visconti. I almost got hard knowing that.

"O'Rourke. Your best is not always what's necessary, or even hard."

It was one of those moments where you're totally exposed, on trial, your whole life depending on the outcome of what you are about to say or do. I thought, at that moment, that just the fact of me realizing the significance of the moment meant I was among the chosen, the elect. With that in my mind, I knew what to say, what I had to say, what any man born, bred, and bound for the Brotherhood had to say.

"It will be easy, sir."

He smiled, that politician smile, shook my hand, maybe even winked, or maybe that wink was really the gleaming glint of the Visconti, and he glided away, confident, actually swaggering slightly. It was I who caused that sinful swagger. It was a mega score. And I've really got to stop all this alliteration. It's unseemly for a man on the cusp of the greatest moment of his life, poised to be admitted into the Brotherhood. I knew it then. Was sure of it then. Oh it had been in the back of my mind ever since Fitzroy told me about it. But not until that day, in that open house, in the presence of the great Flannery O. Flannigan did the idea, the dream, become a real possibility.

My eyes were actually watering. I cast them about the great room (sad but true, the house had one of the most ostentatious ones ever) looking for the ants, who I was sure would bring me back to cold dull reality. No ants. I did see that sexy RE/MAX realtor, such a nice duplex on her, I always thought. I wanted to fuck her, right there, right then, to seal my good fortune. No. Not her. I just knew the other one would be waiting for me later. After the open house. After all had left. The mysterious one. I decided to wait for her.

As if my dirty thoughts dispelled Flannigan's pure air, and let all the scum air rush in at me, who should approach but Fitzroy, who had the audacious nerve to crash my open house.

I won't bore you with the business he had, except to say that it was only an excuse to spy on me. He could easily have told me the next morning, on our way to New Orleans to initiate Phase Two of our Katrina deal. It was time to cash in, and that deal was a main component of my being able to qualify for the Brotherhood.

2

It was a good showing, that open house, one of my best, I thought, as I collected the signs from out front and put them in my car. I went back inside to do my paperwork at the kitchen bar. I knew she would be there, somewhere, preparing for me, waiting for me.

When I was done with the paperwork, I started the search, slowly sneaking into each room downstairs.

This all started after Fitzroy got into the Brotherhood. I would finish up a showing or an open house, do some paperwork, then find her. The first time I thought she was a realtor or buyer who had gotten lost. Except that she was completely naked in the kitchen pantry and gave me the best blow job ever. The second time she was in the pool shed, a garden hose draped seductively around her. She didn't talk much. From what little she said, I knew she was foreign, French or Belgian. She also said her name was Juliette, and that was about it. She would just be there, be with me, then leave.

This time, I found her in the master bath. Oh, sweet Jesus, you know what she did? It was all blue. She had lit these blue votive candles, the kind Rocky, my wife, keeps in her sewing room, next to her bible, that has a red cover. Juliette, she was laying in the tub, with like twenty-five blue candles lit. And you know what she was laying in, in that tub? It sure as shit wasn't water. She had filled the tub half full of blueberries. Fucking blueberries. I didn't know where she got so many in Tucson, but she was laying on a cushion of blueberries. She had them scattered all over her. There was one in that dip in her neck. There were two between her tits. There was one in her navel. She had squished others all over her, so she was, not blue. She was purple. So was I, when we were done. I shouldn't tell you this, but I will, since you should be eighteen or over if you are reading this. She took a plump, tight little blueberry and stuck it down my urethra. Shit. When you use scientific medical terms it sounds like a fucking vacuum cleaner. She took this plump blueberry, took my cock, squished the head, then real fast, she pushed that fucker inside. Just inside. She wanted it to shoot out like a bullet when I came. That was the easy part. The real problem was how would I explain to Rocky all those purple stains all over my body?

I tried to clean up the bathroom after Juliette left. Then I went downstairs and was shocked to see the house, that prime property, was infested with ants.

"What the hell are you two still doing here?" I said to them. "The open house closed over an hour ago."

"We are doing our jobs, Royce," Crystal said, putting a little notepad into her yellow fanny pack.

"What have you been doing?" Chrissy teased.

"My job. Now get out."

"Really Royce, do you want to make a sale or not?" Chrissy asked.

"Yes, but to realtors whose clients belong here, which rules you out."

"Is that so?" Chrissy replied, sounding surprised. "Well look Royce, we've counted at least nine code violations here, so our bid will reflect the cost of attaining the variances and remediation our buyer will incur."

"Bullshit," I said, because it was.

"It's not Royce, and you know it. And Crystal is going to be the new Pima County Real Property Acquisition Agent and will clamp down hard on developers and realtors who sucker people into overpriced subdivisions that go bust, don't provide the promised tax revenue, and destroy the desert environment."

"Like either of you could get appointed to pick up the trash."

"We plan to," Crystal said, quite proud of herself.

"Fine. Submit your low bid and lose. I don't need your business. I'm ascending to a whole different level."

They laughed. At me, Royce O'Rourke. They then crawled out, back to their bicycles. Stupid women. They teased me because they wanted me, but were so out of my league. As if they were Juliette. Or even Rocky.

Rocky was mom's favorite of all my girlfriends in high school. All three of them. There was Rocky when I was a sophomore, then Liberia, yes, that was her name, the first girl I fucked, when I was a junior, who died after the homecoming ball where we broke up and she ran home with Bart Novak, who was drunk and tried to beat a train and lost.

Rocky said I was partly at fault. Gee, I wanted back with her because I needed her comforting arms, but when I asked her to quantify my guilt, like an insurance adjuster, she just stared at me, and when I said two percent me, forty percent Liberia, fifty percent Bart Novak, and eight percent Union Pacific, well, she just stopped talking to me.

By the way, Liberia died instantly. Bart hung on, brain dead for months. I thought that a better outcome than him surviving and being sent to jail, and finding out my dad was a fucking prison guard.

Then there was Marcia when I was a senior, who was in the drama club, which made her uncool. She was also good friends with Crystal and Chrissy Diamond which made her toxic. But she was the gothest of the goth, so I counted her a major asset in my rebellion. Mom wanted like everything for me to go to college. Marcia thought college was a mysterious waste of money and time and tried to get me to do drugs with Fitzroy.

I almost did, but then I got back together with Rocky, because Marcia wouldn't put out, and Rocky got the bug and one day passed me a note in senior biology class asking me if my pubic hair was red too.

She found out after school behind the greenhouse where the corsages for graduation were maturing. I said the only way to know was to look. I unzipped my jeans and dropped my underwear. She saw my red pubes and got an eyeful of my cock growing stiff and I popped her red cherry with my red cock and red pubes right there.

Of course, she got pregnant and mom won in the end because we had to get married after summer break. Dad, of all people, said I had to get a job to support us. Thanks, screw. Mom had started selling real estate when I was a junior, but hadn't made enough even to buy us a house. She said grandma would take Rocky in while I was at college. All I wanted was my own fucking house with my own garage holding two cars, and my own barbecue, and my own swimming pool, and my own god-damned mortgage.

I was this close to joining the Army and fucking them all. Ah, but then I joined with Fitzroy and my path to the Billion Dollar Brotherhood began without my even knowing it.

Dad died before we got married. He was shot in a robbery at a Circle K. He was buying a slurpie and tried to be the big man and stop the robber. How fucking lame. What was even lamer was that the ants were there too, and he had intervened to save them.

Mom and Fitzroy helped me learn the real estate business. By that point even mom saw the advantages of getting quick money over a protracted education. That was cool. Mom was cool. Fitzroy was cool.

Rocky, however, turned out to be all exclamation points and dashes. I managed to evade those when I got home by going straight to the shower to get most of the purple stains washed off me, eating a quick dinner, then heading for bed before everyone else. I had an early flight in the morning, I said, and needed my sleep to be in tiptop billion dollar shape. That turned out to be truer than I knew, for I was about to meet a certain voodoo priestess shaman, whose path I hope you never cross.

3

If you ask me, Royce O'Rourke, Katrina was a bitch, but, the biggest, baddest hurricane of all is Clarrissa. Oh. I'm sorry. Miss Clarrissa, as she calls herself. Two Rs, two Ss. Not young, not old. Big boned, but not fat. Chocolate brown smooth skin. Big black eyes. Nice big tits. An ass you can't take your eyes off of. I think it's OK to end a sentence with a preposition.

So Miss Clarrissa, I'd fuck, oh yeah, at least until she opens those luscious purple lips. God, what a mouth on that bitch. She said "I's be a voodoo priestess shaman and I be runnin' you outta dis place." She said it just like that. OK. So I said "Where is your Ouija board and your crystal ball and your Kewpie doll?" She spat on me, spun around and walked to the bar, swinging that jelly ass. She spat on me, me, Royce O'Rourke. And it wouldn't be that last time either.

It was Fitzroy's fault. I would never go to a bar until after noon, after three preferably, but Fitzroy went straight from the airport to the French Quarter. Looked like Disneyland to me, but he drove past it in the rental car and up to the northern fringe of it where the street looked like some back alley. Figured Miss Clarrissa would hang out in that lowlife place. I complained. I wanted to get down to business. Fitzroy said this was business. I didn't say so, but you can be damned sure it crossed my mind that that town, that street, that place were no way to get into the Billion Dollar Brotherhood.

Fitzroy ordered us scotches and up came this beautiful young black woman who made the drinks, much to Miss Clarrissa's amusement. We made nice with her and had two more rounds when after that, she took Fitzroy aside and left me, Royce O'Rourke, to Miss Clarrissa, who met me by looking down her nose at me in disgust. It was there and then I decided to fuck the attitude right out of that bitch.

Fitzroy came back, coked out of his mind, and drove us to what he called the ninth circle of hell. This is where, four years ago, we came to buy all these houses, damaged by that bitch Katrina. At the time, I was floored by how long those lots had sat like that. Honestly, I thought, those shiftless people had how many months to rebuild that shit? And they just sat in front crying like babies. I, Royce O'Rourke, am no racist, but it says something about those people that they let property rot like that for so long. They must not be historically used to owning property instead of fucking renting it, or working on the grounds of it. Such a thing would never happen in a German or Irish neighborhood, if you know what I mean. I'm just saying, not passing any judgment.

The plan then, was to tear everything down and rebuild. My idea had been to put up new houses way past the lot line to give big front yards and make them all two-story ranches. Fitzroy burst my bubble and told me you can't build two stories there. Soil won't support it. And the lots weren't deep enough for both a big front yard and a big back yard. Oh, it got worse. You couldn't put in swimming pools. What the fuck? Well, at least a deck and a barbecue

I asked Fitzroy, those four years earlier, what the point was, if we couldn't build the American dream there. Ah, then the real plan came out.

Yeah, I should have seen it. Fitz proposed doing neuvo shotgun houses. Recall the historical style but with updated features and amenities. Granite counter tops, stainless steel appliances, parquet floors, big-ass closets, travertine marble in the bathrooms (dual sinks, of course).

Then Fitz dropped the secret surprise. We would build them cheap, overprice them, then use high pressure sales tactics to take advantage of the sub-prime loans the banks were hot to give out. Fitzroy also formed his own mortgage brokerage to speed the process and open another revenue stream.

We got a heavy amount in down payments, a cut of the mortgage payments, and were there, four years later, to foreclose, consolidate, and short-sell the shit out of the place. It was the gift that kept on giving. Genius. Now you know why Fitz beat me into the Billion Dollar Brotherhood.

We visited Fitzroy's mortgage brokerage company, got a list of potential short sells and then went back to the neighborhood to knock on doors. Those that didn't want to sell or buy our loan consolidation services got some scary stories about the joys of foreclosure. We also talked to other homeowners about how the neighborhood was going down the tubes and offered to cut deals, consolidate loans, or just buy them out. It made for a long day, but Fitz was persuasive and, well, hell, threatening, so by the end of the first day, we had nearly half the owners begging us to take over their mortgages.

To celebrate, we had dinner in the French Quarter proper, at a seafood place where I had the best lobster tails ever. It was ruined, however, by, you guessed it, Miss Clarrissa. She sauntered (I've always wanted to use that word) through the restaurant selling roses and telling fortunes. Of course, she saw me and pretended to ignore me. Fitzroy called her over and asked her to read his palm. I could have sworn real fire shot from her eyes when she said "Son, you will dishonor your ancestors for all eternity and you will die at the hands of your brothers next week." Just like that. In perfect English.

Fitzroy was so drunk by then that he laughed it off. I, Royce O'Rourke, was scared shitless. That demon bitch looked so serious I believed every word.

Then she came to me. I held my palm out for her to read. She handed me a rose instead. I thought it unmanly to take it, but she forced me with her eyes. Now, the strange thing is that when I looked at it later, after she knocked on the door of my hotel room that night, after I fucked her, the rose was not red. It was black. Like her skin. Like her so smooth and soft and supple flesh. If only that black rose had been the end of it.

Fitzroy banged on the door the next morning. We had to go back to the ninth circle of hell to save those poor homeowners. As we went from door to door, I thought all was looking good and going my way. Then we saw, parked on one of our streets, a long black Lincoln Town Car with a shrunken head for a hood ornament, images of stars, funny symbols, and satanic pentagrams stenciled along the side, and a fucking voodoo doll tied to the antenna.

We drove over to it, and I rolled down the window to get a better look. Aha. There was Miss Clarrissa, in a leather jacket, trying to comfort a bawling girl who was probably in her twenties, and who looked like the girl who served us drinks and fed Fitzroy coke the day before.

"Wot you be doin' here?!" she yelled at me.

"What are you doing on my street?" I asked.

No one, never, ever, not anybody, I swear, has ever spit in my face. But that bitch did, twice. Fitz had to hold me from flying out of the car and punching that cunt in the face.

"Dat place der. Dat be me daughter's home. Dat land be my home, an' me mother's home, an' her mother's home. An' you tink you kin just swoop in der like a black vulture an' take it from us?"

Fitzroy didn't wait for me to answer. He sped off. But that fucking bitch followed us. Us! Oops. In that voodoo car. Fitz navigated through these stupid curvy streets, streets pretending they were in some decent suburb. And then, we heard a gun shot. That bitch fired on us? Luckily, Fitz hit a major highway named after some French general, and took off, with that crazed demon in full pursuit.

I was afraid to turn around. I didn't want a bullet in my face. But, boy, the one or two times I did, she was so close on our tail I could see the fires of hell in her black eyes.

We crossed the river and she passed us right after the bridge. She shot us a big smile and raised her fist in a funny gesture I didn't get.

She got off into the French Quarter. We kept going. Thank god that evil woman did not follow us to our hotel. She probably would have burned it down.

But she didn't. Fitzroy turned in early and I got bored. Then I thought of my dad.

It's time for some honesty. Yeah, I have to admit it. Not like I haven't been honest so far. I mean, everything so far is true. It just occurred (two Cs and two Rs, right?) to me that I haven't been honest with my real reason, my real motives for wanting to be in the Billion Dollar Brotherhood.

You see, I've always been embarrassed (two Rs and two Ss, right?) by my dad. Not by him personally, but by what he did for a living. As I casually mentioned earlier, but what was in reality very hard to write, my dad was a guard. In a prison. Yeah.

In school I would never say what he did. But they all knew, right? Don't they always? Sure, it was better than being a crook, like those he guarded, but why the fuck couldn't he have been a real cop? Or a bank manager? Or a salesman, yeah, a salesman, good honest work that, like real estate, rewards you for the value of how much you sell, not for just showing up and sitting on your ass.

I had to see a play once because my high school was doing it and Marcia was in it. It was called Death of a Salesman. In my opinion, yeah I'm no drama critic, but I don't use exclamation points or dashes, so there; in my opinion, Willie was addled with two ungrateful, self-absorbed sons, gay probably, and a nagging wife. They killed him. If only my dad had been killed by some cons instead of a robber at a Circle K protecting the ants.

I didn't really mean that. It's just that I was always embarrassed that he didn't make more of his life, bring in more money, drive a cool car, live in an appropriate middle class house, not fucking renting a shack like he did. That's why my mom got into real estate. She wanted something better. He died before she got it.

I don't believe in psycho pop psychology. Even you can see why it was so important for me to get into the Billion Dollar Brotherhood. 'Nuff said.

Now I didn't tell you about the porn I found in his and mom's bedroom. And the whips and handcuffs. Less said about that, the better.

I needed a drink.

So what did I do? Sit in the hotel downtown drinking alone and watching porn on the demand TV like Fitzroy was no doubt doing? No. I'm not my dad. I took a cab back to the French Quarter where life was happening.

It was in full swing. I went into a bar and drank for an hour, watching the babes, hoping to see some tits. Then I went looking for her. She must have been looking for me too because I found her right off. She was standing in St. Ann Street, just off Bourbon. She was outside a shop, staring at me. She didn't scare me, so I went straight up to her.

"You either be brave or be a fool, man," she said.

I told her I wanted another fuck with her. I expected her to slap me or spit on me, but oh no, she led me inside, past some stupid tourists looking at her beads, voodoo dolls, and charms, all made in China, I was sure. That young woman, the one who was in the car and who worked at the bar, was there too, loafing behind the counter. I wanted a closer look at her because I thought she could be Miss Clarrissa's daughter, or sister. I wasn't sure which.

But Miss Clarrissa took me into a back room and had me sit down. She put a purple and green scarf over her head, then took out a deck of tarot cards.

"Now you tell me, Red," she said. I hated being called that. I can't stand it. But I let her.

"Why you be here botherin' good hard workin' folks?"

I told her I was on a business trip and that it was no business of hers.

"You tink so? When you come here from god knows where to steal our land?"

I pointed out that we were providing a valuable service to people who had over-extended themselves. That was probably telling her too much, but she already knew. Plus, I was slightly drunk.

"Here, have some beer," she said, opening a small refrigerator behind her. I thought I saw a shrunken head in there, but it could have been a rotten cabbage.

It was a strange brew. It tasted like beer, but also like, like moss. Not that I've ever tasted moss. I've smoked weed, of course, but not moss. It just tasted like what I thought moss would taste like.

"You tink just because you fuck me you can take me and me daughter's house like you own us?" she asked.

I told her I wasn't taking it. I told her people who couldn't pay their debts shouldn't own homes. Then I got brave and asked:

"So you look like you do a profitable business here. Why don't you help your daughter make her mortgage payments?"

"Dat be none of your business, Red, except dat me daughter and her husband be proud and don't take no handouts, least of all from me."

Funny, I'd finished the bottle before she finished her answer. She handed me another.

"I not be so easily fooled," she said. "You find me a formidable opponent."

I told her I wasn't looking for a fight. I told her that what Fitzroy and I were doing was perfectly legal, that we were properly licensed, and that we paid our taxes. I doubted she could say the same. I may even have said as much.

She shuffled the tarot cards, then laid them face up on the table. It looked like a very old set of cards, but shuffled crisp and tight like a fresh deck. It was getting warm.

"The page, the moon, the tower," she said.

I think I asked if the tower was a reference to my cock. I had a fresh beer.

"Dey have no meaning in isolation. All de meaning be in relation to de adjacent cards. Now be silent."

I didn't know what to say, so that was easy.

She dealt more cards, saying nothing, then she stared at me, with those glowing eyes like an ember in a fireplace that refused to go out. It should be noted that I, Royce O'Rourke, never sell a house where the fireplace doesn't work.

Then she was behind me, unbuttoning my shirt.

"You be on fire. You must be cooled," she said, taking my shirt off.

I felt a sharp pain in my chest and head. I thought I was having a heart attack, but it was that bitch plucking hairs off of me. 'Off of' looks weird, doesn't it? I don't know if you need the 'of.'

Then she was back at her seat with my hand in hers.

"The cards do not lie, but I must check your palm to be sure," she said, seriously.

I think I asked what was wrong. I was still sweating and didn't feel any cooler. It occurred to me that I don't sweat this much in Tucson, where it's a lot hotter than in Miss Clarrissa's voodoo shop.

She put my hand down, then stood. Someone must have opened a door because a rush of wind blew through her hair and a bright light blazed behind her.

I thought I heard the tinkling of little bells or wind chimes. I never stage houses by adding tacky wind chimes like some realtors do.

She spoke in low, profound tones:

"Royce O'Rourke, Realtor. I prophesy you be de king of de brotherhood. I prophesy your ancestors will rise red up and bow before ye. I predict the name and man here before me be emblazoned in words of blood-red fire for the rest of eternity."

All I could think, and maybe even say, drenched in sweat, was ... wow. Me, Royce O'Rourke, President and King of the Billion Dollar Brotherhood. My dad resurrected there at my swearing in to see how it's really done. Me. There. Only question was when. When would it happen?

I wanted to ask her, but I was out in Bourbon Street. The crowds were still thick. Women were showing their tits. And so was I. My shirt. I went back to the shop but it was dark and locked tight. In a panic, I checked my trousers for my wallet. It was missing. Damn that thieving bitch. No. Good. There it was, in the other back pocket. The chocolate voodoo bitch didn't roll me, after all.

Now, I've never been fat. I'm not ashamed of my body at all. But I hated not having a shirt on in public and not being on the beach or mowing the yard. I had money for a cab but didn't want to walk through the hotel lobby like a shirtless drunk. Just a properly attired drunk would do me fine.

Luck was with me. I found a shop in Bourbon and got a Mardi Gras T-shirt. It fit fine. I took a taxi back to the hotel and walked respectably, like the president of the Billion Dollar Brotherhood should walk, through the lobby, into the elevator, and up to my room, where I went to bed. Where I showered first and went to bed. Where I jerked off, showered, and went to bed. I wasn't thinking of Miss Clarrissa. Not of Juliette, not of Rocky. It was Miss Clarrissa's daughter I saw, her firm, tight, soft flesh meeting mine. Problem was, I'd had too much to drink. I could never come. Just as I was about to, there she was, Miss Clarrissa, rising before me, predicting glory for me.

4

We spent another day moving and shaping our destiny, during which I avoided telling Fitzroy what had transpired between me and Miss Clarrissa. On the flight back Wednesday afternoon, in first class, Fitzroy took out his laptop and started figuring our take. He pivoted his screen to me and pointed at the split. Nice.

Fitzroy settled back to sleep, so I took out my trusty Montblanc to do some back-of-envelope calculations on where my share would put me toward qualifying for the Brotherhood.

You see, I have a thing for a good pen. And it has to be a fountain pen. I got a fucking Cross gift set from mom and dad when I graduated from high school. A ballpoint pen and a mechanical pencil. Like what? Was I supposed to go to college and become an engineer? No way. Not me. Not Royce O'Rourke. Not with Rocky. I went straight into the business and scored my first million by the time I was twenty-five. Yeah, I could have used an exclamation point just there, but I didn't.

When I scored that sell to put me over my first million, Fitzroy said I had to start using a Montblanc to sign contracts. First thing I thought of was the ant twins – oh – oh shit, a dash – two, no three. They always had fingers stained with fountain pen ink.

So I told Fitzroy I didn't want inky fingers. God knows Fitzroy had seen inky fingers – Shit! Oh fuck. A dash and an exclamation point. What I was trying to say is that Fitz had been busted before so all ten digits had been inked up and printed. I told him Royce O'Rourke has to have clean hands. So he told me the ant twins were using cheap pens, not a Montblanc. He took me to this pen shop in LA and told me to get a big black Meisterstück, which I did. Then I asked for the cartridges of ink. The store manager almost laughed at me. Oh no. We can't be so cheap and uncool as to use cartridges. I had to buy these two ounce bottles of black ink and fill the pen from the bottle by turning the piston at the top. I gotta give that guy credit. I never had inky fingers with that pen. And when I became president of the Billion Dollar Brotherhood, I would have my own limited edition Visconti.

I finished my calculations right before we landed. Unfortunately, even with the New Orleans money I was still two or three million short of a billion. I had covered Tucson in and out as far south as Nogales, east as San Simon, west as Ajo, and north as, well as far north as not to get into Phoenix. Damn. If I could crack Phoenix, I wouldn't need Fitzroy's New Orleans deal. The Phoenix market was locked up tighter than Rocky's twat, I thought, as I opened the door to the house and saw her filling up another one of her colored bottles.

Rocky collects bottles. Not antique bottles. Her antiquing is quite well developed, but she goes for furniture, and art, not bottles. No, the bottles she collects, and displays, and dusts and dusts and dusts are liquor bottles. She collects clear liquors like vodka, gin, and light rum. Horror of all horrors, she adds food coloring to them so they turn all different, non-alcohol colors. She keeps them everywhere. They're on the mantle, the kitchen counters, the desks, the dressers, the ledges of the windows.

She claims she never drinks from those bottles. She only opens them to add the food coloring. Right. But I knew better. I tried a few, when she wasn't looking, and they were really watered down. Thing is, she never smelled of it. She was never anything less than boringly sober. But she could be annoyingly bubbly and bouncy, even when boringly sober.

"Roar?" she said. She called me Roar, maybe because I like to roar and growl during sex.

"Roar, can you get that box of Bisquick from the top shelf for me?" Not that she's so short, but that I am a tall man. Tall enough to stand among the Billion Dollar Brotherhood.

She was making a coffee cake. Why they call them that I'll never know as I have milk with mine, and she doesn't use coffee in the recipe. It was going to be dessert. Then came the bouncing and the bubbles.

"Randi was teased again at school today. You know. I just told her the old rubber/glue thing."

"Red?"

"Yep!"

And now the exclamation point must be used apropos Rocky. She talks that way.

"Oh!" she said. "I don't get it. But I do! She'll be glad one day. The pool men were here. They were late, again, and I caught Randi staring out her window at them! She's at that age. I had her come help me cut the meat for dinner. Ha! Ha! Ha! She knows that I know – and not a word between us!"

I have to use dashes vis-a-vis Rocky too. Why is it that when I have to qualify something, I resort to French. I wonder if I would have done so before meeting Juliette.

"Anyway, it's natural! I shouldn't discourage it, but you can never be too careful where Mexicans are concerned."

She was blending the butter with the cinnamon and brown sugar with her bare hands. They were all greasy. I thought of the Mexicans. I thought of Miss Clarrissa and her brown sugar walls and her prophesy, so I grabbed Rocky and buried my face in her neck and fondled her tits and pressed tight against her and growled.

"Royce! The kids may come in!" she said.

I let go. I didn't really want greasy coffee cake topping all over my monogrammed Ralph Lauren shirt. Besides, Randi might have come in, and after the Mexicans in the pool, seeing us like that might have confused her.

Roger came rushing in to hug me, his dad. He wouldn't have been phased by me and Rocky. Or even the Mexicans. Roger is twelve, thirteen now, but acts like he's six. He's slow, you see. He's special, you know. Not my fault, I used to think. I mean Randi turned out OK, and red hair like me and smart and clever. Roger has black hair. Where that came from I never cared to know. Of course, Rocky has blond hair.

I made it a point never to go there. He's my son and I'm his father, come hell or high water. What kills me, eats me alive some nights, still, is what he'd do if something happened to me. I worry that he'll never feel the challenge to outdo his father, like I have mine. That he'll never join the Brotherhood and will always be like he was. It's not fair. It's not his fault.

I presented to Rocky my theory that Roger is the reason why the kids tease Randi so much. They know Roger is off limits. Rocky said that's stupid. She said kids don't think that way. I wasn't so sure. Nonetheless, Rocky bubbled and bounced around and treated them both the same, Randi and Roger. She always acted like Roger's normal. Me, I felt, I acted, I mean I really did love him more, not that I didn't love Randi. But Roger needed it and I gave it. He's special. And, I have to admit, since I'm being honest, that it never escaped my attention that Roger just might have made it that much easier to get into the Billion Dollar Brotherhood. It would look good. Add a shine to their halo, especially these days, when special kids aren't hidden away like they were when I was growing up. No sir. They are out there and worth something. Now don't go too far. I never, ever, tried to assign points to him to see how he might tip the scales.

After dinner, and milk and cake, Randi got on the phone and Roger onto the TV, literally. I had to pick him up, and he was getting heavy, and plop him in front of the tube, so he could watch the nature channel. Then I helped Rocky clean up and there came the questions:

"What did you do in New Orleans? Did you go to the Quarter? Did you see tits? Were you a good boy? Did you hear about the Carrs next door? The home owner's association is going to fine them for all that noise! Melany Pruitt across the street is afraid they have guns! She thinks our pool men are illegals, but they are so good!"

And on and on. She doesn't wait for an answer. I wished she'd get a job or something.

All I told her was that Fitzroy and I were in and would realize a tidy profit so we could buy that RV. Where we would have kept it was not clear. We couldn't park it at the house, and rightly so because our housing association covenants strictly forbid it. I pity anyone not living under housing association covenants.

I am a religious, god-fearing man, and I, Royce O'Rourke, was a leader in Flannigan's church. So I know what a covenant is. It's not a law. Not a city ordinance. Not a Federal regulation. It's something higher, handed down by god, to protect the American Dream. To make sure property values keep rising. And the covenant guarantees that all manner of riffraff, undesirable people, and, god forbid, renters, move in. It stops some chump from painting his house pink, from leaving a pickup truck in the driveway, or a sofa in the yard, or a bunch of political signs near the street. Oh yes, it stops those yacks who think it so cool to install some mailbox shaped like a barn, or a dog, or from being some ugly galvanized unpainted USPS tube. And speaking of dogs, it keeps them from running wild and shitting in my yard.

Now, the neighborhood in which I bought our house requires at least fifty percent grass in the front yard. That's not easy to do in Tucson and damned expensive because you have to install these underground irrigation systems on timers and pay to keep everything in tiptop shape. Then there's the cost of the water.

This is how it should be. This is what god decreed a front lawn should look like. Nothing pisses me off more than these new edge of town subdivisions with their oh-so-proper desert landscaping. Dad's rented house had a better lawn, even if it was really patchy.

It is covenants that protect the middle and upper classes and it's covenants that will get the Carrs of the world outta where they never belonged in the first place.

Rocky was still going on. The kitchen was cleared and it was time to put Roger to bed. I do that, did that, kneeling beside his bed with him and helping him with his prayers. He always saved me for last when he was blessing everyone, which still leaves a lump in my throat.

I didn't dare tell Rocky how big the New Orleans deal was. Too many questions. It was our night for sex, so I thought that would distract her. Rocky had a schedule for sex: Every Monday, Wednesday, and Friday. We had to wait until Randi went to bed, but I knew she put a towel under her door, drew the shades and stayed up. Teenagers do that. Doesn't matter, Rocky and I always had quiet sex. Not like Juliette. Not like Miss Clarrissa.

Rocky couldn't know about either. The O'Rourkes represented a proud, happy family, just right for the Billion Dollar Brotherhood. So I had to keep Juliette a secret. So I had to steer Rocky away from asking too many questions about New Orleans.

Too fucking late. Oh shit. She had unpacked my bags while I was tucking Roger in. Rocky doesn't miss a thing. She counted three trousers, three pairs of socks, three used underwear, two shirts, and one Mardi Gras T-shirt. Of course, she packed for me and knew just which Ralph Lauren monogrammed shirt was missing. And I wasn't wearing it.

I played dumb for a bit, then, well, I, Royce O'Rourke, am not stupid. I was about to say that I must have left it in the hotel, but, oh, then Rocky would call them the next day and ask them to try to find it. So, I told her it must have been stolen by the TSA security losers. I told her Fitzroy was missing some stuff when we arrived and that they probably stole my shirt. She seemed to buy it. Except we didn't have sex that night like we were supposed to.

That was OK. I spent the night wondering what Miss Clarrissa would want with my shirt.

5

OK, so I was considering my options – Ah. Damn. A dash. I was considering my options. I had the New Orleans deal. And I had just sold that open house through the sexy RE/MAX realtor by giving her an anonymous tip on what the ants' clients were bidding. But all I could see was that I was still short of the goal. I needed something else big enough to push me well over the edge so I could get into the Billion Dollar Brotherhood.

This idea took on some urgency after Miss Clarrissa's prophesy. You see, Father Flannery O. Flannigan's term as president expired that year. I wouldn't have presumed before, and let me tell you, I didn't buy into Miss Clarrissa's voodoo hocus-pocus crap. Yet, she was so real, and so right there, and so believable, that I decided to ride the chutzpa, as it were, and to think big. That's what got me into the house I owned, in a good upper middle class subdivision, with airtight, restrictive covenants, a wife, and two kids, one special: I got all this by thinking big.

So I would think big and believe I could make it. That's why I went with renewed confidence on Friday to a new listing in Dove Mountain. I had one client who was so right for that house. They fit the neighborhood profile. They were good, clean people. It was a bit out of their price range, but that never stopped Royce O'Rourke. I was going to pick them up, which is the professional thing to do, but they wanted to stop by Sonic on their way home and had arranged to meet me at the showing.

Good god, the ants' bicycles were out front. They rode bikes in Tucson, everywhere, which meant their clients had to drive themselves to each showing. How lame. And the nerve of them, intruding on my appointment, on my time.

And the idiot owners and their amateur housewife realtor did the so 1990s thing of baking fucking bread. Jesus. You know what really works? Honest? Fry some onions and garlic in extra virgin olive oil for a bit, then toss it down the garbage disposal. That smells like home.

The timing was all fucked up and the owners had apparently split after taking the loaf out of the bread machine, so I had to endure the ant twins little upturned noses sniffing about, and sniffing me.

I ignored them, corralled my clients, and did my utmost professional gig, testing the water pressure, assessing the resale value, calculating the closet space. I need not have to tell you that while men pay for the houses, the women buy them.

Chrissy came up to me and punched me real hard in the stomach. Like that hurt. She accused me of stepping on their turf. I pointed out that it was she and her sister who had invaded my time, and told her to buzz off.

Then I smelled it. That hint of some expensive French perfume. She was hiding, somewhere, waiting for me, waiting for my cock.

The ants eventually filed off with their granola client, who, I might add, would never, ever fit in that neighborhood. I sent my clients off to think about an offer. The wife seemed really noncommittal, damn it, but I knew we could outbid the ants. Fuck them.

They practically ruined my day with their eeping about. Eeping. I'm not sure that's a real word, but it's what they do. They don't do it out loud, oh no. They do it subsonically with their ant radar, sending nonsense to each other. Yeah, if I hadn't smelled Juliette, my day would have been a total wash.

But boy, was I ever wrong. We had sex, of course. She was hiding in the garage and made some creative use of some of the hand tools and even a couple of power tools they had in there. Oh, yeah. But then she started talking.

Talking. Why? And in that sexy French accent I only cared to hear begging me to go in deeper and faster. She said she wanted a romantic dinner. What the fuck? She knew I was married.

I started to get dressed, and, wouldn't you know, the garage door started to open. Shit. That sort of cheap chick-flick plot surprise never happens to me. But it did, so I started to run inside, but my pants fell down to my ankles and I tripped and hit my head on a vise mounted on the work table.

I didn't pass out. I was just dazed. I remembered Juliette sauntering out like she belonged there. And, horror of horrors, I saw something that will pollute every nightmare I ever have, and I, Royce O'Rourke, am not the type of man who has dreams, let alone nightmares. (Well I have dreams, but you know, the conscious kind, the dreams of success, the vision to get into the Billion Dollar Brotherhood.) But the sight of those bitch ant twins, eeping and giggling, and eeping, and pointing at me, and jumping up and down, and eeping and eeping, and so fucking eeping is something I still see. I wanted to kill them both, right then and there.

Then I thought of Miss Clarrissa, what she would think seeing me like that, laying on the concrete, my pants around my ankles, blood gushing from my forehead, and those hideous insects eeping at me.

I had to tell Rocky in the emergency room that I tripped while showing the client the garage. The owner of the house and the ants weren't at the hospital, and I was sure Rocky wouldn't check the story out later. Except they brought me in with my pants, and well, the long and short of it was that there was one more missing shirt. I wondered on the way home if the ants took it. Yeah. They probably would bury their insect noses in it and fight over who got to sleep in it.

6

Fitzroy, true to his nature, bought up a ton of those New Orleans mortgages at bargain basement prices, signed up an impressive number of holdouts for our loan renegotiation services, and got a long list of foreclosures to jump on. All in less than a week, thanks to Fitz and his cocaine. So that was looking up.

Rocky dropped one day out of our sex schedule, Monday. She claimed, in sixty sentences, how tired she was, how Roger was getting harder to handle, and that a decision had to be made soon.

Really? Not if I had my way. There was no way the future president of the Billion Dollar Brotherhood would send his son off to some institution, no siree. I let that ride.

But I was worried. With Juliette wanting a romantic dinner, and Rocky putting out less, my sexual future seemed in doubt.

The start of the new week gave me more worries. I had talked my clients into making an offer on that house in Dove Mountain where I hit my head. But I lost. To the ants. As you can imagine, that pissed me off. But what drove me absolutely insane was how those fucking bitch ants got their client in.

You'll never believe it. That's the worst of all: The unfair, underhanded, double-dealing, double-crossing, female, antlike doings. If ever I needed to use an exclamation point, it is right here.

In fact, I'm going to invent my own mark, me, Royce O'Rourke. Right here. Right now. It will be this: ◊. I know what you think that looks like, but that is the last thing on my mind right now.

So, you know how the bitch ant twins got that sale? They dared go behind my back to the neighborhood association and, get this, got them to waive and/or modify their covenants, laws cast in stone, mind you, to allow those granola buyers to put a huge fucking compost heap in the back yard. Yeah. I know. And you know what else? They got clearance to fill over the swimming pool and put a natural desert landscape there. In Tucson. Yeah. Where selling a good upper middle class house without a swimming pool is like selling a house in New England without a furnace. The resell value of that house was going to tank, drawing the whole neighborhood down with it. That's what comes from violating covenants. That's what comes from taking in those who don't belong. That neighborhood association would regret it. And to do it because of those eeping ants? Shit. My hatred for the ants expanded from the size of a modest house to a huge Disneyland castle.

All of this, of course, meant I had to come up with even more to close the gap between what I had sold and earned and what it would take to get me clearly qualified for the Billion Dollar Brotherhood. And who would have thought it? None other than my Roger showed me the way.

You see, when I got home (after I showed a house and had sex with Juliette) Rocky was on a roll. She was on the phone talking a mile a minute with exclamation points as mile markers. Oh, but I never saw her shut up so fast when she laid eyes on me. She just said "Gotta go!" and without missing a beat, hung up and bored into me.

"It's unbelievable! I've always known something like this would happen! I could see it from day one! A mile away! And it's so disgusting! I can't even talk to his teacher about it! I don't even know the words to use. I've told you, haven't I, time and time again that this would happen, that he'd do this, that he needs to be dealt with in a setting equipped to deal with him! I'm not heartless! I'm a good mother. Why couldn't you listen to me? We'll have to order out for dinner. I can't face being seen at the Safeway! I can't face being seen by the pizza man! What do we have – how about bacon and pancakes for dinner? He'd like that, for sure! I can't deal with him. You'll have to do it – and Randi had to be the one to tell me! How's your head?"

"What?" I managed to break in.

"He went missing from school – and ran into some kids from the high school! I'd better set some butter out to soften – close the screen door so the flies don't get in. Randi said they are a strange lot – that group. And what were they doing out of school?! I told you we should have an electric monitor on him or chip in him so we can track him. He wouldn't mind – he wouldn't even know it was there! Sure would have prevented this! Oh, I know why you're against it! You're afraid I'll have one put in you! He was over there! How they got there, I'll never know, but he's up in that old deserted house out east. You know. The haunted house. The one where we – well, you know. And there he was! With that lot. And there he was found!"

Then she lowered her voice, to a loud whisper that probably carried farther than her excited yelling.

"With his pants down! With his underpants down! With two sixteen-year-old girls! Who had their pants down! Randi said they aren't sluts. Well you can guess what was going on! What exploratory playing doctor game he thought it was! Lord knows – those girls had other ideas. I don't care what Randi says. They are worse than sluts. To take advantage like that! It's a good thing they were caught before it got out of hand."

"Where is he now?" I was able to insert.

"Up in his room. I haven't said –"

"Who found them?" I demanded, to stop her verbal joy ride. Had to demand to derail the train. Oh, and I, Royce O'Rourke, know what a simile and a metaphor are. I can use twenty dollar words. And I know I just mixed metaphors there, but at least they both have to do with transit.

"Father Flannigan found them and thank god –"

Her dash, not mine. Shit. I'm fucked, I thought, if Flannery O. Flannigan found Roger there, with his pants down.

Ah, but if Royce O'Rourke does anything, he looks to accentuate the positive. This little rite of passage would give me a reason to make an appointment with Father Flannery O. Flannigan.

And it got better. I tucked Roger in after pancakes, Aunt Jemima, and bacon. The O'Rourke family sometimes did breakfast for dinner.

I will not, under any circumstances, relate Roger's exact words or mock his expression. That is none of your business. I am the guilty one. Well, not guilty, but adult. I'm a free adult male. Roger is, for all intents and purposes (which Fitzroy called 'intensive purposes') a child and will not be trotted out to be displayed, and I will not demean him by attempting to recreate in my words his words and mode of expression. Oh, I know there are those clever people who would, just to show how clever they are, but I, Royce O'Rourke, refuse to display him like a circus animal.

He was my son, and from day one I vowed to protect him with all the power and resources at my disposal.

In essence, he told me he became disoriented, asked these strange sixteen-year-olds for help, and they took him there, in their car, to that deserted place, and he only did what he was told to do. But I also knew that 'boys' like Roger are considered in the ordinary beauty-salon-going, Safeway-express-line enforcing, middle class set to be so cute, until he showed some sign of sexual maturity, then he would be something to be feared, something next door to those people's daughters going out with a black guy or a Mexican. They'd never say it out loud, but they would be thinking it. I knew. I sold them their homes. I was involved in the most critical, most intimate thing to them, their homes, and I knew.

But I'm missing the biggest thing to come out of all this. That deserted house. Good ol' Roger and that house. It's more than a house. There's the huge mansion with a labyrinth basement, unusual for this area, and several out buildings. It is almost a deserted town, a ghost town.

It wasn't until I became a successful realtor that I thought about why it was never razed and developed into an outlet mall or an artists colony. The major problem is access. It is on the other side of the Catalinas and to provide the roads, the electricity, the sewage, the water, oh, the water, would be prohibitively expensive. I like that expression. Some stupid high school legends have it that there is an Indian burial ground under it, that a Mexican witches coven used to use it, that a strange hybrid coyote haunts it, you name it. Thing is, it isn't a viable location. Or so I had thought.

Now, I'm nothing if not creative◊ My dad, one time, when he was drunk, told me that he was driving through southwestern Kansas once, and found a whore house in the middle of nowhere, in a remote town, off a dead-end road. I was disgusted, of course, but the message was not lost on me. Remote places are ideal for such businesses. Obviously, unless you are in Nevada, you can't call them whore houses, but you can open an adult toy shop or something and the unspoken is understood.

Thus was born my master plan, to buy the haunted house and environs, and transform them into an oasis of adult pleasures that would draw men from Tucson, Phoenix, hell, even Albuquerque, or at least Las Cruces. (Why are the place names around here such a bitch to spell?) Insane? I think not. And Father Flannery O. Flannigan would be just the one to help me.

7

It was not hard at all for me, Royce O'Rourke, to get an audience with Father Flannery O. Flannigan. I was not, yet, in the Billion Dollar Brotherhood, but I was known as a successful realtor, Rotarian, PTA, and church and neighborhood leader. I got in fast, too, the next day, after I calmed Rocky down and told her I would talk to Roger's school too.

Flannery O. Flannigan had an office, separate from his church, on Oracle. I met him there before lunch.

I had only been there once before, with Fitzroy, and the place was just as I remembered. Excessively air conditioned, a sign of power. Framed glossy pictures of the properties he was representing, and these were of the best, most expensive places in the Tucson area. He had seven agents working for him, all of them almost as good as me, and worth a hundred ant twins. To maintain his status, Flannery O. Flannigan had just to close the occasional big deal and take his cut from all the deals his agents brought in.

He was waiting for me, a nice gesture, and he invited me into his private office. It was really nice: Plush red carpet, dark paneled walls, a huge mahogany desk with no computer or laptop on it, and a massive leather chair for him. The room was so big it held a regulation pool table. Fitzroy said once that the pool balls were made of gold, but they weren't out. I really doubted that story. Gold pool balls would be too heavy to play right.

Flannigan beckoned me to sit down. I jumped right in, thanking him for finding Roger the other day. I decided to be careful bringing up my idea for transforming that deserted ghost town into a bordello. I hadn't even told Fitzroy yet. I didn't want Flannigan to move in on the idea, and in spite of his being in realtor mode, it just didn't seem right to ask a priest for advice on turning a ghost town into a sex emporium. Not right away, anyway. I had to work up to it strategically.

It occurred to me to ask why he was there in the first place, when he found Roger. But that seemed too forward, for the moment. Shit. Flannigan had this power to make me uncharacteristically nervous.

He relieved me by asking how Roger was doing, how proud he was of Randi's catechism, and on and on. Then he got down to business with a question that surprised me:

"So O'Rourke, why do you think you are a good fit for the Billion Dollar Brotherhood?"

I just said that I had always thought there could be mutual benefits to me being in the Billion Dollar Brotherhood. Benefits to them. Benefits to me. Or something like that.

He just looked at me and cocked his eye. Surely he was not trying to discourage me. To keep me from getting discouraged, I thought of Miss Clarrissa and her prophesy. Then I risked it and told him I had two big deals under wraps and would rake in well over a billion, and that left my membership in no doubt at all.

Then he laughed. At me. At Royce O'Rourke. He said that selling over a billion was not the sole requirement for membership. As if I didn't know that. I went with it. I told him that I was a well respected family man, was a member of the Rotary, was active in my church, volunteered for special needs children (a clever way to bring Roger back into the picture) and that I had big ideas and real ambition. I stopped short of telling him that it was also foretold by a voodoo priestess shaman.

But he went on about the rigorous selection process, the long application, the required supporting documentation, the vetting committee, and the need for a sponsor.

I didn't know why he was still saying all this. I refused to believe he would try to discourage me. That's not allowable. That's inconceivable. Let me explain my situation at that point in my life, where I was coming from, what was going through my mind.

I don't expect stuff to be handed to me on a silver platter. I work hard for what I get. Like I told Flannigan, I do all the right stuff. All the stuff expected of me as a leader in the business community and the community at large. I'm a family man. I sleep around, sure, but only with Juliette, and all the guys do it. Those that don't are losers and followers and Flannigan knows that. He himself is not so innocent in that respect and he knows I know that.

Now I ask you, what else could I do? Then it occurred to me that maybe he heard about my losing that Dove Mountain sale. But that was to the stupid ants. Surely that couldn't count against me. So I told him none of the application stuff was a problem for me. And I told him Fitzroy would be my sponsor, to let him know I was willing to play.

"I don't mean to discourage you, O'Rourke," he said. "But you must also know we have a strict limit on the number of new members we can take in."

"So?" I dared.

"The fact of the matter is we are seriously considering two very unique candidates already."

"Two?" I said. No, it couldn't be.

"I'm not at liberty to say, but surely you know them and when I say two I could just as easily have said twins."

"Not the ant twins◊" I said, yeah, exclaimed in stunned surprise.

"Ants?" he said, clearly puzzled.

"Chrissy and Crystal Diamond?" I asked.

"Ah, well, I can't say, of course, but you are, as always, near the mark."

He winked. Winked. At me. At Royce O'Rourke.

"If it's them, it's the end of the Brotherhood," I said, and emphasized the word 'brother.'

"You think so?" he said. Honestly, you'd think he thought he was the fucking Pope.

"I know so," I rejoined. And continued. "You need men in the Brotherhood who know how to play. How to deal. How to work the system. Not some amateurs with time to kill who are full willing to skirt covenants and bring down property values."

"All true," he said. Then he sighed. "O'Rourke, you are right, and you know I hold you in high regard. But, alas, times are changing, have changed, and we, the Brotherhood, are lagging behind. The old ways of doing things, well, let's just say we need new blood to prime us for the new millennium."

What a lot of New Age bullshit nonsense. I didn't say that, of course. I didn't want to continue this line of the, conversation; argument is too strong a word for it, so I used the reliable O'Rourke rule: Exit with a challenge – best way to push a squeamish buyer into closing a deal he can't afford to close. Oh damn, I used a dash back there.

"That may be," I said. "But it means nothing. No one can be anyone without a proven track record of big impressive sales. I wouldn't move too fast, if I were you. I'm about to, within weeks, unveil two big, new, visionary deals that will lead the Brotherhood on a path to the twenty-second century◊"

I was mighty proud of that, I admit. It was the honest truth, more or less, spoken with force. Flannigan seemed to like it too. He rose up, shook my hand, and said "O'Rourke, I wait with bated breath to see what you reveal."

Semi-score, I say.

I went there to thank him for saving Roger and for insinuating myself into his good graces to get into the Billion Dollar Brotherhood. If I don't say so myself, I admire my success and self-awareness in all that. And it worked to my advantage, after he showed his hand, to keep blind my bordello idea.

But.

Yeah, but.

There.

All about me.

But mostly stalking behind me.

Eeping.

Eeping and Eeping.

Those insects.

Ants.

As much as I semi-scored and should have been pumped to realize my dreams, I was being brought down low, low to the ground, tied from limb to limb, and all over me the ants were crawling and eeping. Eep. Eep. Eep. Everywhere. All on and about me. They were crawling over my face, up my nose, in my ears. Eeping and laughing. At me. At Royce O'Rourke

If I hated them before, I despised and wanted them dead now. No. Not dead. Crushed. Stamped out. Obliterated. Now don't get me wrong. I wasn't planning to go out and get a gun and shoot their smug faces to smithereens. No. That's not me. That's not Royce O'Rourke. What I would do, must do, instead, was make my dreams come true. Cash in on the New Orleans mortgages and turn the ghost town into a thriving adult amusement park. That would get me in, earn me my rightful place in the Billion Dollar Brotherhood. That would make those hideous, evil ants irrelevant. Yeah.

8

When I got to the office, I told Fitzroy about how the ants had bewitched Flannigan and were plotting to get into the Brotherhood. He laughed. I thought it funny telling him too. Stupid covenant-breaking ants thinking they could get into the organization that safeguards the master covenants. Only Fitzroy was laughing because he was coked out. Then he stopped laughing and told me he heard the ant twins were at that very moment showing one of their loser clients a prime property in Saguaro Ranch that I was scheduled to show my client, the one who lost the Dove Mountain bid. Fuck.

I decided to beat them at their own game. I called my clients and told them to get going <u>now</u>. I'm not sure about underlining, so I'll let that stay. They bitched that they hadn't had lunch yet. Jesus. I told them I'd buy them lunch after the showing and that I'd pick them up in ten minutes. I thanked Fitzroy for the tip and told him I'd be back later to go over the details of the New Orleans deal. Right now, the important thing was to beat the ants at their own game and restore the reputation of Royce O'Rourke, who never loses to insects.

Truth is, my clients weren't too keen on that house. It was out of their price range. Ah, but they had nothing to fear, not with Royce O'Rourke on the case. I was pumped. I was on fire. I was primed. I was motivated.

They wanted to stop by Sonic on the way. I wouldn't have it. I wanted those eeping ants to know Royce O'Rourke was on to their game.

Sure enough, they were surprised to see me, Royce O'Rourke, rolling in on them.

One of the ants – shit! (you couldn't tell them apart so it didn't matter which one) glared at me and said I was being rude and intruding on their time.

I so rightly pointed out they did the same to me last week when they cheated and broke long-standing covenants.

She eeped to me that it wasn't their fault. That the seller put the showings too close together so that it was almost an open house, "if not open garage" she eeped, just to spite me.

"How's your head, Royce?" the other one jeered at me.

Fuck her.

I directed my clients to go look at the kitchen, since they were so hungry.

The ant who insulted me grabbed her clients and headed that way too. Ha.

Chrissy stayed behind. I think it was she (HA! Shit. Ha. I used "she" not "her," which is incorrect and something the ants would say) but it doesn't matter which one it was. I mean, take a look at a hundred ants invading the deck of some ill-maintained lower class home, and try to tell them apart. Yeah.

Anyway, she punched me in the stomach and said I was playing dirty pool.

I didn't descend to her level. I just looked down at her petite, insect stature and laughed at her. I told her it was an honest mistake.

Then she realized whom she was dealing with. She eeped in a low voice:

"Royce, we should team up and crack the Phoenix market, don't you think?"

I told her I didn't, surely, need their help and they were too far out of my league to be worthy of my help.

"Well, your loss, Royce, because we are already big in Maricopa County and are going to be in the Billion Dollar Brotherhood while you ply your old, used, tired trade in Tucson."

Those were her exact words to me. To Royce O'Rourke. To the man who is brokering a huge deal in New Orleans, which would make even the biggest deal in Phoenix look like selling a tree house, and who is going to challenge the whole State of Nevada with his brilliant bordello bonanza. I so wanted to say all that to that twat. That fucking bitch. I wanted to say how much bigger I was in all respects to her. I wanted to impress her with the image of me dealing and moving and shaping hundreds of miles away in a really cool city like New Orleans, not fucking Phoenix. I wanted to tell her that I would be the president of the Billion Dollar Brotherhood, that it was foretold, preordained. I thought of Miss Clarrissa. I got a little bit aroused, as much as one could in front of an eeping ant insect, and then I spat in her filthy fucking face.

She looked startled, then like she was about to run bawling to mommy, then really fucking mad.

"Oh, you'll be sorry for that, Royce O'Rourke. You'll be so, so sorry," she said and ran into the kitchen, making one too many a cook.

I had to laugh, except my clients came out, frustrated and wanting food. I forced them to look over the rest of the house. The ants used their subsonic radar to evade me as I took my clients from room to room. Damn. Even I could hear their stomachs growling when we finished. I left the ants to scurry about in their insect insignificance while I drove my clients to Sonic, paid for their lunch, then drove them home.

All while they were eating and on the drive home I played up the advantages of that house. I stressed how the neighborhood would be the most exclusive in Tucson, how the house would appreciate, but only if they got in now, and how loans were still so easy to get. I even told them Fitzroy had a mortgage arm I was sure would qualify them on my recommendation, no questions asked. I worked them hard, doing my damnedest.

And you know what? They wanted to make an offer. I quickly wrote it up in their living room. I decided then and there to add this new tactic to my arsenal. Starve your clients, show the house, then fill them full of hamburgers. That made them very receptive to my charms.

Then I went back to the house, horny as hell, happy to find the ants pedaling away on their bicycles.

I went back in, honestly, to look around to ensure my bid was in order, since I hadn't seen the kitchen. Then I smelled that expensive perfume. I followed it upstairs, but couldn't find her. I looked and looked until I saw her outside in the back, under a mesquite tree. The house was on an acre of land and had a six-foot high privacy wall, so the risk was minimal. I went out to greet her.

She was dressed all in leather, at least where she was covered, and held a whip. I don't get into kink, I really don't, especially knowing about the stuff mom and dad kept hidden in their bedroom. On the other hand, Juliette, the thing about her, she always kept it different, exciting, unpredictable. Not the boring scheduled crap with Rocky, for whom a new set of scented votive candles constituted variety. Juliette tried, not that she had to.

She cracked the whip and ordered me to strip. I did. She put a blindfold on me and told me to raise my arms. I did.

Then I felt cold hard metal around my left wrist, followed by the sound of a series of sharp ticks, then a final, authoritative click. I didn't like that.

She did the same with my right wrist. My mouth was dry.

Juliette gently trailed the end of the whip down my stomach to my cock, which ... well, I, Royce O'Rourke do hereby confess that I, Royce O'Rourke, for the first time, ever, had lost an erection.

That wouldn't do. I tried to take my mind off my dad, doing this to my mom, tried hard, because what Juliette was doing to my cock felt good, so I thought of Miss Clarrissa. I couldn't see her chained up, so I rushed to the ants, the Chrissy one, and thought of her, that stupid, short, upturned nose, buck-toothed, small breasted insect, and thought of me chaining her up like I was.

My dick got rock hard. Yeah, it was working. I thought of myself, in control, as that piss ant was writhing, pulling, and twisting under my dominance. I thought of her disgusting insect shell hammered and shattered off of her, leaving the acrid acid pulp that constituted her being, exposed. Exposed to my power. I pulled hard on the cuffs. I jerked my body about. I even pulled in and made an eeping sound.

Juliette cracked the whip, then brought it down on my ass. I thought, hard, of that exposed, humiliated pulp of an ant feeling my cock beat her down, beating that pulp hard into the ground.

Oh, ah, ouch◊ Juliette was doing something. She was pushing something she had lubed up, the whip handle, up my ass. It hurt. For a bit.

I thought of that vile ant, twisting and writhing, feeling my power thrust in, through, all commanding, the ant feeling totally vulnerable, violated, vanquished, and ultimately vindicated by me, Royce O'Rourke.

Oh, she was sucking my cock now, while bringing her hand around and twisting the whip handle.

It felt so good.

No. The ant can't feel this.

No.

The ant can't have this.

I was now me, and that wet mass of ant pulp was wrapped around my penis, serving me – oh. No. A dash.

I saw her. I tried not to. But she, her buck-toothed, upturned nose face flashed before me, eeping.

I lost it. Limp. That fucking cunt.

Juliette stopped sucking, and gently pulled the whip handle out of my ass. She took off the blindfold, kissed me, then released me from the cuffs, which were on chains attached to ring hooks driven into a large branch of the tree.

I offered to help her take them down, until she told me they were already there when she got there. Oh.

Most homeowners, when they sell, decontaminate the house. You know, they remove stuff they're ashamed of and put in prominent places stuff they think will impress a buyer. Thing is, they usually get it backward. The stuff they hide is usually the crap that will attract people like them. After all, the buyer is looking to move into a neighborhood where the people are like them. And the buyers' income dictates that they look at houses in neighborhoods just like theirs. So more often than not, they are put off by the pretentious crap left in view. If only they could see the real stuff that makes them comfortable. It's the stupid baking bread thing all over again. I mean, who the fuck bakes bread every day? Every week? Every month? But who fries onions for their hamburgers, their sauce, their chili, their hot dogs, their patty melts, their roast? Everyone. Fucking everyone, all the fucking time. That's what sells. That's what works.

Most realtors, typified by the ants, don't know this. They advise their customers to bake bread, paint all the walls white, make the kitchen look like an operating room, make the bathroom look like a sauna no one can afford, snuff out every bit of life to the point where they might as well sell an empty house. All this fucking ant crap about staging, like it's some stupid community theater thing put on by people who spell theater like theatre.

No. It doesn't work. The way I do it works.

Juliette and I were getting dressed, and out came the repetition, most disappointing in her. She still wanted a romantic dinner with me. OK. Sure. What woman wouldn't? But why?

She wanted to talk. I must admit, I love her French accent, so much preferable to Rocky's exclamation points and the ants' pathetic eeping. Yeah, it's nice to hear her say "Go." "Yes." "Cum." "I like thees." "Here." That stuff.

But she didn't want to talk out there in "zee hot zun." She wanted dinner. Twice she'd asked for that. That's not right. She's supposed to appear looking beautiful, fuck me silly, then go away. The perfect relationship. And now she wanted to fuck it up with dinner.

I knew it was a mistake, sure enough. On the other hand, I sensed the risk that if I didn't take her to dinner, she would stop appearing. So I said "yes." I could always tell Rocky it was a business dinner, and if it came to it, Fitzroy would back me up.

She was overjoyed, almost relieved by the news. I set it for next Friday, a sex day with Rocky that would have to be missed, which would serve Rocky right for taking a day out of our sex schedule.

9

My ass felt a bit sore on the drive back to the office. I tried to take my mind off my ass by logically assessing where I was.

Point. I lost that Dove Mountain sale – because – damn! Oh shit◊ Two dashes and an exclamation point to boot. OK. I lost that sale because the ants fucking cheated, and stomped their weak, useless legs, all twelve of them (as ants have six legs each), all over the natural order of things.

Point. I was not happy with the way it turned out with Flannery O. Flannigan and how he thought the stupid ass ants could take my appointed, anointed place, predicted even, in the Billion Dollar Brotherhood.

Point. I had lost trust in Flannigan. But Flannigan was the key to the Brotherhood, so I still had to deal with him, but much more carefully. Good for me that I didn't tell him about my bordello idea.

Point. I must not let any of them get the better of me. I know I'm the top dog and will act as such.

Point. Enough dreaming of the bordello. It was time for action. I would do that immediately.

And when I returned to the office, I did just that. Fitzroy had gone out, which gave me time to work uninter-rupted. I researched the land plots and titles to see who owned the land containing the ghost town. I expected it to belong to Pima County since there was nothing there and nothing to be done with it. Curiously, it wasn't deeded to the county but to something called Monstrance Holdings. How appropriate.

My idea was to approach them, posing as an environmentalist, and take it off their hands. I would say I wanted to make it into a nature habitat to conserve the natural and cultural landscape, yadda, yadda. Why on earth they would want to keep it was beyond me.

I started researching this "Monstrance Holdings" but could find nothing on it, which was strange. It was a strange sounding name, too, like a bunch of monsters owned it. Probably someone's idea of a joke, given the history of the place. Then it struck me that maybe this was a recent acquisition, that maybe someone wanted to turn it into a deserted desert theme park. Nah. Wouldn't work, and I would have heard of it. After all, I, Royce O'Rourke, was plugged in to the market forces. I would have known.

Fitzroy came back. He had just completed a commercial sale downtown, a tiny one, but was pumped over it anyway.

Fitzroy and I shared in the business, but kept a clear accounting of who sold what for tax purposes and then later so we could track for purposes of substantiating our credits for getting into the Billion Dollar Brotherhood, although I was far more qualified, and honest.

We ran an independent business, and were not affiliated with some usurious agency like Century 21, or Coldwell Banker, or Prudential, or RE/MAX, you know. Nothing wrong with them, except they are for loser housewife realtors who know no better and need help with business cards, signs, smocks, financing, and contract arbitration. No one can hope to get into the Brotherhood working in one of those places. I mean, they are the Wal-

Mart of real estate. Fitz and I were among the exclusive boutiques. And I knew for a fact the ant twins started at Century 21 before going out on their own. They tried to hide the fact, but in vain: It was written all over them. And their fanny packs. And their bicycles.

Fitzroy and I ran a lean shop. We had one receptionist, Darleen, a part-time accountant, Andy, and five crack agents. Fitz and I did all the big sales, brokered all the top drawer deals. We were known, and feared, in the market because we swam with the sharks and ran like cheetahs. I wanted to make a slogan out of that a few years ago. Fitz didn't like the idea. He said it was for the Century 21 types, not for an exclusive agency like ours. Of course, he was right. Like he was right about the Montblanc. Like he was right about the New Orleans deal.

Boy, was he ever right about the New Orleans deal. And how◊ Fitzroy also had big news. He had been shopping our mortgages and pending foreclosure deals around and found a channel that would bundle all those assets and instruments for us with a big pool of other ones, with a very favorable profit for us. And they were ready to move fast.

I couldn't believe the luck of it. And you won't believe who the broker was. Never. Never in a million years. Oh, OK. I gave you a big hint earlier. Yes, you are right. It was Monstrance Holdings.

Fitzroy didn't know any more about them than I did. That disappointed me. I mean if Fitzroy didn't know, who would?

Aha. I thought of asking Flannery O. Flannigan. He would know, even if I trusted him less. Plus, oh plus, I could demonstrate to him how big an international player I was to counteract the ant witchcraft that had ensnared him. That meant thinking big, so I hit on the idea of asking him to the house for dinner.

I didn't expect Rocky to be such a bitch about it. She liked him, right? He was her priest. But when I told her that evening, she was all pissy about it.

"This week? Talk about short notice! And who is going to clean the place up? What on earth do I have to wear? We've gotten out of the entertainment circuit. Thanks to you know who and you know what! I have no idea what he likes to eat! And Randi's at the age where – oh, you can just imagine she'd kill to shock him with some pithy insult against the faith."

"I'll ask him on Friday, so we can just do fish," I offered.

So important was this dinner with Flannigan that I forgot I had promised dinner with Juliette on Friday. Funny, but Rocky saved me.

"Friday? Friday? That's the first of the month. He'll have First Friday Mass – yeah, oh make it Friday and he won't show up and we're stuck eating friggin' fish in the desert. If you have to do this, if you have to go ahead with this silly plan, do it on Wednesday or Thursday."

Which meant I would lose another sex night if it were Wednesday. I could see her mind working and didn't bother to point out that First Friday Mass was the next week and is done during the day, if done at all around here.

"Yes! Thursday would be the only chance!" Rocky said. I had just tuned her back in, relieved to discover she had agreed and even arrived at a date on her own.

"And give me time to prepare! We could do shrimp – AJ's has some good sources for that. And then I can slow cook a prime rib! OK. Yes! But you need to figure out how to keep Roger in check. I'll have a little talk with Randi."

I tried to tell her not to worry about Randi. After all, Father Flannigan said how impressed he was with her catechism. Bad move there.

"Impressed? Impressed! He was being extremely charitable! Extremely! You never took the time to inquire, did you – oh no – too fixated on Roger you have been, at your daughter's expense. I know he needs extra special attention, Roar, but – to tell the truth – you are neglecting your daughter and the relationship between a father and his daughter is a special one. She's already turning against me. And where will you be for her? Huh? Roger's hit a brick wall! He's not getting any better – just the opposite! And the older he gets – well! Our guest of honor knows all about that one! The shame of it! And Randi will need you – to be sure! Do you know what she did? During her lessons at the church? She's having her head filled by that damned progressive teacher at school with evolution and the big bang and cultural relativism, and she's questioning Genesis, taking it so literally, like she was at some joke of a Baptist church, and lumping the Catholic faith with these backward religions that haven't reconciled science with faith, talking to her priest as if he were some fundamentalist nut case! Then she went on some feminist rant about no women in the priesthood but plenty of pretty boys! I don't care how much – or little – truth there is in that, but certainly not here! And certainly not with Father Flannigan! I can just imagine how offended he was! You really think he'll come to dinner on such short notice? Maybe I should send her over to the Pruitt's for the evening."

Well, there was some valuable, but oppressive information in that ramble. So Randi tried to show how smart and well-informed she is, and in the process, fucked up my shot at getting into the Billion Dollar Brotherhood. That was not good. Not good. Lucky that I knew then and could be full aware of it to do damage control at dinner with Flannigan.

Then I got another tirade about Roger and how I hadn't talked to his teacher yet. Well, Rocky did accommodate me by agreeing to dinner with Flannigan, so the least I could do was go talk to Roger's teacher. I promised to do that the next day. It was the right thing to do for an ascending star of the Billion Dollar Brotherhood.

10

I, Royce O'Rourke, go to church. I didn't, well, I did believe Miss Clarrissa's prophesy, but only because it had to be true anyway. What I'm getting at is that I don't believe in fate. Yet there it was, staring me in the face when I went to Roger's school the next morning to talk to his teacher.

You see, Rocky always handled parent/teacher conferences. (I'll have to think about that slash mark.) And wouldn't you know, the one time I go myself, there was Juliette, no, not his teacher, his teacher's aide, sitting in the classroom, watching the kids, while I had to talk to the real teacher, an ugly old thing, yes, but very apologetic about Roger getting away. Her aide, you see, wasn't there at the time, and things got busy, and yeah, yadda, yeah. The poor woman had no idea I was fucking her aide when Roger ran off.

She, Juliette, played it cool. She pretended not to notice me, and in fact, distracted Roger so he wouldn't see me. That was weird.

It got me thinking. I mean, did she know? She had to, if she connected me with Roger. Well, well. I was now looking forward to dinner with her.

As to his old crone of a teacher, I could hardly complain about Roger going missing and thereby get Juliette in trouble. I just told her I wanted to congratulate the school on how well Roger was doing and that his progress was due in no small part to his teachers, plural.

Once I got to the office, I put in a call to Flannery O. Flannigan. He seemed quite eager to come to dinner on Thursday. Very eager and pleased, in fact. That boded well for me, Royce O'Rourke. The day was shaping into a mighty fine one.

I wanted to corner Fitzroy when he got in to find out more about Monstrance Holdings and when to expect the New Orleans revenue. I wanted to know that before dinner with Flannigan. And, I wanted in my hands the title for the bordello land so I would have that safe in my pocket for Flannery O. Flannigan.

I was all antsy. Fitzroy was late, probably scoring some snatch, or a hit of coke, keeping me, me, Royce O'Rourke, waiting. I pulled up the MLS listings to kill time. I was in the middle of looking at all the ants' pathetic listings when I heard, everyone heard, the squeal of tires screeching to a sudden stop. A sharp shot. Then another. Then a car door slamming and the squeal of tires protesting against a too fast start.

Darleen screamed. I got up, went to the window, and saw a man laying on the sidewalk, the hot sidewalk, basting in an expanding pool of blood.

Funny. You know who it is, but you refuse to believe it. I knew. I recognized the suit. The hair, what was left of it.

Funny too. Several people had run out to look, got only so close, and stood back, at least five feet from the pooling blood, knowing there was nothing they could do, but wanting, needing to appear to be doing something.

On cue, seven cell phones emerged and the emergency 911 system got those seven calls plus the one Darleen was making, choking with tears.

I just stared out the window, as the seven, in unison, stepped back from the spreading blood. And I thought.

Fitzroy and I had agreed to split the New Orleans deal fifty/fifty. Far be it for Fitzroy to cut me some slack, even though he was already in the Billion Dollar Brotherhood, to give me the lion's share, like a good Brother should. But now that he was laying in a pool of his own blood. Oh, a dash would be really good here, because the name of my bordello came to me just then. The Blood Brothers Bordello. Yeah◊ That's what I'd call it, my bordello. That, and the New Orleans deal, all of it was one hundred percent mine. All the credits for the Brotherhood would be mine.

And then it hit me. Flannigan said they had limited space. Yes. When he was taunting me with the improbable, no, the impossible idea that the stupid slut ants could get in, he said so. He said they had quotas. Well, one vacant space had just opened up. Three, really, as the ants had as much hope as poor Fitzroy to get in now. Not with me, Royce O'Rourke, coming at them so full of power, not with me holding all the cards, the New Orleans deal, the bordello land, oh, yeah, and I'd see Flannery O. Flannigan on Thursday. This was so good.

Police sirens. The wail of an ambulance. The ring of a phone. Darleen handed it to me. It was the agent for that house in Saguaro Ranch. They had accepted the bid I made for my hungry clients. Unfuckingbelievable◊

I called my clients, told them I was coming over. With papers to sign. I was firing on all cylinders. All eight. No puny Japanese hybrid economy car me, Royce O'Rourke.

They started talking and hemming and hawing and I told them to shut the fuck up and wait for me.

Darleen had plucked up the courage to go outside. She was talking to the paramedics who were putting a white sheet over Fitzroy's face. He was put in the ambulance, leaving a lake of blood behind on the hot sidewalk. I made a mental note to have Darleen arrange to get it cleaned up. Blood. Bad for business, the real estate business, that is.

Then another spark flashed in the O'Rourke brain. Miss Clarrissa's prophesy that Fitzroy would die this week at the hands of his brothers. And there his blood was. It had pooled in a shape that reminded me of Miss Clarrissa's ass. So sweet. So hot, on that steaming sidewalk. Was this her magic? No. It was my fortune.

Yes, Fortune. All came to me. All assured my way into the Billion Dollar Brotherhood.

I grabbed my jacket, my stylish linen jacket that proved I, Royce O'Rourke, was immune to the Tucson heat, and I grabbed my Montblanc pen, the one Fitz told me to get, helped me select in LA. I walked out front, patted Darleen on the back, side stepped the congealing muck of blood, and got in my car to make the deal. The deal. It lives. It transcends all. It is eternity. The covenants. The contracts. Business. Rolls on. As did I, Royce O'Rourke. I looked in my rearview mirror, back down the street, at the police cars, at the ambulance pulling out without using its siren, at Darleen sobbing.

Poor Fitz. Poor Fitzroy.

Those stupid clients. They hemmed and hawed some more until I turned on the O'Rourke charm, told them they belonged there, told them the house spoke their name, told them the property values would keep appreciating into infinity, hinted at their increased status in that neighborhood, under those covenants. Oh hell, I pulled out all the stops until they fucking signed the papers. Take that you fucking, covenant-breaking ants.

I signed the contracts, took them to the selling agent for her signature, that hot babe with RE/MAX who was no fucking ant, then headed home to Rocky.

On the way, it occurred to me that I could use Fitzroy's killing as an excuse to have dinner with Juliette. I could tell Rocky the cops wanted background information from me. I wasn't sure how convincing that would be. Cops do work at night. The one inconvenience Fitzroy's death would cause for me was the loss of a reliable, fool-proof alibi. No loss. On the trajectory I was on now, nothing could stop me.

11

As I pulled into the garage, I regretted not having a way to contact Miss Clarrissa. I wanted her to know her prophesy came true. I wanted to hear her reaction. Walking into the kitchen, I wondered if she had a web site. After Rocky went to bed, I would Google it.

Rocky went on and on about Flannery O. Flannigan accepting and what she'd need from the store, how much money it would cost, could I go to AJ's tomorrow and get shrimp, artichokes, asparagus, and frisée, and would I talk to Roger, and how did it go with his teacher, and she had already told Randi to behave and OH! What? – NO! – Oh, my god!"

I had managed to butt in and tell her about Fitzroy being shot to death outside the office.

"Did you see it? Oh my god! How horrible! Who did it? Why? I always knew he was a shady character! But this! Oh Roar, you are so lucky you weren't caught in the cross-fire! – He doesn't have any family, does he? Who's taking care of the arrangements? Did you talk to the police? Do they have any leads? –"

"As a matter of fact," I managed to insert, "I had a sale to close and arranged to meet them Friday. Friday night. They should have some leads by then, and are going to be in forensics all day Friday, but really need to talk to me, since I was his partner."

"What about Thursday?"

"Not with Father Flannigan coming. I'll need all day, and so will you to prepare for that."

"No. I meant should we cancel Thursday?"

"Cancel? Are you mad? No. Fitzroy would have wanted it."

"OK. Oh, oh, how awful – here, hold this, I'll turn on the news!"

She gave me a bowl of potato salad she had been holding the whole time and went into the entertainment room to get the local news. She had to, for there is no great room in the O'Rourke house.

I don't know what's wrong with American culture, I really don't. House after house after house these days has these monstrous configurations known as "great rooms." Fully a third of the livable space is cut open and put under a cathedral ceiling, combining the kitchen, casual dining area, and general living arrangements in the same open space. Yes, oh yes, scum like the ants put in big, bold type in all their listings: "Lotsa Large Open Space!" "Open Layout!" "Huge Kitchen Opening into Massive Great Room!" Yeah, fuck that.

People buying here, in Tucson, buying for the first time, are transplants from LA, San Francisco, Chicago, and other points east. They have no clue what they are in for, coming to these massive open layouts with stucco walls and tiled floors. Oh, but they soon find out. They have to turn the TV up really loud to cancel out the echoes. They have to yell at each other over the dinner table. They have to endure the smell of cooking while watching TV, playing cards, reading a book, or listening to the stereo. They have to endure the clanging and crashing of pots and pans, the deafening whirl of the food processor, the motors in the microwave and convection ovens, and the fucking garbage disposal. Hell, you can even hear the refrigerator refill the ice maker in those echo chambers. And so much for running even the quietest dishwasher if you want to watch TV after dinner.

They are an expensive, impossible to fix concession to a middle class value system that equates large open spaces with a sense of freedom and accomplishment. I always had to bite my tongue when selling one of those houses.

You'd better bet that the O'Rourke family do not live in such a monstrosity. No siree. I spec'd our house to have a formal living room, a theater style entertainment room, a nice dining room with chair rails, a fully equipped, closed kitchen with a large breakfast nook, and real honest-to-god hallways. We live in peace and quiet.

Rocky came back and said there was only a brief mention of Fitz and that the police were investigating. Of course, she had to tell me this because I could not hear the TV from the kitchen, which is as it should be. And the news report was just like I said. That played perfectly into my alibi to cover meeting Juliette.

After dinner, Rocky sat down in the kitchen to work on the menus for the Flannigan dinner. I went to my study, closed the door, and turned on my computer. I searched for "Miss Clarissa, New Orleans" on Google. First thing I got was "Do you mean miss clarissa, new orleans?" No, because that ended up giving me one less result. And that result was the one. It led me to a page with a dark purple background with yellow stars and green symbols. There was a picture of her, and it was she (I got that grammar right), but heavily made up. She had these long, heavy eye lashes, and deep purple eye shadow with silver sparkles in it. Her lips were deep purple, and her skin looked bronzed in a way that accentuated her cheekbones. I was getting hard, so I scrolled down to a blurb of text under her photo:

Suffering under a hex or spell?
Know a loved one with sleeping sickness?
Feel the evil wind at your back?
Need to know the future?
Care to explore your past?
Need amulets of protection?
OR
Has someone cheated on you?
Has someone spited or disrespected you?
Need to put a curse on someone?
Need to zombify a rival or enemy?
Need potions and poisons?

GO SOMEWHERE ELSE.

I am Miss Clarrissa,
Most High Queen and
Voodoo Priestess Shaman.

SERIOUS INQUIRIES ONLY

She had her email address linked under that. And no exclamation points or dashes.

I clicked on the link and, using my secret gmail account, sent her the following message:

"Most high powerful Miss Clarrissa, Voodoo Priestess Shaman. This is red Royce, the man who fucked you. Your prophesy about my friend came true today. He was shot dead outside our office. Twice. Now, the other prophesy, the one about me, is about to come true soon. Very soon.

"You may keep my shirt. Consider it payment for services rendered. For the prophesies, not the sex."

That last bit was cheeky, I know, but she was so pretentious I felt she deserved it.

It was shortly after I sent that email that I saw something that sent a chill down my spine. Another email. From Fitzroy. I sat and stared at it in my inbox.

It was titled "Mine." I couldn't open it. I just stared at the address and the time.

"There you are! Jesus, you look like you've just seen a ghost! What have you been doing in here? It's way past time to put Roger to bed."

Rocky. How long had I been sitting there staring?

"I sold a house today. Just emailing the other agent. I'm done now."

"I have the menus all ready! And I've made a list of things for you to get at AJ's. I can get the rest at Safeway. If you can be home most of tomorrow, especially before he comes, that would be a big help. It would make all the difference, Roar. This is your dinner, really, so you need to help out! Oh, I'll do my best, but it's been so long since we've entertained properly. Not since – well, you know. Who knows, maybe this will start something. Come on. It's late!"

I got up and noticed my shirt had been sticking to the back of the chair, even though the AC was on. Rocky was in front of me, so she didn't notice how drenched I was.

Roger was impatient for me, so I played a little session of our "Who's the Winner" game, in which we play rock, paper, scissors until he tires out. Once he did, we said his prayers. After he asked god to bless me, I had him add "And god bless Fitzroy."

I told Rocky I needed a shower before bed. It had been a long eventful day, so she didn't question it.

I made it lukewarm. I stood in the pounding spray and let it wash over me. It felt so good. I tried to put that email out of my mind and thought positive thoughts. My Blood Brothers Bordello. The New Orleans deal. All of it, and all of it mine. Father Flannery O. Flannigan having dinner in this very house. Yeah. Score. That big Saguaro Ranch sale and losing it with Juliette outside, chained to a mesquite tree. And I was aware of my cock. I made the water hotter and thought of that sexy RE/MAX agent. Yeah. I was hard. I jerked off thinking of her signing the deal with my cock, then sucking it dry to seal the deal. Yeah. Oh, yeah. That was good.

I rinsed off. As I dried, I couldn't help but think of that email. Maybe I saw the time wrong. Maybe I just imagined it being there. I bet anything when I checked, it would be gone. It had to be.

I put on my robe and went back to my office. Shit. It was still there, same sender, same time, same subject. I leaned over the desk, took the mouse and drew a deep breath. I double-clicked it. It popped open:

"Do not think you can take what is mine."

That's it. That was all. From Fitzroy, who was in the morgue when he sent it, calling it "Mine," then telling me not to take it. Holy Jesus, Mother of Mary.

I thought about replying to it, something like "Yeah, sucker, what can you do about it?" but decided I needed a good night's sleep first. I closed the email and shut off the computer. I usually leave it on, but didn't want Rocky or

Randi snooping in on this. I knew Rocky spied on my email, which is why I kept a gmail account and only checked it via web mail using Mozilla, not Internet Explorer, and don't have Mozilla in the "My Programs" list. Still, it felt safer shutting the whole thing down.

Now, I was so secret with this account even Fitzroy didn't know about it. OK, if you must know, this was the address I used on porn sites. So sue me. Now, how did this email, from a dead man, get into an account he never knew existed? Fuck. I needed sleep.

Rocky was still awake. She was putting some aloe lotion on her neck. She dropped her robe down her shoulders, exposing her tits, and asked me to rub the lotion all over her. Damn. I had just jerked off. And got an email from a dead man. And had a big day tomorrow. And was going to fuck Juliette on Friday. Ah, hell, a man's gotta do what a man's got to do. I couldn't just roll over and play dead, and send emails, like Fitzroy.

12

I slept late, for me, the next day, and stopped by the office to deputize Andy into full-time work. I tasked him with changing the sign out front from FitzRoyce Realty to Royce O'Rourke Realty. I liked that. I liked the ring of it. I told him to contact the lawyer to start in motion changing the joint partnership to a limited liability company. I then had a meeting with the agents to reassure them that it was business as usual at Royce O'Rourke Realty and to observe a moment of silence for Fitzroy, then to get cracking ass. Darleen kept sobbing during my whole motivational speech. Winners don't sob.

Then I got a call from Flannery O. Flannigan to check whether the dinner had been canceled in light of recent events. Oh, how I played it. I told him certainly not, and if the O'Rourke family ever needed his compassionate, comforting counsel, it was now. Score!

Fuck! Ah shit◊

Wouldn't you know the exclamation points would come out just as I have to tell what happened next.

And what happened was a detective from the Tucson police came to visit me. I pretended it was Friday evening.

He introduced himself as Detective Payne. He asked the usual crap, who I was, how long I'd known Fitzroy, what our relationship was, did he have any enemies. That last one I was none too sure about. So I said no. He asked about drugs. I said I knew Fitzroy did the occasional hit of coke, but never here in the office and always kept discrete about it, so I had no idea where he got it, as I, Royce O'Rourke, a Christian, a leader in the business community, a shoo-in for the Billion Dollar Brotherhood (well, I didn't say the part about the Brotherhood out loud to him), a family man, very active in his church, I, Royce O'Rourke, never went near drugs.

Then he went over the line. He wanted access to all our business records. I told him no, not at all, under no circumstances. He went on about how they could help solve the case, would be kept in strictest confidence, and would be used only to whatever ends were necessary to find the killers and nothing else.

I told him the records were at the lawyer's office and tied up in the process of dissolving the partnership and re-establishing the agency as Royce O'Rourke Realty.

Can you believe it? He looked at me for a minute as if I were a suspect, as if I, Royce O'Rourke, arranged to have Fitzroy snuffed out so I could take control of the business. It lasted just a second, then he put on his stone face and said he could get a search warrant. I told him to go ahead and try.

Of course there was nothing to hide in the records, but they would soon, very soon, be needed, really, by the lawyer to covert the company to me, and they would be needed, hopefully really soon, by the Billion Dollar Brotherhood to audit my application.

As he talked, I thought of how I had lost my sponsor in Fitzroy. No loss. I could ask Father Flannery O. Flannigan to sponsor me. I knew he would. After Rocky's dinner. And Flannigan would be a better, higher, much more holy sponsor.

He made to leave, to get his search warrant, and I told him to call me Friday, just to add some verisimilitude to my Friday deception. Now, I've avoided tooting my own horn, but I used a billion dollar word back there. Royce O'Rourke paid attention in school.

He left and I went to AJ's, checking to be sure no undercover cops were tailing me, Royce O'Rourke.

I was in the big time now. My own business, sole proprietorship. Talking to a detective, hosting the august Father Flannery O. Flannigan, a clear, clean defeat for those filthy ants, and a clear shot and path into the Billion Dollar Brotherhood.

When I got home, Rocky was in a frenzy, zipping between ordering the cleaning lady around, and tending to the kitchen. This was the one, and only time, I saw any advantage to an open layout.

I set the stuff from AJ's on the kitchen counter and gave Rocky a little kiss. She deserved it. Rocky detailed me to supervising the cleaning of the dining room and answering the door for the florist. She had really knocked herself out for this, and I loved her for it. She was the perfect wife for a man like me, for a man who was ascending and about to grab the prize. How we all would shine. How Rocky, Randi, and Roger would shine with me in my glory. Take that you virgin, barren, hard-shelled insect fucking ants. When did Flannery O. Flannigan have dinner in your pathetic ant hill? Hell. Let termites eat you for dinner, you bitter, dried up old ants.

After the flowers came I went to pick up Roger. Juliette was there with him. Oh, if only I could have banged her there, it would have made for the perfect day. Ah, well, there was Friday. And she pretended to be meeting me for the first time, in front of Roger. What an angel.

I took him home, explaining on the way how important a guest we were having and how super important it is, sometimes, like this time, to just be quiet and listen to what an important man has to say. He did that with me, right in the car on the way home. Super special kid◊

Back at the house, I cranked up the AC so it would be powerfully cold. Rocky would normally complain, as she didn't like it cold. Most women don't. But she was flitting and dashing about so frantically that I was sure she wouldn't notice.

I helped in the kitchen and watched things while Rocky went to shower and change. Then Randi came home in a bad mood. She had been teased again and got in a fight and had extra homework assigned. And she grew even more sullen when I told her under no circumstances could she be excused from dinner to do her extra homework. She would have to do it later or get up early in the morning to finish it. Her only response to that was to slam her bedroom door shut. I thought it best to let her cool off alone. After all, it was nice and cold in the house.

Rocky came out to have me zip up the back of her dress. I was getting pumped. Here I was with my beautiful family supporting me, a successful winner. Next time, I'd be one of the Billion Dollar Brotherhood, and oh, the parties and the guests we would have then. I was practically manic with glee.

I slapped on some cologne, paid the cleaning lady, and helped Rocky set the table.

Precisely at seven, the doorbell rang once. I straightened my tie and got Rocky to accompany me to greet the great Flannery O. Flannigan.

What the fuck◊ It wasn't Flannigan; it was that fucking detective. Holy shit. That was the last thing I needed, and I dreaded Flannigan seeing this loser on my door step.

"Hello, Mr. O'Rourke. I stopped by to ask you a couple more questions."

"Now?" I said. "Now?"

"I thought you were meeting on Friday night," Rocky said.

"Yes, Friday," I said. "That's what we agreed."

"This won't take long," he pressed.

"Long? It's already taken too long," I said. "We are expecting a very important dinner guest right this minute," I said.

"Who?"

The nerve of that fucker. Shit. Now I knew the name of the police commissioner, even if I didn't know him personally, but that idiot detective out there didn't know that, so I was about to threaten to report the douche butt when I heard Rocky tell him what he wanted.

"Yes, our priest, Father Flannigan, so if you don't mind, it's really not a good time now. I suggest you talk to Royce on Friday, like you agreed," she said.

"Flannigan. He's your priest?"

As if the O'Rourke family would receive anyone other than the most powerful member of the church hierarchy around here. Before Rocky could sully Flannigan's name by repeating it to this butt wipe, I had an inspiration.

"You know what?" I said. "We are closing this door. I suggest you go talk to Chrissy and Crystal Diamond. I know for a fact they may know who Fitzroy's supplier was and may even know more than that. You might want to give them some advance warning, because unlike us, they may have something to hide."

With that, I shut the door. Rocky shot me a quizzical look.

"Fucking cops," I said. "That's just how they operate. I promise to come down and talk to them on a Friday night and they sneak to my home and ambush me and my family."

I led her to the kitchen, as I didn't want us to be right by the door, seeming too eager, when Flannigan rang. Once we got there, the doorbell chimed again. This time it was the great Flannigan, entering our house, the one I spec'd, and I quickly checked behind him to be sure that stupid cop had left. He had, and hopefully was heading to an ant hill to interrogate those insignificant insects. I had to suppress the urge to laugh out loud.

"Royce, how nice it is to be in your home," Flannigan said.

"Our pleasure," I replied, correctly.

"And Veronica, how beautiful you look, like a sylph announcing the advent of Spring."

"Oh, Father Flannigan, you flatter me!" she gushed. She scored.

"What a lovely house you have," he said. "Interestingly, not the usual indigenous style one would expect."

"I spec'd it myself," I said with pride.

"Well done, Royce," he said. "It bucks the trend. It's almost Lloyd Wright, but with a Tucson twist."

Score, score, score◊

"Would you like a drink, Father?" Rocky asked.

"Oh, you must call me Flannery or Flannigan tonight, Rocky, and yes, I would love a gin and tonic with a twist of lime."

I figured it best to let Rocky keep charming him, so I went to make the drinks. Good thing too, because I wasn't sure how Rocky would have handled the crisis. We were out of gin. In all her planning and preparations, she had overlooked the alcohol. I can't blame her, really. I mean who thinks of booze when planning dinner for a priest? I stuck my head back in the living room.

"Oh Rocky?" I sang.

She came into the kitchen.

"Where the hell is the gin?" I asked.

"Shit," she whispered. "Oh, wait! She went into the bedroom and brought out one of her colored bottles. "Here, this is gin."

"You've got to be kidding," I said. "It's blue. I can't serve Father Flannigan blue gin like it was Kool-Aid."

"You could run to Safeway, but that would look foolish and unprepared, wouldn't it? I've slaved all day, Royce. This is your problem. My problem is not leaving your guest of honor alone in our living room – unless you want to go in there and I'll run to Safeway."

"No, no," I said. I had a very carefully laid plan and the part in play now was for Rocky to charm Flannigan. I sent her back out with a tray of shrimp cocktails and hors d'oeuvres.

I had to think. Think. Blue gin. With a green lime wedge in it. Rocky and I drank martinis, so I went to the study, got more bottles, and made mine green, hers pink, and Flannigan's blue. Then I searched the fridge and the freezer for something blueberry flavored. I got an erection just thinking about blueberries and Juliette, covered in them. Great. I would serve blue, pink, and green cocktails sporting a hard-on.

Aha. Trust Roger to save the day. There was a box of Popsicles in the freezer and there was a blueberry flavored one left. I unwrapped it and dunked it in Flannigan's drink, swirled it around a bit, and tossed it back in the freezer.

I took a silver tray, put the colorful drinks on it, and returned to the living room.

"Ah, libations," Flannigan said, obviously trying to think of how to forgive the rainbow of liquor. "I heard they were going to come out with flavored gin, like they have with vodka, but I've yet to see it," he said, rescuing me. And this, that gesture, is why Flannery O. Flannigan was one of the winners, one of the movers and shapers, and that he made that gesture, and how he so generously cast it to me, made me think he was already welcoming me into the Brotherhood.

"I hope you like grape," Rocky said.

"Blueberry," I said.

He sipped it.

"It's very subtle," the great man said. "Almost imperceptible. Ironically, the vibrant color betrays a less ostentatious taste."

Oh, to have such a man in my house.

"Mine is strawberry," Rocky lied. "I think I'll try the lemon-lime next."

"Now where are your beautiful children?" Flannigan asked.

"Randi is finishing her homework and Roger is, Roger is watching a show on the saints, I believe," I said.

"Ah, work before supper. Well done, well done."

"Let me get some more shrimp cocktail," Rocky said, departing for the kitchen.

"It's so delicious," Flannigan called after her. Then he said to me, "Rocky is such a wonderful woman."

"She's great."

"I haven't had the opportunity to offer my condolences over the unfortunate departure of your business partner," he said. "Not in person, at any rate. How sad."

"Yes," I said.

"Tragic deaths, deaths by violence, are an especial affront to god. I will not mince words, as we both know Fitzroy dabbled in, in ...."

"Sin?" I offered.

"Yes, well, you could say that, yes. The thing is, his soul has finally found peace, and rest, after such struggles and after such a horrific, violent departure from this world."

"Yes, it's hit us hard at the office. I mean, Fitz and I worked like a well-oiled team and while I'm more than ready to move on all the deals, it's not without a heavy heart."

That didn't come out quite like I wanted, but it made the point that I was moving on and moving fast while still showing decent respect for the dead. It was hard with Flannigan that way. He was a businessman, a mover, and I had to appeal to that. But then I felt I had to soften it to appeal to the priest in him. I wasn't sure which one he really was at the moment.

"Was that a police detective I saw leaving here?" he asked. "I thought I recognized him, Detective Payne."

Fuck. I right there planned to give that cop a piece of my mind.

"Yeah," I said. "We were supposed to talk Friday, but I guess he's eager."

"Any news of who perpetrated such a violent attack on poor Fitzroy?"

"No, nothing, though I suspect it is related to the drug trade here," I submitted.

"Yes. Sad. The church has tried to offer hope and help to those unfortunate souls tempted by vile addictions, but, alas, such is the way of the world and as long as such a commodity is illegal, the black market, and all its ensuing evil, will thrive."

"But isn't that what the Brotherhood is for," I countered, and expertly moved the topic to more important matters. "I mean, at least we can protect our own from this kind of sin by building communities of shared values and filled with homeowners who look after their neighbors."

"That's true where swimming pools and front lawns are concerned, Royce, but you know as well as I, I'm sure, that even in this fine neighborhood, there is behind closed doors a sad dependence on methamphetamines and prescription pain killers, and other temptations, though not in this fine Catholic house, of course."

"Yes, yes," I said.

"Were you, Royce, never able to talk to Fitzroy about his abusive habits?"

As if that were my job? I didn't like that.

"You see Father, I mean, Flannigan, I've known Fitzroy since high school. We shared lots of stuff. I mean, he helped me succeed in this business, but there were, later, certain areas that he made real clear I wasn't welcome to intrude in. And not just the drugs. You know he never married and I did right out of school, and had kids, so I went a different direction. I really think he was jealous of me, and ashamed of his life, and, well, he didn't want me seeing under the hood, you know."

Rocky had come back with the shrimp cocktails during that. Flannigan chose not to respond to my explanation, diving into his shrimp instead. It was good.

Rocky seemed eager not to have to refresh the colorful drinks and move on to the wine instead. I guided Flannigan into the dining room, which looked so clean and wonderful, and felt expensively cold, and I opened a bottle of red wine. Flannigan had taken little of his gin. I wondered how watered down it had been. My martini was very weak. Rocky brought in a basket of bread and asked me to get Randi to help. Oh. Yeah.

I poured Flannigan a glass of wine, then excused myself to get Randi. I knocked on her door, then opened it. She was on the phone, shot me a nasty look, then turned her back to me. OK. Normally I would get Rocky to deal with her. That was out of the question, so I went all the way in, shutting the door, and grabbed the hand Randi was using to hold the phone. She clung to it, but I just had to squeeze a bit, like her hand was one of the ants, to make her drop it.

I told her that her mother needed her help NOW.

Without a word, she got up, then muttered something under her breath on the way out. I thought of checking in on Roger, but no, he would want to come out and it wasn't time yet.

I rejoined Flannigan and poured myself a glass of wine.

"You keep it cold in here, O'Rourke," he said.

I asked him whether he wanted me to turn the AC down. He said no. Score.

Randi came in with a big bowl of salad and set it gently on the table.

"Why Father Flannigan, how are you this fine evening?" she said.

"I'm quite well, and how are you Randi?"

"As long as I have Jesus, I am saved," she said.

That was pushing it, it was. She said it very sincerely, so maybe Flannigan bought it. I knew it was false. She never mentioned Jesus, god, or religion, and had to be forced to go to mass.

"Your children are a credit to you, Royce."

"Yes," I said, scoring. "We are very proud of them and I think they will eventually be a credit to the community."

"Ah, yes, always looking ahead, aren't you O'Rourke," he said.

Score◊

"No sense in looking back," I added.

Until one has to, of course.

Rocky returned and told me to get Roger to the table. I fetched him and led him to the dining room. Flannigan was seated in Rocky's normal place at the end of the table, she next to him, then Randi across from her. I put Roger next to Randi, then asked Flannigan to pass the salad. After he took his, he asked Roger how he was doing.

Roger just stared at him. Damn. Now, I have stated before I have no intention of exposing Roger to anyone. He is a special boy and has done well in spite of his condition. I will go so far to say he is able to talk in complete sentences and to carry on a basic conversation, just like the one Flannigan had initiated. So I didn't know what had gotten into him.

Rocky gave me a look as she passed the salad to me. I told Roger that Father Flannigan had asked him a question and that he should answer. I held the salad because I didn't want to confuse him.

He just looked at me, as if I had told him to bite Flannigan.

I could hear Randi sigh.

"You know Father Flannigan, don't you Roger?" I said, spooning some salad on his plate, and passing the bowl across to Randi.

"But he's not in uniform," Randi said. "Roger probably doesn't recognize him dressed in street clothes."

"How insightful you are," Flannigan said to Randi. "I shall have to reacquaint myself with Roger tonight, as a friend, not as his priest."

"One in the same," I said.

Flannigan smiled at me. Score.

"Shall we," I said, picking up my fork. I was so eager for Flannigan to taste Rocky's salad. She always put fresh greens and exotic herbs in it.

"Royce!" Rocky said, folding her hands.

Damn. I had been thrown off my game by – NO. Ah shit. No. Not by Roger. Somehow, this was the ants' fault, and damn it, that idea made me make a slight giggle.

"Father, will you do the honors?" Rocky invited.

Flannigan said grace and we tucked in. All of us, except Roger. I didn't need this and didn't want to have to remove him from the table.

"So Roger," Flannigan started. "I am Father Flannigan. You remember me from church, don't you?"

Roger nodded yes.

"And can you tell me the name of our church?"

Roger nodded yes.

"What is it, Roger?" I prompted. He looked at me.

"Eat your salad, Roger," Rocky said.

"Yes," Flannigan added. "Enjoy the bounty of our lord, and of your mother," he said, great man that he was.

Roger did as Flannigan told him to do, thank god. Roger, whatever else one might think, was instinctively drawn to what is good, and powerful, and important.

During the salad, Rocky initiated some small talk about church activities and charities. I let that flow on, an unequal flow, as Rocky chattered too much, and bided my time. Finally, Rocky got up, signaled to Randi, and they cleared the salad plates and withdrew to the kitchen. You see now the advantage of the house as I spec'd it. They could chatter in there, and I could even go in to manage a crisis in privacy. Let the ants chatter and echo in their great open wastes of space, dwarfed by their own eeping insignificance.

"Now, Roger," I said, "please feel free to talk to Father Flannigan."

He looked at Flannigan, again, then at me, and finally said "But ...."

"Yes?" I asked.

"You said to be quiet and listen to what an important man has to say."

Ah.

"Indeed I did," I said, meeting the proud smile of Flannery O. Flannigan with a wink. "But when he addresses you, you must respond to him."

"Like I do you?"

"Yes, quite like that. Right."

"Well then, Roger, tell me about your school and how you are doing," Flannigan asked.

"I like school," he said.

"I'm sure you do," Flannigan said. "What do you like about it?"

"I like my teachers," he said.

"I'm sure they like you too," Flannigan smiled. "What is your favorite subject?"

Roger paused.

"The things you learn," I prompted him.

"I like art," he said.

"Yes, art is important," Flannigan encouraged. "Did you know, Roger, that through most of history, there were no printed books for everyone, and most people couldn't read. It was art that told them the stories of god."

"I like to draw things from outer space," he said.

Well, god was in outer space, so I figured that was OK.

"What do you draw from outer space?" Flannigan continued.

"Constellations."

"Which ones? I like Orion," Flannigan said.

"I just drew the Ant Nebula," Roger said proudly.

Funny, him saying that. The Ant Nebula. I doubted the ants rated a nebula, except for the nebulous masses in their own heads.

Rocky returned with the big plate of prime rib, followed by Randi, who officiously set chargers before everyone.

"Oh, this smells delicious," Flannigan said, of course.

I did the honors and cut the slices, loading the plates, and passing them to Randi, who set them on the chargers for everyone. I liked Rocky's idea to use chargers. I never saw the point of them, myself, though Flannigan must have seen them as a sign of the good breeding of the O'Rourke family.

After the vegetables were passed, and the wine glasses refilled, I was all set to get to work.

"Delicious, Rocky," I said.

"Yes, the best I've had in a long time," Flannigan added.

"Why, thank you," she said. "My pleasure to cook for someone who enjoys it," she continued, somewhat clumsily. Ah, that was my opening.

"Flannery O. Flannigan is one who enjoys the finest things in life," I said, raising my glass to him.

He smiled.

Randi sighed. I hoped Rocky was kicking her under the table. Flannigan, however, noticed it and looked at her. Before I could avert disaster, Randi spoke up.

"It's just that a priest takes a vow of poverty, dad, so how can he enjoy the finest things in life?"

She had escalated, lobbing her second volley. I wanted to kill her right then and there.

"That is very true," Flannigan said, coming to the rescue, "and it heartens me that Randi is so aware of propriety. I think what your father meant, however, is that I appreciate the gifts of our lord, those which strengthen and nourish us so we can rally our strength and do the works for which we are chosen."

Ah. need I say more? I didn't have to there and then. I just wanted to ricochet past Randi's remark and back into my plan.

"Precisely," I said. "We all, all of us in Father Flannigan's congregation, benefit from his experience, wisdom, and rock strong faith."

"You flatter me, Royce," he said.

"I must confess, I do," I continued cleverly. "What I value most in you, beyond your spiritual guidance, is your knowledge."

Randi choked on her food, intentionally, I was sure.

"Father Flannigan is a Jesuit, Royce," Rocky said. "Of course he's knowledgeable."

"My my, this must stop or I will be too proud to enjoy myself. Let's talk of the O'Rourkes now," Flannigan said.

Damn.

"I know Royce appreciates your guidance and compassion in the wake of that horrible thing that happened to Fitzroy," Rocky said.

"Indeed," Flannigan said. "A sad loss."

Fitzroy? Fitzroy? He was yesterday's news. Why did he have to –

Then, oh fuck. A dash. Then I remembered that email. I saw a way back in. It was risky, but I had to do it.

"Father, and I call you that because I want to cheat a bit. I want to ask you a spiritual question."

"Yes?" he said, holding a delicious bit of red meat on his fork.

"Do you believe, I mean, is it possible, for the dead to speak to us, to communicate? To send a message?"

He set his fork down. I think everyone did. I knew it was risky.

"Why do you ask that?" he said.

I bullshitted that since Fitzroy had died, I had been thinking of such things.

"Well, I'm sure Randi could tell you that it is a complicated topic. I would advise that perhaps, in some cases, the souls of the dead can transmit impulses or messages of love, but are quite unlikely to appear to you, or call you on the telephone."

"That's what I meant, I mean the impulses," I said.

"Have you had any impulses, Royce?" Rocky asked.

"Maybe," I said.

"From Fitzroy?" Randi asked, spiteful child.

"No," I said. "Oh no. I was thinking more of my own father. I've been thinking of him, lately, with regard to my future, and I sometimes think he is, well, if not guiding me, rooting me on."

"That would be his love for you, and you are lucky to have and to feel it, Royce," Flannigan said.

"I thought so," I replied. Then I cut to the chase.

"Switching from spirituality to business," I said, pouring another glass of wine, "have you heard of Monstrance Holdings?"

"Monstrance Holdings," he repeated.

"Yes. They bought the mortgages on that New Orleans deal I'm working on."

He smiled. "You have never heard of it, Royce?"

"I researched it, and couldn't find any record of it."

"Perhaps it's new, or maybe something else."

"Yes. That's what I thought. That's why I figured you'd know, that you'd be the best one to ask."

"Hmm. I suppose the first thing I should ask is if you know what a monstrance is."

"I checked and I couldn't find anything," I said. I didn't like him turning this into a guessing game. I thought, expected, the president of the Billion Dollar Brotherhood to be more direct, more businesslike. He was stuck being a priest.

"I know," Randi said.

Oh shit.

"Please elucidate, Randi," he said, encouraging her insolence.

"A monstrance, as opposed to Monstrance Holdings, is the vessel used in the church to hold the Eucharist. Monstrance Holdings, therefore, is a bit of a redundancy, but also an ironic play on words."

"Well done, Randi, well done," he said.

I started to say I didn't know what all that had to do with real estate, until I saw the look in Flannigan's eyes and realized he was Monstrance Holdings, the devil. And tricking my own snotty daughter into figuring it out for me. Maybe, of course, this was a test. I sallied forth.

"So you bought the New Orleans mortgages?"

"Not me, I mean not my own firm, directly. Monstrance Holdings is a vehicle to broker deals in which, well, the buyer wishes to remain anonymous."

"Is that legal?" (Need I say who said that?)

"Randi!" Rocky shouted. "You apologize to Father Flannigan this instant!"

"That's quite alright," he said, but Rocky kept glaring at Randi. Roger looked like he was ready to cry.

"I apologize, Father Flannigan," Randi said.

"I accept," he said, smiling.

Such drama. My mind was elsewhere. I was trying to figure out who would have bought all those mortgages and foreclosed houses in New Orleans. Who was using Flannigan's Monstrance Holdings to conceal himself? Only Fitzroy and I knew about it. And then Flannigan. Maybe he was concealing himself, crafty devil that he was. Or, no. It couldn't be.

Then I remembered how Fitzroy knew the ants were showing that day when I was also showing the house in Saguaro Ranch. I didn't think about it at the time, but there, at my own dinner table, it struck me as odd that Fitz would know the ants' schedule. It would be just their style, just their cheating ways. All three of them.

"I think I know who those buyers are," I declared.

"I imagine you do," he smiled.

That cinched it. Those fucking insect bitches.

"Then there's the land past the Catalinas, where the ghost town is. That's listed as belonging to Monstrance Holdings too," I observed.

"Why would you be interested in that worthless land?" he asked.

"Yes. Why would anyone? And why would they use Monstrance Holdings?"

"I cannot speak to the motives of anonymous trusts, except to say it is a tenet of the Billion Dollar Brotherhood not to leave any land, no matter how useless, to government ownership. I am glad to see you share that sentiment."

"Indeed I do," I said. "And I would like to see about acquiring that land for a more profitable commercial use."

He seemed honestly surprised.

"That land? Profitable? You must see something in it no one else does."

"I just may, and it will be a deal that will be talked about for years to come," I boasted.

"We must talk, O'Rourke," he said. "In a more professional setting, of course. Your interest in that land intrigues me."

"Me too," Rocky said. She had been admirably quiet during all this. "I don't even know the details about the New Orleans deal. I thought you and Fitzroy were only licensed in Arizona."

"It's complicated," I said, annoyed by the disruption.

"Well, at least there can be women realtors," Randi said, lobbing another rude volley at Flannigan, though I wouldn't have been surprised to see the ants outside the window prompting her. No. They were eeping for Detective Payne.

"Randi!" Rocky said firmly. "Help me clear the table."

She did as she was told, leaving just us men. I apologized for Randi. Then I told Flannigan that I would stop by his office the next day to discuss Monstrance Holdings in more detail in a businesslike setting. I fully planned, without telling him, to shake down those ants to see why they were moving in on my New Orleans deal. I'd have bet anything they were the ones holding the ghost town too. I was wracking my brain trying to think if I ever told Fitzroy about the ghost town. My thoughts were interrupted by the arrival of the girls with dessert.

"Ah," I heard Flannigan say. "That looks like blueberry pie."

Blueberries. I started to get hard.

"Blueberry!" Roger shouted, and got up and bounded into the kitchen.

"I always say I'm going to enjoy blueberry pie until I have to have dentures," Rocky said. She cut the pie and

Randi put each slice on a plate, each one having one of those lace doilies, and passed them down.

Then, a loud disturbance from the kitchen. Pots crashing. Dishes breaking.

"Noooo!" Roger yelled.

I was up first, caught a look from Rocky, dared not to look at Flannigan, and met Roger coming out of the kitchen, in a rage, holding the blueberry Popsicle I had used to flavor Flannigan's gin.

"It's ruined!" he cried.

Of course, I refuse to egregiously exploit Roger by relating what it took to get him under control, except to say that I was able to get him to bed only after he showed me his picture of the Ant Nebula, in which I could clearly see the Diamonds' insect faces.

After I got him to bed, and had him bless Father Flannigan, I returned to the adults only to find Flannigan about to leave.

Damn. Oh well, I got done what I wanted to get done, so good riddance for the time being. I promised to stop by his office the next day.

Rocky said, after he left, that she was too tired to clean up and would do it in the morning. I suggested Randi, but Rocky told me she had skulked to her room to do her homework and would be up all night on it. Yeah, sure. On the phone, maybe, to tell all her friends how she insulted the great Flannery O. Flannigan, and how it took ... well, how Roger put an end to the evening.

I was wired, so I sent Rocky to bed and cleaned up myself, doing a damned fine job of it.

Then I went to my office, to my computer, to see if there were any more emails from Fitzroy. No. But there was one from Miss Clarrissa.

"All my prophesies come true, Red, so no news to me. What makes you think I care about your dead friend or you? Both of you came here to rob and steal from me and mine. Go away and don't bother me. You are an ant to me."

That was worse than an email from Fitzroy. An ant? Me? Me, Royce O'Rourke? After hosting Flannery O. Flannigan at a successful dinner in a heavily air-conditioned house I spec'd myself? Me? An ant? That bitch. I was tempted to reply and tell her how successful I had become. No. I decided to wait. I wanted to do that in person, with her on her back, legs spread, receiving me. Yeah.

I turned off the computer and went to bed. I kissed Rocky. I whispered to her how proud I was of her. How she pulled it off perfectly. I really valued that. I'm not sure she heard me, but it counts more if she didn't, doesn't it?

13

Ah, Friday. Yeah. A great day. I strolled out into the sun that morning, took both kids to school, like a good, responsible father, then cruised to the office, and there it was. The sign:

Royce O'Rourke – Realtor

Fuck. They got it wrong. It was supposed to be "Realty." And what the fuck was up with that god damned dash? I felt like ripping it down with my bare hands. Then I saw the stains on the sidewalk. Traces of Fitzroy's blood. Two phone calls for Darleen.

A minor setback. All of Tucson seemed to know Royce O'Rourke was on his game and to duck and cover. I fired up the sales agents and instituted a new incentive program. I also required each agent to attend a seminar on leadership, motivation, focus, management, or acting. They all had the mechanics of selling real estate. Now, since their leader was about to become president of the Billion Dollar Brotherhood, they had to up their game. And I put acting out there because sales is acting, the houses our sets, the sale the drama. Oh, how my agents' plays would outclass something like Death of a Salesman.

I called our web guru to jazz up the web site. I thought about calling a contractor to redo my office by breaking down the wall between Fitzroy's office and mine. I planned to install a shower and a wet bar. Yeah. That was the future. On speed. The best way into the Billion Dollar Brotherhood was to act like you were already in it, something the measly insect ants could never do.

But I had a big day ahead of me. I had to take on the ants, go sky-high with Flannery O. Flannigan, then have dinner with Juliette. Just as I was about to head out to confront the ants, I got a call from the lawyer. Now I was fully expecting to hear of his progress in converting the agency to my sole ownership. Imagine my surprise when he went into a hushed discussion of how the records were all out of order and showed sloppy signs of fraud – ah, a fucking dash. Fraud, his word. And a lie.

It was perfectly legal what Fitz and I did: Putting our clients' assets and incomes in the best possible light so they would qualify for the highest possible mortgages, stating our own revenue and profits in a way to minimize socialist taxes, providing escape options for clients in over their heads, and moving money around to make it work for the benefit of homeowners, communities, and the nation at large. Everyone in the business did that. It's how the world works, and he should have known that. I told him I'd send Andy over to work it out. Honestly, as if that shit lawyer wasn't paid a generous enough retainer. I had to get cash to give Andy to line his lawyer pockets. I had heard there were quite a few lawyers in the Billion Dollar Brotherhood. I fully planned to reverse that policy when I became president.

Then, just as I was about to leave again, that detective from the Tucson police showed up. Shit.

I was not surprised he had no new leads. He asked again about the records. Putz. I told him my stance had not changed and that I was surprised he didn't have a search warrant. He said he was going to be nice and ask again, but would now definitely get one after I was so helpful by putting him in touch with Chrissy and Crystal Diamond.

I pressed him on what they said. He shut up fast and made to leave. Then he turned and asked me if I had heard of the Billion Dollar Brotherhood. Stupid moronic Tucson cops. I remember, even now, exactly what I told him:

"Of course I know of the Brotherhood. Only the select few know of it. They are the untouchables. They make and shape the world economy. They can buy and sell you and this shit city a hundred times over. So go get your search warrant. Just try to take on the Brotherhood. We like a good laugh every now and then."

He almost snickered, almost smirked. Clearly he was in over his head. He looked plain stupid. One day I would own him.

I waited for him to leave, then set out to seek the ants. I knew where their stupid office was, on Speedway, in a strip mall between a tacky pizzeria and a FedEx, which probably constituted their support staff. I had to laugh just at the thought of it: Ants in a strip mall on Speedway, thinking they could get into the Billion Dollar Brotherhood.

About three blocks away I saw them, riding their bicycles, the two of them side by side, wearing those flat oval helmets, yellow, which, combined with their yellow fanny packs, made them look even more ridiculously insect like. I slowed behind them, followed a bit, then laid on the horn, hoping to scare the shit out of their ant asses.

The silly things pulled over to the side, looked at me, stuck their tongues out at me, then took off again. I beat them and was laughing at them as they rode up to their office.

"You'll never make the quick sale on those things," I chuckled, pointing at their bicycles.

"We're not talking to you, Royce," Crystal said.

"Not after you spat on me," Chrissy said.

"I had to stop her from taking revenge on you," Crystal eeped.

"I may still," eeped Chrissy. "You deserve it, Royce."

"I thought you weren't talking to me," I teased.

"Well, maybe we should talk," Chrissy eeped. "I mean we are willing to interview you for a junior agent position. I'm sure you need the work with Fitzroy out of the way."

Bitch. That was a funny ant way of referring to Fitzroy's death as if I benefited from it.

"I wouldn't work for you two any more than I would have you work for me," I said.

"No chance of that, Royce," Crystal spat.

"No chance of you two cheating me again," I said.

"We don't cheat," Chrissy eeped. "Nor do we cheat on, which is more than you can say."

"And talk about cheating! FitzRoyce wrote the book on that one," Crystal eeped.

"Clearly you can't distinguish between your trickery and our expert deal making," I said.

"Get out of our way," Crystal said. "I'm sick of this kindergarten talk and we have work to do."

"Yeah, we don't want you in our office," Chrissy added.

"Fat chance of that. Me? In your office," I said, putting air quotes around the word "office," like I just did now. "No way would I expose my feet to your cheap linoleum and my head to those crappy ceiling tiles, and my ass to those dated plastic chairs. Is that your air conditioner there, rattling and dripping rusty condensation on the side-walk?"

"Better than blood, Royce," Crystal said.

"Let's cut to the chase, girls," I continued. "I know all about Monstrance Holdings and I know all about you moving in on my New Orleans deal and another deal of mine."

"Bullshit," Crystal said.

"As usual," Chrissy eeped.

"No use denying it," I said. "I'm about to go meet the owner and manager of Monstrance Holdings to reject your offers."

"Be our guest," Crystal eeped.

"Insane as usual," Chrissy added.

"Typical of you insects to resort to name calling. It just makes your denials all the more unbelievable," I told them.

"Insects?" Chrissy said. "Watch it Royce. You've got a lot of nerve to insult us."

"Yeah," eeped Crystal. "We are on our way into the Billion Dollar Brotherhood and we'll see who the insect is then."

"Dream on girls," I said. "I'll see if they need janitorial services and let you know. I should have known trying to talk to you would be a waste of time. Just like you both are a waste of time and space." I liked that part.

"Buzz off, O'Rourke," Crystal said.

"I pity you," Chrissy eeped. "You are a joke and the joke will be on you. Insects? You are the insect, Royce, the roach. Spitting on me like some twelve-year-old. Even your own son would know better, you sad loser."

"What a joke," Crystal said. She took Chrissy's arm and they started inside.

What the hell? They dragged Roger into this, so I spat after them, hitting the back of Chrissy's cheap ant sandals. She spun around to me.

"That does it. You'll be so sorry Royce O'Rourke, but you'll deserve every bit of it."

She turned and shut the door.

They didn't fool me. An evasion is as good as an admission in my book. Well I, Royce O'Rourke, had slept on it and knew that as partner, I had the right to reject any sale of our projects to Monstrance Holdings and as sole owner and proprietor, I had total control. At least Flannigan had to give me more detail. I was mad at Fitzroy, who must have known it was the ants who moved in on the New Orleans deal. The whole thing still didn't make sense to me. It was so fast. And with such secrecy. Wouldn't the ants want to trumpet this buy to the world? On the other hand, it could have been their final gambit to get into the Brotherhood. Just like them, too. Move in on our profits and try to increase the take for themselves. That, of course would benefit Flannigan's Monstrance Holdings. I had to admit, to myself, it was a clever move on the ants' part. Yes, indeed. Thwarting me, increasing their holdings, and lining Flannigan's pockets. Damn them. And damn Fitzroy. I had to up my game. I had to impress Flannigan.

I drove to his office, and sign of good signs, he took me right away, leading me into his freezing suite. Yeah.

"So, O'Rourke," he started, pouring me a gin and tonic, real gin, not blue, and full strength. A class act, Flannigan was.

"You know I'm intrigued, and you know that new, fresh ideas are what the Brotherhood is all about."

He poured a drink for himself and gestured for me to join him at the conference table.

"That's what I'm all about," I followed expertly. "But first things first," I challenged. "I know Fitzroy offered that New Orleans mortgage package only provisionally," I lied. "I have the papers, and think the deal is way too low. Not only that, but I also question the potential buyers' ability to maximize profits on the turn around."

"Do you?" he questioned.

"I do. You know as well as I that banks hate foreclosures and short sales and will draw things out forever."

"That's true."

"So why would Monstrance Holdings want that deal?"

"Monstrance Holdings has no say in the matter. It is a service; it has no vested interest in the profit or the value proposition."

"Shouldn't it?" I ventured.

"Perhaps. But in this case, I gather the buyer is not interested in profits, at least, profit, financial profit, is not the primary motivator."

That was just one more bit of proof the ants were behind it. They only wanted the sale to up their ante for admission into the Billion Dollar Brotherhood.

"I understand that, I do," I said. "I just think the buyer could increase the value without sacrificing their other goal."

"That may be true, but both you and Fitzroy signed the agreement, did you not?"

So maybe we did. I remember Fitzroy rushing some papers for me to sign when he told me of the sale before he went down. So what? I decided it was worth it to push Flannigan a bit more to show him I was for real, that I was a player, a mover and a shaper.

"That's possible, but I'm finding, going through all the files, that much of Fitzroy's contracts are questionable, to put it kindly," I said.

"You don't mean to suggest Monstrance Holdings is dealing in bad faith?"

Oh, that was rich, coming from him. Faith.

"Of course not," I said. "The questions are unilateral."

"That does not entirely surprise me, but I can assure you Monstrance Holdings does its due diligence before committing to a contract."

"Yes, yes. All I wanted to say was that I would like to make a counter offer for the property."

"I don't follow. Counter offer to your own sale?"

"Ah, not quite. FitzRoyce sells to Monstrance, representing its client, and Royce O'Rourke Realty, counter offers what Monstrance's client offers."

"But...."

I had him◊

"I know it's unusual, but I'm not converting FitzRoyce. I'm dissolving it and putting all its assets in an escrow account. Royce O'Rourke Realty will be, is, soon, very soon, a separate, independent agency."

"Interesting, if improbable," he said.

"But it benefits us all," I pressed. "After all, the FitzRoyce escrow account will need to disburse its assets and what better mechanism than Monstrance Holdings?"

"So then, if I follow, and I must admit I'm having some trouble doing so, the agent buying the New Orleans mortgages does so through Monstrance Holdings, who buys from FitzRoyce, which is dissolved and put in escrow, then Monstrance Holdings buys the escrow, and in effect buys its own offer, which Royce O'Rourke Realty counters with a higher offer."

"Yeah."

"But ... Monstrance Holdings ends up owning what it is buying. And –"

"And profits not only from the sales, but think of the tax loopholes."

"Well, O'Rourke, this is either the most brilliant or the most criminal scheme ever."

"Criminal? Not me."

"Of course not. Honestly, I will need to think this over. Ha. I may even need to draw some schematics to follow it. I must admit, it seems rather circular."

"You did a sermon on circles a few weeks ago."

"So I did."

"Everything is connected," I said. "Everything circles back eventually. Like all decisions have an impact. I was just over at the Diamonds' office on Speedway." I couldn't resist taking a swipe at the ants then. "Honestly, it escapes me how they can do business from such a tacky place."

"They succeed in spite of their obstacles."

Damn. He would defend them.

"I suppose," I said, "so far as it goes. But I doubt they can move to a higher level from there."

"Time will tell, but let's talk about you O'Rourke. As I said last night, I am eager to hear of your plans for that deserted lot on the other side of the mountains."

I had to be careful here. I couldn't tell him too much, in case he wanted in himself. And there was the delicate matter of discussing a bordello with a priest. Except this was Flannery O. Flannigan, who wore so many hats. I tip toed in ....

"Yes, it's true the land seems useless for most purposes. I mean there are issues with access, water, electricity, sanitation, the usual."

"Indeed."

"So my mind went to what would draw people for just a couple of hours at a time, something that they didn't plan for, but needed, something they would pay good money for."

"Yes?"

"I'd need to get an easement to build a modern access road to the closest interchange on I-10; that would be the biggest cost. As to water and sewage, realize no one would actually live there, or spend the night, well, not all night, that is. I know we could truck in what water is needed. The girls themselves could rough it a bit, until I turn a profit and can reinvest in the infrastructure."

"The girls?"

"I could get some high efficiency generators for electricity, in combination with solar power, and that would do for lights and air conditioning."

"What exactly would go on there?"

"I'll put two huge ads, lighted billboards on both directions of I-10. That's really all the marketing necessary."

"Again, why would anyone stop there? What would be the draw? Surely not a casino."

"Oh no."

He would press the point. I had to improvise.

"I mentioned the girls. Well, you see, this plan has a humanitarian side to it. The illegals. I know the church is against just sending them back. They are god's creatures and need our help. So we would give them work at my establishment. Non IRS work. They would work in shifts. Be bussed in. At the center, they, the girls, would, uh, well, perform is not exactly it, but provide a service."

"A service?" His eyes widened.

"Yes. A service. A prayer service. Truckers, tourists, businessmen would see the billboard on I-10, pull off, drive to this secluded location, park, and pay for personalized, customized prayer sessions with these young, beautiful children of god."

"Pay? For prayer?"

"A special kind of prayer. A sort of ministering to the special needs of men, and it's men who would come, you know, and these Mexican beauties, good Catholics, would minister to their needs, you know, their special needs."

He pretty much had the long and short of it, though I shot my load sooner than I wanted.

"I think I follow you, O'Rourke," he started. "Officially, of course, it's not something I, or you, or anyone in the Brotherhood would acknowledge or put their name to."

"No, not officially."

"Quite. But as you describe it to me, and the fact you haven't named it explicitly tells me you have the necessary circumspection to pursue this in the proper manner."

Score◊

"Obviously, the obstacles are considerable," he continued. "The permitting alone will be very tricky, and as you point out, the infrastructure needs to be provided."

"All obstacles that can be surmounted," I said. Surmounted by me, Royce O'Rourke. No pissy ant could even approach me in this.

"To be sure," he said, as if agreeing with me about the ants.

"There is one obstacle you can help me with," I pointed out.

He knew what I meant. We were clearly on the same level, the same Brotherly wavelength.

"Yes, the title," he said. "Which is now in the hands of Monstrance Holdings."

"Better than Pima County."

"True. I tell you what Royce. I will make some discrete inquiries with the title holder. As you now know, the only role of Monstrance is to hold the capital. It does not usually involve itself in the actual use or any future transactions."

"You think the owner will sell?"

"As to that, I cannot say. I should emphasize it's not that I don't know. It's only that I am restricted by confidentiality clauses."

Yes, of course he was. He understood. He knew how to play, unlike those cheating, covenant-breaking ants.

"Have you developed a revenue model yet?"

"I have started, but need to factor in the cost of acquiring the property, which will be a big part of the initial investment."

"Yes, yes, of course."

"But let me tell you. I know these places do really well. You don't need a lot of initial investment. Just have a shop up front that sells ... penances, you know, and the prayer rooms in back, and there you have it."

"I worry it won't be close enough to the interstate."

"Ah, the billboards. In fact, having it well off the interstate provides much needed anonymity, or confidentiality, which is essential."

"True. Well, let me make my inquiries and I will get back to you Royce," he said getting up.

Wow. This was moving now. Fast. And then ...

"And O'Rourke!"

"Yes?"

He walked over to a carved wooden filing cabinet, and pulled out a large package. My god, it had the emblem of the Billion Dollar Brotherhood on it. I felt a rush of a thrill, almost like right before an orgasm.

"This is the application packet for the Brotherhood. I need you to fill it out."

Score◊

"I'll get it to you on Monday. I'm just, well, Fitzroy was going to sponsor me ...."

"No matter. I will sponsor you."

Oh, score, score, score◊◊◊ Game, set, match. Royce O'Rourke, unstoppable. Royce O'Rourke on the rise. Royce O'Rourke ruling. Take that, fucking ants. My first ruling, as president of the Billion Dollar Brotherhood, is to reject your applications. Or if you insects get in before I'm president, I will eject and excommunicate you post haste and with extreme prejudice.

I took my leave of Flannigan with a renewed sense of purpose. I proudly carried the application to my car, set it squarely on the passenger seat, then drove back to the office, where I searched online for porn shop suppliers to get a sense of how much it would cost to stock the bordello with condoms, dildos, cock rings, whips, chains … shit. Don't go there, Royce. It was amazing what was out there. I thought I should find a similar setup somewhere to stake out what sold. Yuck. I should avoid such alliteration. It's almost as bad as exclamation points and dashes.

Then I had to figure out what to tell Rocky. As little as possible, except for the stuff about the Brotherhood. She wouldn't get that, but she needed to know. I had never heard of them having a ladies auxiliary group, but they might. Oh, maybe the ants could join that. No, that would mean some poor man somewhere had to marry then, and god forbid, try to penetrate their hard shells. I thought they should move to Utah, where only one man could marry them both and save another man from a similar fate.

Andy popped in. Whatever he had to say, I resolved that no fucking lawyer was going to ruin my great day. All he could tell me was that the lawyer refused his cash bonus and wanted to talk to me. Shit. I decided to nip this in the bud right away, so I drove over to his office, patting the Billion Dollar Brotherhood application to give me authority and strength. His antlike secretary made a fuss about me not having an appointment. She dared talk to a member of the Billion Dollar Brotherhood like that. Like her boss was at all important, let alone important enough to keep me waiting. He must have heard me, because he came out and let me into his office, fully proving he was keeping me waiting for no reason at all.

He went on and on about the state of the books and the contracts, about the disrepute (is that a word, even?) of our finance and mortgage partners, and then accused Fitzroy of embezzling from the shared profits. As if I didn't know that. The upshot of all this was that it would take some time to straighten things out, delaying the conversion of FitzRoyce to Royce O'Rourke Realty.

I had to impress on him how big a priority this was and told him to put more resources on it or I'd take my business to a law firm that could handle it. He must have known that I, in that time of transition, was more likely than usual to change lawyers.

That was a setback. I felt I needed full ownership to impress the Brotherhood. Well, I decided to gloss over that in the application, and would still insist on my new sign, without the dash.

14

The day clicked on and I soon found myself at dinner with Juliette. We chose a place off the usual circuit, just in case. I pretended that I was at the police station talking to that stupid detective. It was weird. I had never really talked to her before. I wasn't sure what to say or how to act.

We didn't say much at all until after the waiter took our orders.

"Royce, we have our fun, yes?"

"Sure," I said.

"And you like me? No?"

"Of course I do. You know it."

"I like Roger, your son. He's zo sweet."

"Yes, he is."

"I weesh he were mine."

So would Rocky, I thought. She'd gladly give him away, but not me.

"I'm very proud of him," I just said.

The food arrived. I had a steak and she did the fish. She took white wine. I cleverly got beer. It would be believable for Rocky to smell beer on me, but not wine. I mean it's conceivable I would talk to that cop over a beer. But not wine. That would be too weird.

"I like you Royce. You are zo hot with the sex and cool as a man. No strings. I like that."

"So do I baby."

"Then you won't be mad when I tell you I am pregnant. With my very own Roger."

Shit. She should have known better. She should have been more careful. Christ. She's fucking French so she should have had the morning after pill they invented. Well, there were other ways. And her very own Roger? What was that all about? In fact, that's the first thing I said:

"There's only one Roger."

"I know, but, if I'm lucky, mine will be like him, zo sweet, and special, and innocent."

Lucky? Like him? I could tell from the code words what she wanted. Sick. I mean, yeah, if it happens by accident. If it's god's plan. That's one thing. Then you have to love it. There's no choice. It's automatic. But to try to have one? To gamble that it's me with the faulty genes, not Rocky, what the hell was she thinking?

"I know what you are thinking. I'm not some beech. I will take it, mine, and not involve you, eef that's what you want."

"You don't have to. You can get rid of it. You don't know what you're in for."

"I work with children, special children, all the day long. I know what I want. And I don't want rid of it."

Fucking great.

"Eef you want to help, fine. I will not cut you out. It's up to you."

Damned right it was.

"And what if it turns out to be not so special?" I asked. "What then? Give it up and try again?"

"That ees cruel, Royce. I would never do that."

"Okay, okay," I said and bit into my steak.

I had to consider this. There was no way Rocky could ever know. As to the Brotherhood, I gather a mistress is okay and if any accidents occur, well, as long as one cleans up after them properly, no harm, no foul, as they say.

"You know I'll do the right thing, with financial support," I said. "Anything beyond that, well, I have to think about it."

"I need no help, Royce, and said I will be discrete. You know you can trust me after all the fun we've had. You just let me know, and I will be agreeable."

She was trying hard, that's for sure.

"Just keep its father a secret for now," I said, "and it might be best to leave town before you start to show. I could see about getting you a place in Phoenix."

"I will take care of that," she said. "Oh, I will miss dear sweet Roger."

It struck me, then and there, that our little trysts would soon be coming to an end. I smiled at her.

"We can still have fun for a little bit longer," I said.

"Yes, yes," she agreed.

We had kept our voices down throughout all this, even in that place. There was a stupid birthday party across the room, being noisy and taking pictures, so that gave us cover.

But, oh, wouldn't you know it, just as I congratulated myself on our discretion, I was cursed to hear that familiar eeping sound. I looked in its direction. Sure enough, those insect ants were leaving the place. I excused myself from Juliette, and rushed over to them.

"You know, I'm tempted to file a restraining order against you two stalking me," I said to them.

Chrissy turned to me.

"Us? Stalk you? Don't you have that backwards, Royce?"

"The only backward thing here is you two."

"Is that so?" Crystal said.

"I'll have you know, Royce," Chrissy eeped, "we come here every week to plan, prioritize, and strategize. It's all too clear you followed us here, like you ambushed us at our office, to try to gain unfair advantage."

"As if," I said. "As if I needed to."

"Well then what does bring you here?" Crystal sneered.

"None of your beeswax," I said. I wanted to use "ants wax" but ants don't make wax. They are far too useless for that.

"Is that your wife over there?" Chrissy teased. "Doesn't look like her."

"If you must know, it's a client. You know what that is? Someone you sell a house for or to?"

"Shame on you, Royce O'Rourke," Crystal eeped.

They were pissing me off.

"Come on Crystal," Chrissy eeped. "This place used to be more respectable."

"See ya, Royce," Chrissy sneered.

Bitches. Fucking ants. That was no coincidence, I was sure. They must have gotten wind of my eminent admittance into the Billion Dollar Brotherhood and were running scared, just as if I had lit a match and smoked them out of their anthill. Run, ants. Run.

I went back to Juliette, so beautiful, so exotic, so un-antlike. We finished dinner, went to an empty house I had on the market, and got it on in the massive, open, empty great room, my roars and her moans echoing about us. A sweet end to a totally winning day, except for the ants.

Rocky was none the wiser when I got home. I made up that I met the cop downtown, then that we went for a burger and beer. She wanted to know what he wanted to know. All I could say was not much and that they still had no leads.

After tucking Roger in, I checked email. Nothing from Fitzroy. Nothing from Miss Clarrissa. I decided to reply to her insolent email to me:

"Bitch. You think you are some special queen with your cheap voodoo crap made in China. Get used to the fact that I own you and yours and all there is for you to do is wait on your back for me. I'll be back soon."

That was probably inviting a little war with her, but so be it. I did want to fuck her again, and it turned out I would be back ....

15

I spent the weekend working on the application for the Billion Dollar Brotherhood. That surprised me a bit. You'd think I was applying to be President of the United States of America. They wanted a twenty-five page questionnaire filled out, full personal financials, full business financials, a detailed inventory of all real estate transactions over the last twelve months, five references, a twenty page essay, details of my last physical, a full biography to include ancestors as well as current wife and children, any misdemeanors and felonies, all political and religious affiliations, and a list of any other organizations I belonged to, etc. Jesus. Why they needed all that was beyond me. I mean what happened to the days when just the recommendation of another man was sufficient? What happened to developing a social standing, as I had done, known to all, and have that be your bone fides? I couldn't believe Flannigan expected me to fill all that out.

It took all day Saturday just to do the questionnaire, which was far worse than filling out my tax returns. By Saturday evening, I decided to show some leadership and do just what I wanted to do, like I always did with my tax returns. Let the ants follow the form, dot the i's and cross the t's. That was their losing, follower ways. I was a winner, so I would make my own way. Besides, I had Flannigan as my sponsor.

On Sunday, Flannigan did a sermon on brotherhood, which I took as a positive sign from god that my destiny was sealed. I spent the rest of the day finishing the application, what I would of it. The best part of it was in the biography where I was supposed to describe my family. I loved that. I wrote how great Rocky was. How she did it all, caring for me and the kids, being active in the church, the PTA, and the neighborhood organization. How she kept the house so clean and classic, keeping the property values up. I told about Randi, how she excelled in school, was captain of the swim team, and a regional math champion. I predicted a career in medicine for her. And then there was Roger, how special and sweet he was, how he succeeded in the face of a cruelly dealt adversity, how he surpassed all expectations and would be an example and model to all such children. I didn't put in how Juliette would be able to use him as an example to her child, should he turn out the way she strangely wanted.

The hardest part was telling about my parents. Oh, my mom was a piece of cake, how she picked herself up after dad died and got her real estate license and supported herself. I said as little as possible about my dad. I said he was a distinguished civil servant for the state. 'Nuff said. I certainly did not say he was a, gag, a prison guard. Fuck that losing shit.

There was one last thing I needed: An 8 x 10 glossy glam shot of me. So on Monday, I put on my best suit, stopped by a professional photographer, paid extra for same-day service, and enclosed the picture in the huge package. I drove over to Flannigan's office after lunch and was disappointed he was out. I had to leave the package with his secretary.

As I handed it to her, I paused. I regretted not sealing it with wax and the O'Rourke coat of arms. Oh, yes, my father, when I was just a child, sent money in to some mail order rip-off firm to get the official O'Rourke colors and coat of arms. I knew it was fake, even then, and had always wanted to go to Ireland and get the real deal. I hadn't had time to do that yet, so the wax seal was probably a bad idea. Surely the ants wouldn't have a wax seal. But seal or not, I didn't want to leave it with Flannigan's secretary. I wanted Flannigan to have it directly, so I apologized, took it back, and headed out.

When I got to the office, Darleen was frantic. I thought it was about the sign, or that cop and his search warrant. No. Once I had calmed her down, she told me it was Rocky. She had been calling nonstop. Sure. She had called my cell several times already, but when did she not? And I was on a sacred mission that morning, so I ignored her calls.

Darleen said Rocky insisted I return home right away. Then I panicked. What if Roger ...? So I got in my car and headed home. On the way I called Rocky. All she would say was that she'd tell me when I got there. I had a sickening feeling. Had she committed Roger finally? Had Juliette kidnapped him?

I pulled into the driveway, leaving my car there without opening the garage, and rushed in the front door. Then all hell broke loose.

"Good. I wanted you home before the kids got home! I don't want them to be here to witness this," she started.

She was all flushed and disheveled. I wondered how much she had been drinking from those colorful bottles.

"How could you? What have I done to deserve this? This? On my front door step? You the big man can't work it out with me and have to take up with some whore who leaves her calling card on my front porch in the middle of the day where the whole world can see it! The pool man!

The mailman! The termite man! What the hell were you thinking?"

What? Juliette would never ….

"Royce! Talk to me! Explain yourself, you bastard! How long has this been going on? Tell me! Tell me, then get the hell out!"

Then she broke down in tears. I wasn't sure what to do, so I played dumb.

"Rocks, I don't know what you are talking about."

"Oh, you don't, do you? Liar. Lying comes so easy and natural to you, doesn't it? Well, the pictures don't lie!"

She took a manila envelope from the coffee table and threw it at me, then ran into the bedroom.

I pulled some papers out of the envelope. It was a much smaller package than my Billion Dollar Brotherhood application. Oh god. Pictures of me and Juliette. There was one of her naked and me getting up with my pants around my ankles. It was in a garage. There was one with me chained to a branch of a mesquite tree and Juliette in leather with a whip. Another was of us fully clothed in a restaurant, and one of us all naked and purple in a bathroom. They weren't glossy, professional photographs like the one I got for my application. They looked like pictures from a cheap digital camera or cell phone printed out with an inkjet printer on regular typing paper. Cheap. There was something else in that envelope. My shirt, the one I lost in that garage at Dove Mountain.

I put them back in the envelope. It was addressed to "The Poor Wife of Royce O'Rourke, Adulterer." That was written in block letters in a purplish Sharpie ink. I took the pictures back out. Did Juliette do this? No way. Who? Oh, shit. Those fucking degenerate bitches!

Fuck. Well, if I ever needed an exclamation point, it is here. Those cunt-faced ants. I knew they were there for that garage one and at the restaurant. And they must have stalked me and snuck in to snap the others. How badly they must have wanted me. But, Jesus, couldn't they do the time-honored, decent thing and just blackmail me with them?

Oh, it had insect ant marks all over it. The cheap pictures on cheap paper. The plain manila envelope they got from the FedEx next to their strip mall office on Speedway. The purple Sharpie. Hell, they probably pedaled it over to my house on their damned bicycles, carrying that filth in their fanny packs. I bet anything they were hiding across the street, just waiting to see Rocky pitch me out of the house, and poised to take a picture of that too, with a cheap dime store camera they kept in their stupid fanny packs.

Well, I would show them. I went back to the car and got the Billion Dollar Brotherhood package. I scanned the block for signs of insect ants, their dirty slimy antennae quivering near the ground. I saw nothing, and went to Rocky in the bedroom.

She was laying face down on the bed, her head buried in a pillow. I sat next to her, stroked her hair and started talking.

"I'm so sorry, babe. You see, she kept stalking me, she did. I resisted until one day, I was weak, and I gave in. I'm not proud of that."

She reared up.

"Oh Royce, I'm not stupid. You don't think I don't know who that slut is? I've met her. She's Roger's fucking teacher's aid!"

"I found that out, Rocks. She had this camera hidden and then showed me the picture from that one time. Then she said she'd send it to you and show it to Roger if I didn't give in to her demands."

"What? Do you expect me to believe that?"

"Yes. Honest. You know how much I hate kink like in that one picture. Do you think I enjoyed that? She kept threatening to send you each picture, each time, and to start picking on Roger. I finally had enough and broke it off, and look what she does, the bitch."

"That's so, I mean, why didn't you tell me sooner? That's at least four separate times! Take another look. Sure looks to me like you were enjoying it!"

"It's over. It's done. It was just kink. I hated it. It's in the past."

"The past is so present right now!"

"It doesn't have to be baby. Look. Look at this. It's done. I filled it out and put a real picture of me, who I really am, in it. Do you know what this is? This is the golden key to our future. A better future. The best. The one I want to share with you. This is the key to it all. That cheap joke in the living room. I'll burn it. It's gone, over, like she is. This package means I'm in. I'm in. You're in. We're in. The Billion Dollar Brotherhood. My dream come true. A better place for us. Not just for me. We can get a new, nicer, bigger house in the Catalina Foothills or in Saguaro Ranch. Way up in the mountains if you want. We can get horses. I can put in fewer hours. Rocks, I don't expect you to forgive me, but don't throw all this away because of that cheap teacher's aid. I got rid of her. This is just her way of striking back."

"You think you can excuse all this just by getting into that stupid club? Are you insane, Royce? And don't touch me."

I took a deep breath.

"Rocky, it's not just a club. It's not like the Rotary, or the Moose, or the Elks. It's a power syndicate. It means we move from the upper middle class to way beyond the system. We go into that top one percent."

"I don't care about the money."

"But ...."

"I care more about having a husband I slave for be faithful to me."

"Oh, baby, I was, for so long. I'm a man. I'm weak. I failed once, and that bitch used me. It's over. I hated it. It won't happen ever again, I promise. And listen, Rocks, I'm not kidding. I met Flannigan today and he practically inducted me into the Brotherhood then and there. I've never told you much, but Christ, there are senators and university chancellors, top judges, key movers and shapers. And they want me. I'm telling you, no way will I ever stray in that company. It's our future. Think of the house we could have. A live-in aide for Roger. Horses, trails. You'll love it."

She widened her eyes.

"You can't bribe me out of this. I have to think about it. I wanted you out of here. I may still, but, oh, I don't know."

"I understand, baby, I do."

"If that French bitch was blackmailing you, you should have her arrested."

"No, we don't want this public."

"Oh! No! I'm sure you don't!"

"I'm thinking of us."

"You said she threatened Roger? After what she left me, you'd better go get him, to make sure she really left."

"Oh, baby, I will. I just want to be sure you're okay."

"Really? Just go. Go now and get him. Take your time. I'm not sure I'll let you back in."

I thought it best not to push her so I took the Brotherhood package, collected the ants' disgusting work, and went to get my son.

His school had another hour to go. I wanted to get there right after school got out so I could talk to Juliette. How to kill that hour? Oh, it crossed my mind to go after those evil cunt ants. If I hated them before, now, well, I couldn't judge how I felt. I was mainly relieved that Rocky didn't kick me out then and there.

However.

There was something deep in the pit of my gut. Something alien to me. Something thick and concentrated and dark and oozing with slime. Something slowly smoldering and growing. It was a big ball of ant poison, just concentrating itself to spew its lethal bile all over those malevolent cancerous insects. I wished Fitzroy were still alive. He would have known some "people" to send over to their cheap, tacky strip mall and deliver a potent, lasting message to them.

Funny, I had driven right by their strip mall. I saw their bicycles outside. I thought about letting the air out of their tires. Or running over their cheap Wal-Mart bikes with my car. The black ball inside told me to wait. So I drove over to that RE/MAX realtor who won my big open house offering.

I went inside, invited her out, drove behind the building, and fucked her right in back, up the ass, in the back seat of my car. That felt so good. That reinflated me.

I drove to Roger's school, waited the few minutes it took to clear out, then went inside. His teacher was on her way out of the classroom, and stopped to say hello to me and to tell me Roger was waiting.

Sure enough, he was there with Juliette. He ran to me. I told him to have a seat and to draw me a picture. Juliette gave him some paper and colored chalk, then took me to the front of the classroom.

We kept our voices low, just in case, but Roger was engrossed in his picture and would not have understood anyway.

"She knows about us," I whispered, "my wife."

"How?"

"We were spied on. By an enemy of mine. They sent her pictures."

"Pictures? How?"

"By cheating. Look, she recognized you. You need to get out of here. Resign. Go to Phoenix."

"Oh, Royce, no, I'm not ready yet. I won't show for another two or three months."

"She won't take me back if you are still here."

"Oh, I see. I comprehend. Eef she still doesn't take you, we could ...."

"It's too soon for that. I need to stay married for a year or more, at least."

"A year or more?"

"It's complicated. We'll see how it goes. Do you have money?"

"Some, but I can't just walk out on zee children."

"You have to. Give it until the end of the week. Turn in your notice now. I'll get you a place in Phoenix. I'll help out. You can trust me."

"Thees is all zo sudden. I don't know."

"Just do as I say. I'll get some cash and come by later this week."

"It's zo fast. I don't know."

"Start seeing yourself in Phoenix. It's bigger. It's got so many kids who need you."

"I, I will try."

"Dad! Look!"

Roger was holding up his drawing. We both went to him.

"It's the Ant Nebula!"

Oh, god. When would I be free of those accursed ants? ◊

"That is very good, Roger," Juliette said.

I took Roger by the hand and led him out. We waved, both of us, to Juliette. She stood there holding his picture. She had this funny look on her face. Kind of contented, but sad, too.

When I got home, Randi was in the kitchen, eating a Pop-Tart.

"Nice move, dad. Pictures even. I expected you'd be more discrete, what with Monsignor Flannigan darkening our doorstep these days."

I couldn't believe Rocky told her. I was so dumbstruck I didn't even think to scold her for her sassy tongue.

Then Rocky came out. She looked better than when I left her.

"Now that we're all together, I have an announcement to make."

Shit. Oh shit. I glanced into the dining room and noticed there was a little less red in one bottle.

"Your father, my husband, has been unfair and unfaithful to me," she started. "I have honored my vows to him all these years and today I find a gift from his, his friend, indicating he has betrayed us all. Now we are good Catholics and your father promises he is about to join a secret society that will dramatically increase our standard of living. For this, and for other reasons, I am considering letting him stay with us. But we will put it to a vote. Each of us will vote on whether he stays and also prescribe a punishment, starting with Roger."

Oh, that wasn't fair. He looked very confused.

"Roger," Rocky said, "do you want your father to stay in this house?"

"Yes. Can he leave for work?"

"Yes. Now if daddy were bad and needed to be punished, what would you do?"

This was insane.

"I know," he said. "He should talk to Father Flannigan."

"Very good, Roger," she said.

I was so proud of my son.

"Randi?"

Oh great.

"Well," she drew out, looking at me, and grinning. "It's really cool these days to come from a broken home ...."

"So you vote him out?"

Jesus, this was turning into one of those cheap antlike reality game shows.

"I didn't say that," Randi said. "I think he should stay, but only if he buys me an iPhone and has no say in what I do or don't do."

"Randi!"

"I submit to that," I said.

"Very well," Rocky said. Then she looked at me and called out my name. I didn't know I got a vote too.

"I just want to say," I said, "that I was very wrong, and am very sorry, and I love you all." I managed to choke up, during that part. "So, if you'll have me, I want to stay."

"And your punishment?" Randi asked.

Hmm. I was saving all thought of punishment for the ants. Then there was the problem that I was the perfect father and husband. I took out the garbage, helped clean up after dinner, helped the kids with their homework, kept the cars running, made a great living for us all, so what more could I do? I looked at Rocky. Aha.

"My punishment is that I have to get you one of those Roomba vacuum cleaners."

"Cool," Randi said.

"Not enough," Rocky said.

"OK," I admitted. Then I poured it on. "After I get into the Billion Dollar Brotherhood, which is a sure thing now, and after we move into a house in the mountains, I'll get everyone a horse."

"A horse!" Roger said.

"Not enough," Rocky cried.

Shit. What more could she want? I even said as much.

"Make him wear a chastity device," Randi said.

Jesus. I couldn't believe that came out of my own daughter.

"They don't make those for men," I said.

"Oh yes they do," Randi disagreed.

"Really?" Rocky said. "How?"

"Use your imagination, mom. He can pee in it, but anything else, well, there's no room for it and you can get some models that will make him hurt like hell."

Where the hell did my own daughter get this stuff? Shit. I thought that very moment that Randi could work the front counter and gift shop in my bordello.

"What's a chastity?" Roger asked.

"Never mind, Roger," Rocky said. "I have an idea. Your father and I will sign an agreement. A post-nuptial agreement."

A post-nuptial agreement? Was I in a soap opera now?

"You, Royce, will sign an agreement that if this ever happens again, you leave and leave everything, every dollar, quarter, dime, nickel, and penny, and even the shirt off your back to me."

Fuck. Oh well, I planned to be more careful in the future, and had no desire to give up this family I worked so hard to get. But I was worried about Rocky. Not only did she drink during the day, but she apparently had started watching the soap operas.

"Deal," I said.

"Then I vote yes," Rocky said, tearing up.

"Yaaaa!" Roger yelled.

"I want that iPhone tomorrow," Randi demanded, heading out.

I moved to Rocky to hug her, but she ran into the bedroom and shut the door. OK. Fair enough.

I decided to make dinner for everyone. It was the least I could do. As I fried up some onions, I figured I'd have to get a different lawyer for this post-nuptial agreement, preferably one out of town and who was at least seven degrees removed from the Brotherhood. It also occurred to me that the more I delayed, the more likely Rocky was to drop the whole thing.

I found some steaks in the fridge. I decided to tenderize them. As I beat down on them with the meat hammer, I thought of the pieces of meat as the ants, after I sucked them out of their protective exoskeletons. It felt so good to beat them into bloody pulps. That tight slimy black ball in the pit of my stomach turned and spun about with unbridled glee.

Dinner was a somber affair, no one saying much. I made things easy for Rocky by sleeping in my office that night. It had what Rocky calls a "day bed" so I was comfy. I had trouble sleeping, however. I realized that in all the drama of the day, I had forgotten to go back by Flannigan's to turn in my Brotherhood application. That could only mean I had to seal it with wax.

A good sign. Rocky came in much later, after I had nodded off, took my hand, and led me back to our bedroom. I held her tight, with love and appreciation. She must have known I never did that with Juliette. Or Miss Clarrissa. Or that RE/MAX chick, if she knew about them, which she didn't.

I guess this is as good a time as any to pose that eternal riddle known to all men: Why do women get so bent out of shape when we get a little action on the side? I mean every guy does it. As long as we don't bring babies and disease home, who cares? After all, the women get the kids, the house, the paycheck, and everything else. And as long as we go home and do our duty by family and wife, who is really hurt? It's not like we men love and pay all the attention to the extra piece on the side. I'm just saying.

I remember, way back, seeing a documentary on TV about genes. It showed that men had tons of sperm that didn't care where they got shot, as long as they got shot, and by that I don't mean in your underwear during sleep or in an old sock. Women, on the other hand, have a limited supply of eggs and one egg needs so much time, attention, energy, and protection to be viable. The upshot of all this is that men are programmed to spread their seed far and wide, while women are programmed to trap a man into staying with her, supporting and protecting her, at least until her children can repeat the process. That's the natural order, except for ants. It's just that non-ant women have to create this whole familial, religious, social, and legal apparatus around them to enforce the deal, and all that takes such an investment that they start to believe the fairy tale. And the fairy tale is reinforced by novels, chick flicks, and Lifetime movies for women. The sad thing, really, is that they are taught, brainwashed, and programmed to go all haywire if their guy gets some on the side that they are willing to chuck all that investment to redress the supposed betrayal.

Now how would business work if it were run like that? Or the government? Or the Billion Dollar Brotherhood? The smart women are the ones who knew how to judge the transgression against everything else, and decide to shame the man a bit, to make him more attentive for awhile, then move the fuck on. It appeared Rocky was such a smart, judicious woman, which befit a husband about to be inducted into the Billion Dollar Brotherhood.

16

The next day I went to an office supply store and got some sealing wax. They also had some stamps, most of them stupid flowers, animals, zodiac signs, and other crap the ants might use if they had the class to do such a thing. Luckily, they had letters of the alphabet and I debated between an R and an O. I identified more with the R and bought it, even though the O was a circle.

I stopped by the office, melted the wax over the package flap I had already licked and sealed, waited a bit, as per the instructions that came with the wax, then I set my R in it and pulled it back up. Nice. It looked singularly appropriate.

Just as I was about to head to Flannigan's that fucking Tucson detective came in with two uniformed cops. Shit.

So he had a search warrant. Big fucking deal. I told him all the papers were with the lawyer. He wanted my and Fitzroy's computers too. I told him to see the lawyer first, but oh no, mister big shot, couldn't succeed in high school, wouldn't matter in a roomful of people without his fucking badge, told me to step aside while one of the uniformed cops moved in and grabbed my laptop. Fucker. The other cop dared, that cockroach, to touch my Billion Dollar Brotherhood package. I slapped my hand down on it and told him to back off, that it was personal, not business, and not covered by his sloppy search warrant. The cop looked at the detective, like Doofus looking at Dumbass, like Chrissy looking at Crystal, then backed off. I grabbed my application, and told them I had to go.

On the way out, I told Andy to call the lawyer and tell him to package up all the stuff and have it ready because we were switching lawyers. I thought that might work. Mind you, there was nothing there incriminating, nothing to hide, but it was private business property and definitely not the business of the Tucson police.

I raced over to the loser lawyer's office, busted in, and demanded our papers. He wasted time by saying what I was doing could be construed as criminal failure to comply with a search warrant. I told him to bill me, then toted four boxes to the back of my car. The putz refused to help me because he didn't want to be an accomplice to a crime. I told him he was fired as of Andy's call, then hightailed it out of there before those nosy cops arrived.

I drove to Flannigan's. I was safe there, at the epicenter of world power. He was out, again, but I felt safe giving my sealed application to his secretary. Then I did something very clever. I told her I also needed to drop a copy off at Flannigan's lawyer's office, but had lost the address. Succumbing to my charm, she gave it to me. Ah, downtown. Of course.

Back in my car, I drove to Flannigan's lawyer's office and spent the next two hours insisting on seeing a partner, telling him of the billions of dollars in business I was bringing, and convincing him to take my boxes of papers as his team's first assignment. I told him I needed them cataloged and reviewed. He seemed reluctant until I dropped the F-bomb, and that I was there on Flannigan's personal recommendation. Oh, yes, well, of course, now he would have been willing to stash a dead body for me. He even sent some clerks to the parking garage to get the boxes out of my car.

Score. And, I was truly acting like the president-elect of the Billion Dollar Brotherhood. Awesome. And part of being such a mover and shaper meant faithfully executing my familial duties, so I pulled Roger, then Randi, out of school and went to the AT&T store to buy Randi her iPhone. Wow. She had her usual air of nonchalant entitlement, lacing it with guilting me the whole time, until the store clerk activated her new toy. Oh, a daughter never loved her father more than in that moment. I decided right there that my first act as president of the Brotherhood would be to commission special iPhones with the BDB logo and give one to every member.

Then it was off to the mall to get a Roomba for Rocky. I felt bad about Roger, so I got him a Wii. Randi didn't even pitch a jealousy fit over that. Excellent.

When we got back home, that detective and one of the cops were waiting in the driveway. Shit. Well, I was practically in the Brotherhood, so I could handle that situation. I sent Randi and Roger in with all the goodies we got and marched over to them.

"Does your search warrant give you the right to harass my family?" I said.

"No, O'Rourke. But it does give us the right to arrest you for obstruction of justice."

Shit.

"I'm not obstructing anything. I let you steal our computers. Though what they or I have to do with Fitzroy's murder is something you'll be hearing about from my new lawyer," I said, taking out the new lawyer's business card and handing it to him. "You'll find what you are looking for there."

He looked at the card, then back at me.

"Moving up in the world, aren't you?" he said.

Insolent shit.

"That's my business. Now unless you have a search warrant for my house, for me, and for my wife's twat, you can get off my property."

He glared at me, that, that, oh what was his name? Payne. How appropriate. As if his puny Payne glare could burn through me. He gave up, got in his car with his sidekick, then headed off to whatever hovels those two could afford to live in. As for me, as for the O'Rourkes and their iPhone, Roomba, and Wii, we were moving up.

The next day Rocky insisted I take time out of the day to see a lawyer about her post-nuptial agreement. So much for her forgetting that insane idea. I had to call that new lawyer to recommend a different lawyer for this delicate alcohol-induced bit of Rocky exclamation points and dashes. I looked for his business card. Shit. I had given it to the retard; oh no, I won't use that word, to that doofus detective.

But wouldn't you know it, just as I was about to get online, the lawyer called my cell phone. He sounded confused and a little upset. Seems Tucson's finest were there with their dime store search warrant. I told him it was okay. I told him it had to do with Fitzroy and was routine, and one reason I went to him was that the other lawyer was making a mess of it. Blah, blah. He said he would comply but would recommend the cops waited until they finished cataloging it all. Ha. Truly a top flight lawyer, indicative of Flannigan and the ways of the Brotherhood. In fact, I reconsidered taking Rocky's nonsense elsewhere, not with that class of service, which would undoubtedly fix things in my favor. So I told him I also needed to see him today with my wife, who was so upset by Fitzroy's death that she worried something would happen to me too, that I would disappear, and therefore felt she needed some legal protection beyond the usual last will and testament. Of course, he made time for me, and off we went.

Randi saw herself to school, but one of us always had to take Roger. I made sure to be the one to walk him in so Rocky wouldn't see Juliette. Then I drove downtown to sign my life and all worldly goods over to Rocky.

Timing was not with me. As Rocky and I waited in the impressive, understated reception area, those fucking cops came out with the four boxes. Jesus, it took two uniformed cops and that idiot detective to do what I was able to do all on my own. And apparently they did not heed my new superior lawyer's advice. And then, that putz Detective Payne had the gall to talk to me.

"Good morning, O'Rourke, Mrs. O'Rourke."

"Did you get what you came for?" I asked.

"For now, yes."

Fucker.

"Get what?" Rocky asked.

"Some of Fitzroy's papers," I said.

"What are they doing here? I thought Fitzroy used that other lawyer."

"Who made a mess of things, and who is not trust-worthy, which is why I transferred them all here to ensure this detective was able to get everything," I said.

He admirably kept quiet.

"Do you have any leads on who killed Fitzroy?" Rocky asked.

"We're working on some, ma'am."

"Aren't you the detective who was at our house last week?"

"Yes."

"And who met Royce over a beer and hamburger on Friday?"

"Yes, ma'am."

Well, I thought I should revise my opinion of Detective Payne, a little bit.

"I'm sorry I couldn't offer our hospitality when you came by."

"That's quite alright, ma'am."

"Who else have you talked to?"

"I'm not at liberty to say, ma'am, although we did find some good information from the lead your husband gave us."

"No way," I said, involuntarily or reflexively, I'm not sure which.

"Why do you say that?" he asked. "Certainly you would not send us on a wild goose chase in our effort to solve your business partner's murder."

Shit. Now the new lawyer was standing in the reception area, hearing all this.

"Not at all," I said. "It's just that the ant, the Diamonds could only have peripheral knowledge of any important thing happening in this town."

"On the contrary," he said. "I found those ladies to be quite well informed and connected. They certainly knew a good deal about Mr. Fitzroy, and about you, Mr. O'Rourke."

"I suppose they are the ones who told you to impound all of Fitzroy's files?"

"Among other things," he said, looking strangely at me.

I had to cut this off.

"We have our appointment now," I said, taking Rocky's hand and introducing her to the lawyer. Detective Payne left. Good riddance.

And during that meeting with the lawyer, I was so distracted that I gave every advantage to Rocky. It was the fucking ants' fault I was even in such a position. It was the ants who set that detective on me, to harass me and my family. It was the ants who were cheating their way onto my turf. I saw those pictures they took of me and Juliette. I saw their ant legs hold up a cheap camera and I saw their ant antennae quiver with delight as they printed out the pictures and bought that envelope at FedEx, and rode on their bicycles to my neighborhood, to my home, to my front porch.

"Did they what?"

Rocky was looking at me.

"Are you paying attention, Royce? What do you mean 'Did they ring the doorbell?' What doorbell?"

I had to work hard to focus on the rest of the meeting. The lawyer said he would have all this typed up then have us back in to sign it and have it notarized. Done.

I drove Rocky home. We were both quiet on the way. I guess we each had our reasons. I was almost totally consumed with how to get back at the ants. She, she must have been thinking of how she owned me. I even said it aloud:

"Well baby, you own me lock, stock, and barrel now."

"Yeah."

That was like world record for Rocky: A one word response.

"That Roomba ought to be fully charged now. Why don't you take it for a spin while I drive to the office to catch up on some stuff."

"Okay."

Boy, she was on a roll.

"Royce?"

"Yeah?"

"Never mind."

I had pulled into the driveway.

"Love ya, babe," I offered.

"You do, don't you?"

"You know it, Rocks."

She smiled, a bit, and got out, and went inside.

Strange.

I drove to the office. No new sign, still blood stains on the sidewalk. My tax dollars at work.

And work had piled up, what with all the time I had taken with lawyers, the Brotherhood application, and buying love for my family. I had wanted to figure out what to do to those ants, but I had contracts to review, payroll to process, commissions to calculate. That took the rest of the day and the next. I had called Flannigan to be sure he got my application. He had. He also had no news on the land for the bordello.

So I worked and worked and worked. With Fitzroy gone, there was so much more to do. I just told myself that once the bordello deal went through, and once we finalized the New Orleans sale, I'd have enough extra revenue to hire some more help.

And money became a small concern. I couldn't draw out money for Juliette on any account Rocky could see, so I had to do it on a corporate account, something Fitzroy had done countless times, so I knew how to do it.

On Friday, I picked up Roger and had him wait in the car while I talked to Juliette. We stood in the parking lot. I told her I had found a place in Phoenix for her, an apartment for the time being, and gave her a check for twenty-five thousand dollars. She seemed reluctant to take it.

"I'm not some mistress to be bought off," she said.

"I'm not buying you off. I'm investing in my child," I said.

"That's sweet. You are sweet. But I talked to the principal and I can stay, even as an unwed mother. So it is all OK, you see."

"No it's not. Rocky, she, she won't have you near our family."

"I am no harm."

"But she is. She'll be so pissed. She'll be so jealous. She'll think we're still carrying on."

"Can't we?"

"Not right under her nose."

"But we have been."

"But she knows now. It's not safe. I didn't tell her you were pregnant. If she sees, she'll know."

"I see."

"So take the check and go to Phoenix, or France."

"France? Zo you want me far away."

"Look, you said over dinner you would move. I'm agreeing to help out. It's only fair."

"Give me the information on the place in Phoenix. I will go up this weekend and look at it."

"It's in here with the check, who you go see. Pack a bag. You know, I'm expanding into the Phoenix market, so I'll be able to see you, and it will be much safer."

"OK."

"Good."

That part about expanding into Phoenix wasn't really true yet. Once I got in the Brotherhood, Phoenix, shit, the whole world was mine.

I gave her a quick kiss, and got back in the car with Roger, who had been growing impatient.

Women. I hoped she wasn't going to be difficult. She was lucky she had me. I didn't blame her. I blamed the ants. They exposed us and I still hadn't figured out how to get revenge, other than scotching their chances of getting into the Brotherhood. I decided I'd visit with Flannigan after church on Sunday to poison them in his mind. Then I'd see him again on Monday. Yeah.

I worked from home on Saturday. Rocky loved the Roomba and even agreed to get Roger a cat, since the little robot could clean up the cat hair and Randi showed her YouTube clips of cats riding on it.

Roger with the Wii? A natural fit. Had I not the issue with Juliette at the school, I would have recommended they install one there. It seemed a perfect rehabilitation tool, and certainly kept Roger active.

Randi had already downloaded dozens of applications to her iPhone and could not be detached from it. I was so the hero for providing those things. Randi even told me, out of Rocky's hearing, that I should have an affair more often.

On Sunday, I managed to get some time with Flannigan after church. I started by asking about the bordello deal, but, of course, I didn't use that word. He told me he should have an answer by Monday afternoon. Good.

Then the not so good.

"I gather you have switched to using my law firm, Royce. Wise move."

"Yes, they are much better organized and totally more professional."

"To be sure. I was a bit discouraged that the police made a visit on your behalf."

"Fitzroy."

"You need to disavow that association, Royce."

"Yes."

"And you didn't complete all the requirements of the application."

"Well, I thought what I did was sufficient."

"Did you? I want you to pay a visit to the Diamond sisters and have them help you finish. Their application was a model for all and I think they could help you."

That black slimy ball in the pit of my gut started spinning again.

"Well, yeah. I'll see about that," I said.

"Royce, be aware. A new age is upon us. Aligning yourself with the Diamonds is the way. I may want their input on that little project of ours. We'll discuss on Monday, the four of us."

"Oh, sure."

He had to visit with someone else, and good thing too. I couldn't take much more pissant talk. Me, Royce O'Rourke, guided by those bitches? No fucking way. And "that little project of ours?" Did he assume he would have more to do with it than selling the title? And poisoning it, infecting it, with those stinky ants? That sacrilege annoyed me no end.

I drove the family home, had lunch, then had to go host an open house for one of my agents, who couldn't make it. Sure. Fine. Maybe that would take my mind off the ants.

17

It was way out on Redington Road, past the point where it went from pavement to gravel, almost to where it turned into a dirt mountain pass. Set far off the road, it was an empty, secluded house. The owners couldn't keep up with the mortgage payments, and were desperate to sell it before the bank foreclosed. They had headed back to live with their parents in Kansas. It was a risky venture for us. Since it was an empty house, we had to incur the cost of staging it on top of everything else. I was heartened to see my man did a good job. Not a loaf of bread in sight. But he did put in some nice touches, like fresh flowers, a telephone and flat screen TV (both disconnected), and some colorful coverings to hide some less than quality furniture. Nice.

I had decent, if not impressive traffic, and even got a couple of bites, but both seemed put off by the asking price.

Then, just as I was about to close it up, after everyone had gone, who would show up but those evil ants. Both of them. With no client in tow.

"Oh god, we didn't expect you here," Crystal said.

"Downsizing?" Chrissy eeped.

"I think this house is out of your league," I said. I wanted to say so much more.

"Yeah, it is, but we're taking on some charity cases, being good Christians, and we thought this FitzRoyce dump might be the right low end solution for them," Chrissy eeped.

"Let's look at the upstairs and get away from him," Crystal said.

"You won't find anything to take pictures of up there, to send to my wife, you cunts," I said, feeling the black ball in my gut start to spin.

"You what?!" Crystal demanded.

"You heard me, bitch. Home-wrecking dyke."

"Fuck you Royce. Let's go," Crystal said to Chrissy.

"No. Go check out the upstairs. I want to see how this worm wiggles out of blaming us for his infidelity."

"Waste your time. Go ahead," Crystal said, and crawled away.

"So you did do it. You pedaled all the way to my house and left those pictures for my wife?"

"How did that feel, Royce? That will teach you to not spit on me."

"You fucking infinitive-splitting cunt. I'll have you know it didn't work. I'm still married, which is more than you and your dyke sister can say."

"We aren't dykes, Royce. Though I know thinking we are probably turns you on. We are decent Christians. And you know what? Father Flannigan knows our hearts, and he knows yours too, and he knows you have a black heart and are a small, puny, insignificant man, who will never get into the Billion Dollar Brotherhood. You are just a tool and a cog with ridiculous pretensions. Flannigan, us, most of the real dealers around here see you as the joke you are."

"Joke? Me?" I said. "That's a laugh coming from you."

"Is it? You still don't get it. Did you know Flannigan has already pulled the strings to get Crystal on the county property acquisition board? Did you know he has raised hundreds of thousands for me to run for office? What has he done for you? Think about that. Think about how every organization needs its grunts to do its dirty work. How else do you explain Fitzroy? How else do you explain yourself?"

The slimy black ball was spinning out of control. How dare an insect eep to me like that?

"Ha ha! Your face is as red as your hair, Royce! You know, even Fitzroy was more useful than you. You can't even do the dirty work against your own wife without getting caught. But what to expect from the son of a prison guard? If you do get in the Brotherhood it will be as the court jester. The trained circus dog who jumps and barks for our amusement. The comic relief, except you aren't even funny Royce. You are just a worthless juvenile pathetic little unfunny joke."

The ball spun free. But all I could do was spit in her alien ant face.

She slapped me.

I slugged her, hard, right in the kisser.

Now, my mother always taught me never, ever to hit a woman. But I ask you. Based on the evidence you've seen so far, was this a woman before me? Was this a voluptuous center of sweet warm soft flesh? Was this a vital, living, breathing, beautiful woman before me?

No. This was a sick, cancerous, insect ant. And I had lit the match, and smoked it out of its anthill.

It stared at me. With its bulbous compound eyes, and its swelling pincers. It started to quiver and shake. Then it reared its ugly head and eeped at me.

"You fucking bastard. I'm calling the cops. You are going to jail, Royce O'Rourke, for assault."

Not so fast. I grabbed the insect and started to crush and squash it.

It eeped a pitiful squeal.

I put my hand over its mandibles.

That spinning slimy ball spun before my eyes. I trapped the insect head in my right arm and put on all the pressure I could muster. That thing, that piece of dirt, violated the natural order of things. It broke the covenants. It made a mockery of Juliette and of Rocky.

And yet, it struggled. It struggled against the natural order which was reasserting its rights. I relaxed a bit.

It tried to break free.

Aha. I held it tighter and brought its eeping ant skull down hard, very hard, on the granite kitchen counter in the eeping open great room.

The insect went limp, then, exterminated, slid to the floor.

I looked down at it.

Then I heard a high-pitched eep echo in the open space. There it was. The other ant. Terrified.

It tried to run, but I caught it and got it down on the floor. It struggled and writhed beneath me.

I pulled off its exoskeleton and mercifully gave it what it had always wanted.

Me. Hard. My cock.

And damned right. Damned good time for it. This monument, which exalted the great Miss Clarrissa, and Juliette, it tamed that vile insect beneath me. It brought the natural order to it. It restored the balance of time and space.

The insect writhed and gasped for life. My hands, my strong hands, enclosed the skeletal space between the ant head and body cavity and clasped hard, choking the cancer out of my life, as I filled the dying shell of the insect with my power, my blood, sacrificing all so that the Brotherhood could be cleansed of its insect-infected infestation, restored to its natural state, that safe, sane, comforting, calm place of peace.

Yes.

Yes.

Yes.

It was done.

It was good.

It was limp, lifeless, beneath me.

I stood.

I started to laugh, to bellow, uncontrolled, but it didn't sound like my own voice echoing in that open great room.

I spat on the dead ant.

I went to the other dead ant. I wanted to pee on it. To wash it away.

Then I got dizzy.

I may have fallen down.

On the floor.

In that great open space.

Because.

There were two things there. Two things that didn't belong.

Two things that had to go.

Two things that had to go away.

Who am I? Where was I? Everything had gone from great and open to all closed in about me.

Oh my god.

What have I done?

Oh shit.

Oh fuck.

That black spinning ball. It had gone, leaving me alone, by myself.

OK. Now I had to make it go away. Reverse it somehow. Make it so that it never happened. I thought of torching the house, making it look like some termites or ants had started a fire and got trapped in it. No. I needed the sales revenue from that place.

Then I saw those colorful coverings over the furniture. I took one and rolled a squashed ant up in it. I did the same with the other. Funny thing about it all was how automatically it happened. It was like I was prepping a house for a big showing.

I went into the garage and opened the door. No one was out there. Good. Except there were two bicycles out front. Ant shells. I pulled my car in the garage, brought the bikes and my open house signs in too, then closed the garage door. I managed to get both bikes in the back seat of my car. I opened the trunk.

I went back in the house and scooped up one ant roll, carried it out to the garage, and put it in the trunk. I repeated the process for the other ant roll. I couldn't believe how relieved I felt closing that trunk.

Back in the house I looked for evidence of ant infestation. Ah. There was a yellow ant fanny pack that had fallen off one of them. I scooped that up. Strange. There was no blood. Not on the floor, not on the counter. I took some paper towels and wiped them off, just to be sure.

I went upstairs and did a quick sweep. Fine. Fine. OK. Good. Blood. What? I thought I saw blood in the master bath. I froze. Was Juliette there? Did she hear the whole thing? Did she see it? She was supposed to be in Phoenix. I couldn't go in. I couldn't face her.

I'm not sure how long I stood there, thinking of nothing, except how the Roomba would have been nice to have to sweep up traces of ant hair and ant fibers.

I finally went in. She must have heard me come in anyway.

Only she wasn't there. Good. I felt relieved again. The red I saw was on the mirror. It was lipstick. It said:

"Royce O'Rourke, Adulterer. Don't buy from that cheater."

Cheater? Not me. Never. But those ants, that's all they knew and here was the proof, the evidence. I thought I should leave it, as it would justify my actions, but I had to make the house presentable. I ran downstairs, got more paper towels, then went back upstairs and wiped the mirror clean.

I brought the used paper towels back down, set them with the others I had used, then went to double check the doors. I should have done that first thing. I locked the front door, then went to the sliding glass doors that led to the back yard and pool. I secured those. Then, oh shit, had they got out of the car and come in to haunt me?

No, it was Juliette.

"How did you get in?" I asked.

"The front."

"When?"

"Why? You never used to care."

"How long have you been here?"

"A few minutes, just after you went upstairs. I was going to follow you, but I found a nice big closet een the bedroom over there."

She put out her hand. I took it, as if the open house had just ended. She led me to the bedroom, which was really a den with a big storage closet.

We got into it, or tried, as I couldn't get into it.

"Is it because I am with your special child? Are you now afraid to go there?"

"No, I did Rocky when she was pregnant."

"Is it because she knows? Are you afraid of the spies?"

"What spies?"

"Those that sent the pictures."

"No, not at all."

She kissed me, then went down on me. I closed my eyes tight and thought of Miss Clarrissa, and how I could use her magic powers now. Juliette tried, then abruptly stopped.

"Have you replaced me already?"

"No," I said.

She got up.

"You have been a bad boy."

Oh my god, I thought. She had seen it. But if she had, why didn't she try to stop me? Unless, of course, all she saw was me stomping out some insects.

"What do you mean?" I asked.

"You have been with someone, someone else already, Royce."

"No."

"Don't lie. I can tell. But I don't complain. I have what I want."

I did up my pants and asked her why she wasn't in Phoenix. She said she went on Saturday and liked the place, but was evasive about when she would actually leave.

I didn't have time really, under the circumstances, to pin her down, what with two dead ants in the trunk of my car.

She seemed unhappy, and left out the front door, which I had to re-lock. I did another sweep, a quick one, then went back to the garage, opened the door, ran back inside to collect the used paper towels, then back to my car, which I pulled out into the growing darkness. I got out to shut the garage door, then back in my car, and started to drive, cursing home owners who leave a house to a realtor and fail to provide him with the fucking garage door opener.

I just drove, turning south on Houghton, which led me to I-10 East, where I got off at the Benson exit and took

Ocotillo Road to the dangerous dirt trails that eventually took me all the way over to the haunted house where my bordello would be. My bordello, not those ants', not Flannery O. Flannigan's. I kept a flash light in the trunk, as all good realtors do, took it out from under the two ant rolls, then shut the trunk.

There was a back entry to the old house. But it wasn't safe there; too many kids came to the haunted house during the day to lose their virginity. I headed for the out buildings, checked a few, but turned back. None of them offered a decent place to dispose of two insects. I didn't know what to do. Then I remembered the old house had a basement, which was the scariest part of it because it was closest to the mythical Indian burial ground. It also was a bit of a maze.

Back in the main house, I found my way to the basement, poked around, but with just the flashlight; it was impossible to dig a, well, to dig. I was lost. God damned ants. Plus, the longer I took, the more questions Rocky would have. I went back to the car, took out one ant roll, and carried it back to the house, down to the basement and left it in a corner. I went back to the other ant roll and put it in the opposite corner. I would have to come back in the morning to deal with them properly, before they started reeking of ant death stench.

I drove back to town and almost got home when I caught a glimpse of the ant exoskeletal bicycles in the back seat.

Damn.

I detoured to a car wash, transfered the bikes to the trunk, threw away the used paper towels, washed all the dirt from the road off the car, then drove home. At least the car was clean. Me? I felt scrubbed.

18

Rocky gave me the third degree, as I had missed dinner and not called. She, of course, started to accuse me of seeing Juliette again. I told her, once I could get a word in, that I had an offer for the house and wrote out the contract right there, then called the agent back and spent the rest of the time negotiating.

"In the past I would have believed that. Not now. Where's the contract? Show me."

I told her I had run it back to the office.

She just stared at me, then went to the bedroom, shutting the door behind her.

I didn't bother pursuing it. I was desperately hungry, but had no appetite. I forced myself to eat a sandwich which I promptly threw up. I went to my office den and laid down. I was tired, but couldn't sleep. I couldn't get that haunted house out of my mind. I kept going down to that basement, caught between those corners. Then I started to cry. I hadn't done that, well I can't ever remember doing that, not even when my father died. Not even when my mother died.

I tried to sleep again, but couldn't. I got on my computer and checked the web site for the local news. No reports of missing ants. Then I checked my email; maybe Miss Clarrissa had responded to my saucy reply. It sure would have been nice to be in New Orleans right then. Nothing from her, but, oh, would the horrors of that day ever end?

There was an email from Fitzroy. It was titled "What is necessary." I fully expected the body to say "I saw what you did." No. All it said was "Is not easy."

Really? Was that so? I had just fucking killed Chrissy and Crystal Diamond with my bare hands and it was easy as pie. Easier than dealing with Juliette, or Rocky. Easier than selling a house. Easier than that fucking Billion Dollar Brotherhood application, on which the ants no longer were in no position to mentor me. And now there was plenty of space for me in the Brotherhood. You bet it was necessary. You bet it was easy.

The room closed in on me and I passed out.

I woke up, automatically, no, as if summoned, by a dark duty. It was three-thirty in the morning. I showered, got dressed in jeans and a T-shirt, took a suit, shirt, tie, and dress shoes, and put them in the car. I took down a shovel from the wall and got the battery powered emergency light and thew them in the trunk.

Then I drove, and drove, back to that place, the haunted house, my future Blood Brothers Bordello. Ha◊ Yes◊ My juices were flowing again.

Just that one little task to complete, then me, dressed nicely, to see Flannigan to rule far and wide and large.

I parked the car. The sun was rising. I lugged the flash-light, shovel, and emergency light to the main house and crept down to the basement. Funny. I couldn't find them with the flashlight. I turned on the emergency light and flooded the space with its white glow. Nothing. I aimed the light at each corner. No rolls of dead ants. What the fuck?

Maybe it wasn't there. I left the emergency light on, and took the flashlight to look down a passage that led to another room in the basement maze. Nothing. Then another. Nothing. Now I knew that the night before I went no farther than the main basement. I didn't go into the maze. So I went back to the main room, fully illuminated. Nothing. I panicked.

It was all too strange. Did I imagine or dream what happened the day before? Impossible. Then I froze. Oh shit. What if the police found them, during the late night, and called in the coroner, who took the ants to the ant morgue? The colorful coverings were gone too. I didn't get it.

I went back to my car and took out the bicycles. I carried them both back to the main basement. Still no ant corpses. Shit. Did this mean they were back in play and would show up at Flannigan's to spite me?

All that stuff I brought and for nothing. I couldn't exactly bury the bicycles. Aha. I went back to my car, got a mini tool set, another prerequisite for being an ace realtor, and then saw an ant fanny pack which I must have missed the night before. It might have identification, so I hid it under the spare tire for the time being. Then, I went back to the basement, and took the bicycles completely apart. I spent the next hour tossing the parts in the desert around the out buildings. I saved the four tires and tossed them out of the car on the way back to I-10.

I got to the office before we opened for the day, changed into the suit, and got some breakfast, which I kept down. Then it was off to Flannigan's, right on time at ten o'clock.

He greeted me in his office, which was set up for a continental breakfast, for four. He had never gone to such trouble for me, and I resented that, after treating him to such a nice dinner.

We made small talk. He was obviously waiting for those ants to arrive. I wouldn't have been surprised if they had. I was so unsure of Sunday, of what had happened. It was strange. The whole day seemed a blur, except for that part of it which invaded my consciousness in excruciating slow motion and close up. The ant faces, just after they had eeped their last. Maybe it was all just a movie I had seen.

"It's not like the Diamonds to be late," he said at ten-fifteen.

I told him that, in my experience, they were most unreliable.

"I am a trifle concerned, however," he said. "Crystal was supposed to call me last night but she did not. And I tried to call both Crystal and Chrissy, but they never answered."

"Maybe their phones died," I said, immediately regretting my choice of words.

"I tried their office phone, their home phone, and their cell phones."

So, he had all those numbers. Stupid man. Why have such contact with insects? All they could do was eep over the phone. Well, they used to be able to do that.

"Royce, I need to ask you something, in confidence," he finally said, after waiting for eeping ants another ten minutes. "Can I trust you not to relate any of this outside this room?"

"Of course," I said. "I'm very discrete by nature and always keep my oaths."

I liked that last bit. It sounded appropriately archaic, and fittingly apt for two men of the Brotherhood. I imagined oaths were very important in the Brotherhood.

"Good," he said. "Royce, why did you send that detective to talk to the Diamonds?"

What? He knew about that? One would have thought those ignorant ants were already in the Brotherhood.

"Honestly?" I said.

"Of course."

"I just wanted rid of him, and they were the first thing I thought of to get him away."

"Why is that?"

"Why is what?"

"Why, when you wanted rid of the man investigating the death of Fitzroy, did you send him to the Diamonds?"

That was rather carefully put.

"To be honest, again, I've never liked them that much and thought it would annoy them. It was kind of a joke."

"Nothing more?"

"Nothing."

This was weird.

"I see. Well, not a funny joke. I think it upset them. Perhaps that is why they are not here."

That was below the belt. And so weak. I called him on it.

"With all due respect, sir, I don't believe that and I don't think you do either. If they are so worthy of being in the Brotherhood, surely they would not fail you because of a quarrel with me."

"Yes, O'Rourke. True enough and truly spoken."

"Why do you ask all this?"

He paused. He looked at the door. He even went out to ask his receptionist if they had called. Then he came back, shutting the door behind him.

"It's only, how shall I say, it's that they thought of Fitzroy as you think of them."

"And they think of me as they thought of Fitzroy? Is that it?"

"On the contrary. In fact, if I may say, they are very, uh, smitten with you. Both of them, and that has caused some friction between them," he said, picking up speed and self-encouragement as he went. "And that, I fear, is why they may be no-shows today."

He seemed rather proud of that. I didn't believe a word of it, well maybe. The thing is, I hated them so much, despised them, that it never occurred to me that they might have actually liked me. Oh, sure, they may have wanted me sexually, wanted my body, like Juliette did, like Rocky did, like Miss Clarrissa did. I must confess I am a bit of a stud. That's embarrassing to say.

And to be honest, thinking of it now, here, after all that's happened, with a clear mind, I can see now that, maybe, their insults and taunts were a kind of frustrated flirting with me. Frustrated because they knew I was beyond them, not just in business, and life, but beyond them as a man, a physical man. How Crystal ant must have enjoyed it, become complete, in her last moments. With me.

But as to Flannigan, then, it didn't gel. Even if the ants were "smitten" with me, as he had put it, that still shouldn't have stopped them from their business duties. I said as much to Flannigan, who agreed with me, naturally.

"It looks like they are no-shows," I said. "That shouldn't stop us, and to be honest, I do not intend to cut anyone into this deal. I want to be clear on that."

"I see."

I hate that kind of response: "I see," "Whatever." What a put down. What an insult. It only meant he had nothing more to say, or nothing more he wanted to say.

"So let's get to it. Do you have a price for the haunted house land?"

"The party holding the title is willing to sell," he said. "They naturally are curious as to the intentions of the buyer, but I, of course, told them nothing of your intentions."

Good, except it occurred to me that the party was no longer in a position to sell.

He named a price which was twice what I was willing to pay and ten times what the land was worth. Time for me to stand taller and stronger than usual.

"Look. I don't intend to waste time haggling over the price. But no one has been able to make a go of that dump and their asking price, to be blunt, is a joke, and an insult."

He didn't react, so I named a price, half of what I ever intended to pay and said that was my best, final, and only offer, and it was good for ten business days.

He took all that in like the quintessential businessman he was and said he would write up an offer. He knew I was as tough as he. Tougher, if he only knew what I had done to those puny ants, who were slacker no-shows. It would be interesting to see how he handled this situation. If he had no contact with his sellers, would he go ahead and sell their title to me anyway, pocketing all the money for himself? That's why I set a time limit. He would know within those ten days that the ants were not just no-shows, but also never to show again.

Then I pinned him down on the Brotherhood. I told him I didn't need the ants' help and that I would turn in all the required parts of the application by the end of the week. He said that was fine. That worked for me. He would know by then that the ants were out of the picture and that there was plenty of room for Royce O'Rourke in the Billion Dollar Brotherhood.

I took my leave trying to figure out what his game was. Oh, on Sunday he was all ready and willing to thwart me, to belittle me. Oh, Royce, you must have the ants take you by the hand, lead you to the penalty box, and walk you step by step on how to fill out a fucking application on paper, which wasn't even online. Oh, Royce, surely we need the expert help of the ants to do a simple title trans-action. Yeah, right. And now that the ants were no-shows, oh, he'll insult me by seriously putting forth a nonsensic-ally inflated offer for dead land, thinking I'm so weak I'll be taken in by a bad faith series of negotiations. Now if I were such a weak little ant, why did he give me that applica-tion? Such a reversal didn't fit. It wasn't like him, unless he really was in control of their transactions and through Monstrance Holdings would funnel all the New Orleans and bordello money to himself. That made more sense. That was the Flannigan I knew.

I wished, for a moment, I had only subdued the ants, pinned them to a white foam board in an insect display case so I could open the lid, when I needed to, flick their antennae to wake them up, and interrogate them as to their connection to Flannigan and what his motives were. Ah, how Detective Payne would love to be able to do that. As for me, even if I could, my time was deflected by having to go back to that application and do every stupid, fucking, ant-inspired requirement.

Andy finally got me a new laptop and copied the backups to it. I had him prepare a bill for the hardware and his time and sent that to the Tucson police department. That should teach them.

And my luck kept on the upswing. The new sign arrived for the office, corrected to "Royce O'Rourke Realty." Score. If only those blood stains would fade away.

Juliette continued to annoy me. She just said soon, maybe, I have to think, yadda yadda. It made it so easy to be faithful to Rocky. What used to be the perfect sexual relationship had turned into a growing entanglement. Leave it to kids, and money, to ruin it.

Then, on Thursday night, I finished every single requirement of that stupid application, and I also marked the fourth day with no mention, anywhere, not in the newspaper, not on the TV, not by a visit from that detective, nothing to do with those exterminated ants. It was as if no one, other than Flannigan, knew they were missing, and apparently he hadn't bothered to report it.

Given all that, I celebrated by cooking the family a nice barbecued dinner, drinking liberally. After everyone went to bed, I repaired to my office and looked at porn online. Rocky hadn't put out since those damned missing ants left their disgustingly cheap photos. After I jerked off, I took a shower, then went back to my computer, opened the last email from "Fitzroy," and replied:

"To hell with you. Oh. No. You're already there. Leave me the fuck alone. I'm so beyond you. I'm in the Brotherhood. I am about to broker the biggest deal the Brotherhood has ever seen. And I'm not doing it crooked like you. Miss Clarrissa was right about you, and she was right about me. She foretold your death and she prophesied my success. So stew on that while you burn in eternal hellfire. FitzRoyce is no more. It's Royce O'Rourke Realty, now. And if you are really not in hell, why don't you come knock on my window, Fitz?"

That should show him. Or whoever was sending it. I wondered, as I laid down on the day bed, if it had been the ants. No, they couldn't have sent that email on Sunday any more than Fitzroy. Gulp. It hit me then that maybe it was Flannigan, who seemed to have his fingers everywhere. Oh great, and I had just sent that boasting to him. I should have known better than to email a ghost when I was buzzed. Who else? Randi? It would be just like her. Juliette? No. Then I thought maybe Miss Clarrissa had been sending the emails. That was intriguing. But why would she care? It didn't seem her style. She was more direct. The more I thought about it, the more it made sense Flannigan was sending them. And I had sent that response.

Oh well, what more could he expect, sending me an email from a dead man? Maybe, if I allowed myself to think about it, not rationally, but spiritually, metaphysically, maybe it was possible that Fitzroy could have sent it, straight from hell. If that was the case, then I expected to start receiving emails from the ants, if they were really dead. I just wasn't sure. All I was sure about was that as I dozed off, I heard a knocking on my window. Just three evenly paced, deliberate raps that got increasingly stronger. I froze. Maybe it was Fitzroy, or the ants. It didn't repeat, at least not in the hour or so I laid there, frozen, pinned to the day bed.

19

The next day I sealed up the revised package and took it to Flannigan's office. He was there, and invited me in.

"The seal is a nice touch, O'Rourke," he said, setting my application on his desk. "And I have good news for you."

It was about time.

"The title owner of the land for your, uh, project, accepted your offer."

Impossible, I thought. I said "Excellent."

"The only thing is that the party will not be able to conduct the transaction for another week, which fortuitously will give you time to liquidate or transfer whatever assets you need to raise the cash."

Ah. The time it would take him to convert the title to himself.

"That works for me, sir."

"Well, good, then. Oh, and I should be clear, the party does want cash, not a check or a wire transfer."

Of course, no trail to be traced back to him.

"One question," I said.

"Twenties and hundreds will do," he jumped ahead of me.

"No, I mean sure, but what I wanted to ask was how long it would take for the application to be reviewed, for the final decision to be made."

"For the Brotherhood?"

"Yes."

"Oh, very soon, I should think. The only hitch is the Diamonds. I still have yet to hear from them and am most alarmed."

"Have you talked to the police?" I ventured.

"Oh, no, I don't think it's my place. I mean, it might, well, let's just say the Brotherhood has greater resources than the Tucson police."

That was a tortured response, for him.

"I understand," I said.

"However, if you hear of them, or from them, you must let me know immediately."

"Sure, but I'm not likely to hear from them."

"No, no I suppose not. Well, time will tell. I must say, if I may, things are looking good for you, O'Rourke. Quite good indeed. Shall we have a drink on that? I know it's early in the day ...."

"Sure," I said, pumped.

So far I was doing my best just keeping up with him. Not that I, Royce O'Rourke, couldn't keep up with Flannery O. Flannigan: It was the subtext, the undercurrent, the not said. I knew the ants were dead. Did he? How could he make an offer on their behalf while despairing of their absence and lack of communication? Complicating my ability to track all this was the missing ant bodies. Did he find them and take them? He was out there, before, with Roger. Then there were the Fitzroy emails I suspected him of sending. You can see how many rooms I was exploring simultaneously while trying to remain focused on the deal.

So overloaded was I becoming that as he handed me the gin and tonic he had prepared, I decided to risk it, to go the O'Rourke route and up the deal.

"You know, Father, I have such visions for the Brotherhood. For being in it and for furthering its cause. I know you said it needs fresh blood, something new, something like the Diamonds. But what is that other than tired political correctness? From what I know of those girls, they play on the same turf we all do, but on a smaller scale. Oh sure, they add the woman factor. They add the lesbian factor, but it's the same stuff in a different, smaller package."

"Now, Royce, they are not lesbians."

"They don't have to be. They give the appearance. I'm all for having them in, if they ever show up. Look, you yourself told me to disavow the likes of Fitzroy. I have. I have always been more above board. And I want to be clear. When I say above, I mean above the petty drug dealing, shady deals, and what not. I'm willing to do big stuff, real big stuff. I have already. I can do what is necessary and it comes easy to me."

"Necessary? Easy? Royce, are you, are you speaking .... No. Never mind. It is enough. It is good. Oh, Royce O'Rourke, cheers! I see a new day before us."

Score◊ Score◊

And I was right. I had slipped in those enigmatic lines from "Fitzroy's" email and, by doing so, definitely elicited a telling reaction from Flannigan. What that reaction told was up for grabs, I realized after I left him.

As I drove back to my office, I decided he must have known about the dead ants, perhaps even got the Brotherhood to stash the bodies. Even more important, he seemed to be signaling to me that it was OK, even a good thing, that I exterminated them. So all that talk about them being the new blood, maybe that was all just a test, a challenge for me. It followed, then, that what had just transpired was some kind of validation for me, that I realized what had to be done, did it, and would be rewarded. I got a thrill thinking about how that elusive, elliptical exchange with Flannigan was emblematic of how they must talk in the Brotherhood, how the movers and shapers speak in their own special code.

Back at my desk, going over the commissions, it dawned on me that I, Royce O'Rourke, had just spoken that special language with Flannigan, and not just spoken it. I was damned fluent in it. It came naturally to me, like I was a native, like I was born with it. I felt changed. I felt more like a Brother than ever before. That led me to dreaming of the day, which was prophesied to come soon, where I would ascend above Flannery O. Flannigan, and it would be him coming to me.

I allowed my little fantasy to rise to the heights where I was in the presidential regalia, sitting on the high throne. I didn't even know if there really was such regalia and throne, but there certainly was in my fantasy, which I intended, one day, to make reality. And I would decorate the throne room with Chinese-made tchotchkes from Miss Clarrissa's shop. They would shine, tinkle, and glisten like Christmas as all those assembled, including Flannery O. Flannigan would bow, kneel, and prostrate themselves before me. I, sitting on my throne in my regalia, would bless them all and bid them enforce the covenants which protected our property, our wealth, our class, our way of life.

As they sallied forth on their quests, I looked up into the steely eyes of Detective Payne. Who the hell let him in?

"I'm sorry to disturb you, Mister O'Rourke," he said.

He didn't scare me.

"Have a seat," I said.

He took out his notebook.

"I won't take much of your time."

"Much obliged."

"We were hoping to find something in Mr. Fitzroy's records to help us identify his killer, or killers."

"And did you?"

"Perhaps, among fairly strong evidence of massive fraud, against his clients, and against you."

Like that was big news to me.

"Well, you can hardly prosecute him now," I pointed out.

"No, but his, your firm, may be held accountable."

"That firm no longer exists."

"And what is this?" he asked, ridiculously gesturing around the office with his arm.

"This is Royce O'Rourke Realty. It is not, never has been FitzRoyce. And it is funded entirely by my honest revenue."

"You were not a co-owner of FitzRoyce?"

"That arrangement was very vague and complicated, but really, why does that interest you? You are a homicide detective, not the fraud squad."

He actually laughed.

"True, but fraud can point to motive. And the Tucson police does have a fraud squad, if you will. But for the moment, that doesn't interest me as much as the whereabouts of Crystal and Chrissy Diamond."

He paused, whether for effect or a reaction, I couldn't tell, nor care less. I stayed calm, sitting on my throne while this supplicant blabbered before me.

"Have you seen or heard from either of them in the last few days?"

"No, I haven't. I usually don't talk to them personally at all. Our only interaction is professional."

"Have you talked to anyone in the business who may know of their whereabouts?"

"No. Except, yes. I met with Flannery O. Flannigan earlier this week, Monday, and funny you should ask about them, because Father Flannigan and I were expecting them to join us, and were surprised when they didn't show up."

I felt safe telling him that, even a bit cocky to drag my servant Flannigan into it. Of course, I didn't tell him I had just come from Flannigan's.

"Monday? What time?"

"The meeting was at ten in the morning."

"And they were supposed to attend, or may have just stopped by?"

"I believe it was Father Flannigan's intention that they attend, and when Father Flannigan expects something, well …."

"He definitely invited them?"

"You'd have to ask him."

"What is your relationship with them?"

"As I said, it is purely a professional relationship. You could say we are competitors, somewhat, except that I deal exclusively at the high end of the market, whereas they do not."

I impressed myself. I was starting to talk like Flannigan.

"And how would you describe Mr. Fitzroy's relationship with the Diamond sisters?"

I wanted to tell him they were all three dancing and fucking in hell. I just told him, instead, that I didn't know. Sure, I had my suspicions, and if I could open that insect display case, I would have tickled them awake and demanded they tell me how Fitzroy aided and abetted their treachery against me. Lacking that, I asked the detective why he was so interested in the ants.

"No reason. They did give me some information and I wanted to follow up with them. Then they go away on vacation, it seems."

"Well, I'm sure they'll be back."

"Yes. And if you hear from them, please contact me immediately."

"To be sure," I said. "And, by the way, thanks for what you did."

"Did?"

"In front of my wife. At the lawyer's office downtown, you covered for me."

"Ah. Perhaps you were with one of the Diamond sisters that night?"

"Think again, sir. As I told you, our relationship is strictly professional."

"Who were you with?"

"What, are you vice, as well as fraud and homicide now?"

He got up. I had played it perfectly, I thought. I imagined he was trying to trip me up, asking me repeatedly about the ants, hoping I would slip and refer to them in the past tense.

"Good day, Detective Payne," I said.

"Mr. O'Rourke," he said, and walked out.

Good riddance, again, but then I had to, well, not worry, as that is something an ant does, not something a shining knight of the Billion Dollar Brotherhood does, not at all, but think it through, as befit the future president of the Billion Dollar Brotherhood.

So, why was he asking about the ants? Who reported them missing? Surely Flannigan didn't. No, that couldn't be. Yes, then it struck me. What if Flannigan had ordered the hit on Fitzroy? And maybe those sneaky ants, who had Fitzroy trapped in hell under their quivering antennae, maybe they found out and were blackmailing Flannigan. Like they found out about me and Juliette and took those pathetic pictures. And Flannigan killed them. Not me. Or could I make it appear that way, if such a contingency became necessary? Then it all fell into place. I stood up. I could frame Flannigan for the extermination of the ants, thereby securing the presidency of the Billion Dollar Brotherhood for me.

Then I sat back down. That could only work if it were true that Flannigan knew they were dead and arranged to have their ant bodies disposed of, and rapped on my window that night. Flannigan. How could he have known? No one saw me kill them and take them to that haunted house at that ungodly hour. The only other person there, after the open house, was Juliette. I wondered if Juliette could be in the Brotherhood and was really a double agent. No. Impossible. I looked back down at the commission sheet. The numbers came into focus. It's not that they didn't add up. No. They were just too complex to resolve without some calculus or trigonometry. Or maybe I just needed some corroboration to be sure.

I needed someone to talk to. My priest? At confession? Ha. No. I would go to Miss Clarrissa, that Voodoo Priestess Shaman. That was clarity. I got online and booked a ticket to New Orleans for Monday.

Score◊

When I got home, I told Rocky all about the New Orleans deal, how we, with all the best intentions, sold scores of houses to people after Katrina, who really didn't qualify by our standards, but did by the banks', and how we tried to make amends by short selling, yadda, yadda. And how I had to fly down there on Monday to help those poor people refinance and move into smaller homes. She was cool with it, then took me by the hand to show me how clean the floors were and said Roger still wanted a kitten, and how cool it would be to make a video of the kitten on the Roomba, and post it on YouTube, and how everyone on YouTube would be able to see how clean her floors were, and how she loved me, and had Juliette left town yet, and whether I wanted pot roast or beef steak for dinner, and how wouldn't it be nice to leave hot, dry Tucson to live in New Orleans. I didn't need to check the colored bottles.

So that weekend, we all four of us went to the animal shelter to get a kitten. Well, excuse me, but you'd think we were there to adopt a baby from China. We got a pretentious lecture from some pasty white, unwashed vegan granola renter about people who got kittens because they were cute and then couldn't handle them when they grew up. I told her to fuck off, which pleased Randi no end, and drove the family to the mall, where the pet store was only too happy to sell us the kitten of our choice. God and the Billion Dollar Brotherhood bless capitalism.

20

On Monday, I had time to drive to the office to give marching orders to the agents, then drove to the airport where I had to connect through Denver to get to New Orleans. I took a cab straight to the French Quarter and walked to Bourbon and St. Anne.

I strode to Miss Clarrissa's shop and crept into her lair. Her daughter was behind the counter, reviewing some papers, as there were no customers. She looked up, pretended not to recognize me, and looked back down. I ignored her and headed toward the back of the shop where the beast lay waiting for me, but I wasn't able to find the door from the last time. Surely this was the right place.

I spread apart some colorful, fluffy boas, looking for the door.

"She's not here," a voice came from directly behind me.

It was the daughter.

"When will Miss Clarrissa be back?" I asked her.

"That's not for me to say," she said.

"Oh, come on. You recognized me. I know it. And I know your mother. Now where is she?"

"You put on such airs, Red. What gives you the right to stroll in here, ignore the merchandise, and demand an audience with the most esteemed voodoo priestess shaman, Miss Clarrissa?"

"Because I want to fuck the shit out of her, and because she stole my shirt, that's why."

Her eyes widened.

"You do have a high opinion of yourself, just like Miss Clarrissa said."

"Do you always call your mom 'Miss Clarrissa?'" I asked.

"In front of you, Red, yes."

"I'm not 'Red.' I'm Royce O'Rourke."

"Whatever, Red. Miss Clarrissa is actually out of town right now. She won't be back for a few days. You should have called first to make an appointment, as she is a very busy business woman."

"Serious? You're not shitting me?"

"Watch your language, Red."

"Stop calling me 'Red,'" I ordered.

"As you desire. Perhaps I can help. What did you come for?"

"A fuck and a chat. Care to oblige on the former?"

"Let me call my husband, all six foot seven, two hundred fifty pounds of him. We'll see what he with his uncontrollable temper has to say to that."

"That's OK. Just a suggestion."

"I ought to throw your ass outta here anyway. You are still on my shit list for what you did to my neighborhood, Carmine."

"Who?"

"Scarlet ruby red Royce. You think you and your buddy fucked us over real good, don't you?"

"You fucked yourselves over real good. No one forced you to sign those papers without reading them."

"I beg to differ. No honest man would use all forms of trickery to rebuild homes at twice the price they were and lure the former residents in with the collusion of the banks who say 'Oh, honey, don't you mind, we'll just raise the points a bit to get that monthly mortgage payment down; y'all just sign here and shake my hand like a brother and all will be ruby red like Royce O'Rourke.'"

I actually clapped three times for that performance.

"You speak better than your mother," I said.

"You don't know shit how my mother speaks except how she speaks to you."

"So if I'm so evil and caused you such harm, where are you living now? With mom?"

"That's none of your business, Red. But if you must know, my mother, who is Miss Clarrissa to you, set us up real good and real honest in a real nice neighborhood full of red and white people like you, so you can sleep pretty tonight."

"I have no regrets," I said.

"I bet you don't," she retorted.

"Look, uh, what is your name?" I asked.

"That's my business, but you may remit all payments to Mrs. Risa Sclar, as long as you address me in person as Princess Risa."

"OK, Princess Risa, I will remit no payments, but you can hardly blame me for the bank insisting you pay your mortgage."

"Fuck you, Red."

"Now you sound like your ma."

"Fuck you again. I know good and well you and your partner were paying off all the parish leaders, sending kickbacks to several banks, who wrote unfair loans. You are guilty as anyone in that amateur fraud."

"At least I didn't steal the shirt off your back like your ma did to me."

She stared, smoldering, at me. I got rock raging hard. She cast her eyes up and down me, smirked, then looked me in the eyes.

"Wait right here," she said.

She stepped outside, looked both directions, then shut the door, and locked it, flipping a "Be Back Soon" sign toward the street. Then she went back, back into the mess in the back of the store.

I was tempted to follow her. It didn't feel right, so I looked over the merchandise in the shop, the laces and chains of colorful beads, the neon day-glo gowns, the cheap imports from China. I made mental notes of which ones I would use to decorate the throne room of the Brotherhood, and also decided I wanted my bordello to look just like this, the gift shop, at least. Oh, not the actual stock, but the exuberance of color and the profusion of the tightly packed merchandise.

Princess Risa came back, holding what looked like a doll, and two bottles of cold beer, one of which she gave to me.

"Cheers, Red," she said.

"What's that?" I asked, pointing at the doll.

"You."

"Me?"

"See?" she said, holding it before me.

I took a swig of the beer then recognized the doll was made out of my shirt.

"Hey," I said. "I recognize that pattern. It's the shirt Miss Clarrissa stole off my back."

"Indeed. And look what she did with it. Look at the care she took. Look, and see, how the pattern matches all around and how she magically was able to get your monogram right perfect where it would be – here over your black heart."

I took another swig of the beer. I noticed, as she held it close in front of my eyes, several arcs of single hairs carefully glued across the chest of the doll, and on its head. I tried to point.

"Yes, you see. You see the red hairs. This one here from your head; this one from your chest; this one from your pubes. All taken with love and all transferred to this effigy with care."

"Why?"

"Don't touch!" she warned me. I must have tried to take back what was mine. "It might burst into flames if you touch it!"

"No," I protested. My throat was parched. I took a big gulp of the beer. It seemed the more I drank of it, the thirstier I got.

"See this?" she said, with a long silver pin in her other hand. "Lick it."

I refused.

"It's sweet, like Miss Clarrissa. Just give it a little lick."

"I'll bleed."

"Not if you're careful. Give it a lick, but don't swallow."

I did. It was sweet, but freezing, like ice, like a Popsicle, a blueberry Popsicle.

"Now, stand firm Red. I'm not supposed to do this. Miss Clarrissa would be flaming mad at me, but I like you, so watch me."

"Yes, Princess Risa." I was wholly incapacitated, involuntarily surrendering to her.

"See the sleek, cold, sharp silver pin? See the arm of the doll? See how the pin gets close, dances above, then –"

I was on the floor, clutching my right arm, my beer spilled on the floor, pooling around me like Fitzroy's blood. My arm was on fire, throbbing in piercing shards of pain.

I saw her leaning over me. She held the doll before me, then with an exaggerated gesture, pulled the pin out.

It was like I was on fire, then submerged in a cold calm pool.

"Get up, Red Royce," she commanded.

"Now you see our power. Now you know how close you came. See this pin? I could stick it right here, in the ROR monogram, and give you a heart attack right now."

"No, please," I begged. Me, Royce O'Rourke, begging? Believe it.

"I ought to make you lick that beer off the floor, but I won't," she said.

"Thank you Princess Risa," I said. This was so fucked.

"So what did you want to talk to Miss Clarrissa about, Red?"

"Stuff."

"Stuff," she said firmly. Then she took the round, bulbous head of the pin and started circling it around the crotch of the doll.

"What stuff?" she asked.

I was hard, again.

"Stuff about the bodies."

"How dare you talk to me with your pants done up. Drop them and take it out!"

That wasn't hard. It was necessary, and easy. She took the doll and teased my cock with it.

"What about the bodies?"

"Who took them?" I said. "Where did they go?"

"Maybe you took them," she suggested.

"Where did I put them?"

"Let's see," she said, then dropped to her knees and put her sweet, hot mouth around my cock.

"I don't know where I put them," I said.

She got up, went behind the counter, and got a purple candle, which she lit with her finger, no match, no lighter. She was so beautiful.

"What bodies?" she asked as the light from the candle cast alluring shadows about her face, highlighting her high cheekbones, making her look like some lost, exotic queen of a secret sisterhood.

"The ants," I said.

"Ants?"

"Two of them. The Diamonds."

"The diamond ants."

"I thought, I mean, they tricked me. They made me think ...."

"That you killed them?"

"How do you ... ? NO. No. I didn't. Flannigan did it."

"Did he?"

"I say so."

"Then so it must be."

She held the candle over my cock and let the hot wax drip on it. It stung at first. A good sting, then it felt better. I wondered if my Billion Dollar Brotherhood application felt like that when I sealed it with my initial in wax.

"You lie," she said.

"Yes."

"Lies are good, yes?"

"Yes."

She went down on me again. While she was at it, she held the candle up, letting the wax drip on the base of my cock while she toyed with the head.

She let go and stared up at me.

"So the diamond ants, you lost their bodies?"

"Yes."

"Red, I worry."

"Worry?"

She caught my cock in her lips, then pushed in, taking it down her throat, and thrusting back and forth until I couldn't stand it. Then she put the candle out right below my balls, shoving the lit wick into that area just below, the wax flowing like lava there, and I shot strong and full into her mouth. She let go, took up the doll, and spit the cum on its back. She cleaned her mouth with its head.

"Do up your trousers, red stud," she said.

I did.

"Do you still worry?" I asked her.

"Yes."

"Worry about what?"

"I worry those diamond ants you talk about; I worry they may be zombies."

"Zombies?" I said. I had almost laughed. Almost. She still held such a commanding presence I didn't dare.

"Yes, zombies. They can exist, not like in the movies, but a powerful enough force can conjure them. Thing is, you have no such power. But the dead don't walk away on their own unless they are zombies."

I shuddered. It occurred to me that it could have been a zombie that rapped on my window. At the same time, it occurred to me that this was a totally irrational idea, but in those surroundings, everything seemed possible, including zombie ants.

"You go now, and beware of zombies," she ordered. "Walk bravely. You dare tell Miss Clarrissa about this, I'll take that pin and stick it through the head, and then drive it into the chest, giving you a heart attack and a brain aneurysm all at once. You clear?"

"Yes, Princess Risa."

"And do note duly that I did not steal the shirt off your back."

"Yeah."

She went to the entrance, flipped the "Be Right Back" sign around, and opened the door.

"You leave here, turn left, go half a block, and you are back on Bourbon. Get a cab there. I'll tell Miss Clarrissa you called."

I managed to get back to the airport without losing my shirt or being stalked by zombies, or chased by Miss Clarrissa or Princess Risa. I had come for Miss Clarrissa, and didn't get that. Princess Risa was far from a poor substitute. She was, it turned out to be, a fine hostess. There must be something in that beer. I made a mental note to email Miss Clarrissa to ship a case to me so I could use it at the Billion Dollar Brotherhood.

Yes. But zombies?

21

Zombies. The whole idea of it seemed more ridiculous as the beer wore off. And as the flight leveled off, I relaxed and gave it some serious thought. I mean, she was able to make my arm hurt using that voodoo doll and silver pin. It didn't hurt anymore, and it did stop hurting when she pulled the pin out. Now, I asked myself, how else to explain the ants disappearing? OK. I wasn't sure I killed them. Assuming I did, and I did leave their ant carcasses rolled up in the basement of the haunted house, over an Indian burial ground, and no one else knew of it, no one saw me, then how else to explain their disappearance? How else to explain the police not finding a trace of them? Then there was that rap on my window. I know I didn't dream it. It could have been a zombie ant.

Yet, there's no such thing as zombies, except for the one that finally got me a gin and tonic at 35,000 feet. As I drank, I examined my beliefs. It's true, I was expected to believe Jesus rose from the dead, not quite like a zombie. God was a real force, if not corporeal in everyday life. There was an afterlife. Everyone believes that. So why couldn't there be zombies? If Jesus could turn water into wine, why couldn't Princess Risa work magic on a voodoo doll? And the church still believed in demonic possession. Maybe a zombie was just a minor demon possessing a corpse.

I didn't want to dwell too much on it. The events in my religion took place two thousand years ago. Such things weren't supposed to happen in the modern world. I decided to relegate the idea of zombies from a certain reality to a metaphysical possibility. I chuckled that Flannigan would approve of that conclusion. Still, there were the ants' bodies, the emails from Fitzroy, that pain in my arm. Flannigan was the most logical answer, but he didn't cause that pain.

We arrived in Denver and I changed to Tucson, resolving to relocate the headquarters of the Brotherhood to a city with major direct air hub services like New York, Chicago, Atlanta, or Los Angeles. Oh, angels too. If there can be angels, can't there also be zombies?

On the Tucson flight, I came back to direct, close reality. If I did kill the ants, then my whole career, future, and chance to get into the Billion Dollar Brotherhood were at risk. It didn't get me anywhere to question whether the victims being in a zombie state negated a murder charge. On the other hand, it occurred to me that timing is all. When I got into the Brotherhood, I would be safe, as Flannigan hinted at our last meeting. The Brotherhood was teeming with lawyers, judges, congressmen, movers and shapers, all knights of the round table, all disciples at the last supper, who would never let some puny putz detective pin a murder charge on their president, Royce O'Rourke, for snuffing out two insects, when they were ranging across the desert as flesh-eating, window-rapping zombies. Even if their non-zombie corpses were found rotting in the desert, the Brotherhood would find a way to protect me because it operated under a covenant that was above the common law.

After the flight landed in Tucson, I drove home to tell Rocky all was set in New Orleans to bring in even more money. I made sure to admire the clean floors, and patiently waited by Randi's computer to see the clip she uploaded showing the new black kitten, which somehow got named "Zombie" while I was gone, ride on top of the Roomba as it spun around the floor. And, wonder of wonders, Rocky put out that night. I thought Princess Risa must have been playing with the crotch of that doll because it was better than it had ever been, with Rocky.

At work the next day, however, I couldn't get my mind off of two basic facts. First, I didn't trust Flannigan. He clearly wasn't honest with me, preferring to play games, so I couldn't assume he was serious about putting me in the Brotherhood. What if he really believed the lie that I was a joke and was willing to see me take the fall for removing the ants?

The other thing that preyed on me was the possibility that the dead ants could really be zombies. If they were zombies, where did they hang out? I thought of going by their office, to see if there was any trace of their being there since that open house. Then that funny thing happened where your mind clicks on something deeply important, but totally forgotten. It stood to reason that Detective Payne would continue searching for them, especially when they failed to return, at least in human ant form, as opposed to zombie insect form. And, his detection would turn back to me, and where I was and where the ants were last. I was sure no one else was in the open house when the ants showed up. But what if they left some record in their appointment book or with their clients? So I thought about two things: Their office and that ant fanny pack I had hidden under the spare tire. And one might lead to the other. Plus, maybe I could find something there to implicate Flannigan in their deaths.

I raced out to my car, drove it to an alley, then got out and recovered the yellow fanny pack dropped by Crystal

Ant. Yes. There was a big ring of keys. I took the keys, then stared at the fanny pack. It wouldn't do to have it. Detective Payne might get closer and closer and get a search warrant for my car. Aha. The best place to dispose of it was in the ant hill. So now I had to go.

I drove to the ant strip mall, to the back of the building. I knew the ant office was next to the FedEx, so I tried key after key on the adjacent door until one worked. I opened it, slipped inside, and went to their desks, stupidly pushed together so the ants could eep across to each other. How lame. I tried one of the computers. Stupid ants. They had invoked the password protection on the screen saver. I tried "billion," and "dollar," and "brotherhood." No. I tried "Crystal," and "Chrissy," and "Diamond," and even "zombie." No. Then, for shits and grins, I tried "Royce" Bingo. Well, Flannigan was right. They were "smitten" with me. And I bet the password for the other computer was "Orourke." Bingo. I found the appointments in their Outlook calendars and sure enough, there was one for my open house, so I deleted it on each computer.

Then I got nosy. I started scanning through their email. There were tons of messages from Flannigan, which spanned the last six months. Bitch ants. They had been cheating and colluding and conspiring against me for that long. They deserved what they got. And Flannigan? I didn't know what to think of him. I rarely emailed him, but I had private face-to-face meetings with him in his luxurious office.

Oh, but as I read through the eepmails, damn those ants, they did too. And they got a tour of the Brotherhood "headquarters," as they called it. Fucking cunt bitch ants. And fuck Flannigan for stringing me along, making me redo that application. My blood was at a high boil just at the point it became clear what they meant by a term they kept using: The vermin issue. They, the fuckers, meant Fitzroy, and, of all people, me.

Of course Fitzroy's ways were criminal, but not genteelly criminal enough for them. They had code names for us: Weasel for Fitzroy, and, for me, and my blood boils now, even now when I think about it, as I write about it, as I take back every apology I ever made, as I invalidate every bit of contrition I ever showed, for me, they, those insects and that black viper priest, they called me a rooster. A red rooster. Red O'Rooster they called me. Burn in hell zombie ants. Burn in sulfurous air and hot streams of steaming magma, and acrid tongues of flames. And as if that weren't enough, it soon became clear what they were getting at.

You see, the scorched ants applied five months before, keeping it, with the help of Flannigan, a huge, special secret. Oh, he treated them like fucking royalty, until they were just about in, then he turned dark and demanding. He had them completely under his power and he set forth a final qualifying task for them.

That task became clear to me in a sequence of emails:

"My Dearest Crystal and Chrissy.

"I am edified that you understand our particular, strange, ineluctable need. You demonstrated at our last meeting a keen insight into the mystery which we all try to understand.

"Now that you understand, equally, and as I do, I ask you to delay no more. What must needs be done must needs be done. You have nothing to fear. Only inaction will undo you.

"The vermin is dumb and of the devil's making. Deal with it. Soon.

"FoF."

And the ants' reply?

"Eep Eep Eep."

In English:

"Right. Understood. Will act soon."

Then another one:

"My Dearest Chrissy and Crystal:

"Ah, I am never wrong. You are brilliant and insightful.

"However, I must say no. The rooster is not the threat the vermin weasel is. The weasel carries germs and disease and rabies and must be dealt with.

"The rooster, on the other hand, can continue to serve for our amusement."

The ants' reply?

"Eep. Eep, eep."

In English:

"Ha! Yes, we agree."

In Royce O'Rourke:

Me? A toy for their pathetic fun? Their amusement? Ah, how amusing was it for you, Crystal Ant, when I took you down, penetrated your mushy ant nothingness, shot my life force of power into you, and used my strong bare hands to choke the death into you? And you, fucking Chrissy Ant, did you glean amusement from your ant head being bashed by my brute force on that counter in that open kitchen at that open house? How much fun was that? Are you laughing at me now? No. You are crawling in the dark: Undead, tormented, zombies. Nothing will free you, nothing will amuse you but the fires of hell.

And Flannigan? His time would come.

The third email cinched it:

"My Children, My Lambs!

"Yes. I am heartened and thrilled that you will exorcise the demon weasel tomorrow. And my congratulations on your resourcefulness with a certain new mode of transportation for the deed. As to the red rooster, it will be instructive for it to be near the exorcism.

"Take care. When done, hie thee rapidly to headquarters for debriefing.

"Remember, what is necessary is not always easy. Go with God, as after tomorrow, your path to the Brotherhood is assured."

There was no response from the vermin ants. And, as you may have guessed, the date of that email was the day before Fitzroy was gunned down in front of our office, in front of Darleen, in front of me.

So, the ants had to kill Fitzroy to gain entry into the Brotherhood. And what would my assignment be? The RE/Max agent? Oh no, I had already accomplished my task, by exterminating those murderous ants. And there was now no question of it. I had to frame Flannigan for the murder of Crystal and Chrissy Diamond, thereby removing him from the Brotherhood, and opening the path for me to ascend as beautiful Miss Clarrissa had prophesied.

The rest of the emails, I won't recount, as they made fun of me. Actually, I'll recount just one, so it is clear that those hideous evil ants asked for what they got:

"Eep! Eep eep eep eep eep eep eep eep."

In English:

"Hey Chrissy!

"Look, I know Red O'Rooster spit on you, and I know how disgusting that must have been. But! Listen to me. I think I have a better solution.

"Sure, Red is a joke. It's almost sad to see how he huffs and puffs and can't even blow a shingle off the roof, let alone the whole house down. The thing is, why do you let such a joke of a man, such a loser, get your goat? Lookit. He comes from white trash. His father was a prison guard and his mother did him the massive disservice by making him think he could sell real estate!

"All you will do is hurt his wife and kids, who don't deserve that, especially since they have to live and deal with him.

"I know it's none of my business, but I think you should send the pictures to Father Flannigan instead. That would cement the image Flannery has of him as a stuffed shirt, a Fitzroy wannabe, who lacks the intelligence to rise to Fitzroy's level of deceit and criminality.

"And please don't be mad at me for accusing you of being in love with him. But if it ever went anywhere, you'd end up just like his lush of a wife. And don't get me started on his corrupt genetic stock ….

"What I'm getting at is I think you should wait. Wait for the right moment. And the right opportunity.

"And finally, why do we waste so much time on a loser like Red O'Rooster? We should be focusing on running you for city council."

Now, let's get this out of the way. To knock Roger like they did in that scum-ridden eepmail, to insult him like that, well, that alone warranted their execution. Fucking bitch cunts.

As to the rest, there it was, just as I always knew. Two frustrated women who could never get laid, least of all by me, agreeing to murder a man for Flannigan and perpetuating a mutual delusion about me, their better. I could go on about how all this was worse than anything I ever did to them, but I won't. You get the picture and the joke, I hope, of those two running for any political office. They were not even fit to be dog catcher. Now, all I could think of was how to frame Flannigan for their extermination and crush three ants with one foot: Remove the threat of a murder charge against me, remove Flannigan from the Brotherhood, and pave my way to the presidency, as Miss Clarrissa foretold.

By the time I endured all the ants' eepmail it was time to pick up Roger, and talk to Juliette, again, damn it.

We had Roger draw another picture, and I told her in no uncertain terms that she had to move to Phoenix. Now, why was it that every woman on the planet had it in for me that day. She gave me "sheet."

"I have decided to stay here een Tucson, Royce. I have a good job here. I love my students. I have been here a long time and they say they will make me a teacher next year. A full-time teacher. They have accepted my credentials from France."

Shit. I told her no. I said:

"Look, Juliette, you said you'd be cooperative, that you wouldn't make trouble. Well, you're making trouble now. The only way to be cooperative is to cooperate by moving to Phoenix."

"I didn't like it there. I will never move there. I will not leeve een a place where the sheriff wears pink underwear and locks people up een tents een the hot zun and makes them eat baloney, and puts them een gangs een chains. Only een America could that happen. It would never happen een France."

I could have told her my father was a fucking prison guard and that the prisoners deserved what they got, but I didn't. I told her instead she'd get no money or support from me.

"I don't care," she said. "Eef you want to be that way, fine."

Then I told her I'd tell the principal of the school that she had been leaving during the day to have sex.

"And will you tell her the sex was with you?" she countered. "How would your wife like the whole school and the whole town to know? I have to say, Royce, you are giving me wrinkles on my fronthead."

Then I told her I was fed up with this. I was probably too harsh, as the libelous ant eepmails was gnawing at me. I said:

"Look. This isn't fair. If you don't move, I'll expose you for the whore you are and demand custody, sole custody, of that child, on the grounds you are an unfit mother. Then I'll turn you into the INS and have you deported. And you know where they'll take you first? That jail in Phoenix where you'll be kept in a hot tent, in the sun, and have to eat baloney, and be in a chain gang, and have to dig graves for car crash victims."

She started to cry, then stopped, then looked like she could take on Wellington's army. Suddenly history replayed itself and she was Chrissy Ant slapping me across the face.

I reached for her throat, I did, and to this day I don't know whether I stopped because I realized she was not an insect ant, but a beautiful woman, or because Roger started wailing and crying and throwing his chalk at us.

"Now look what you've done," Juliette said, rushing to Roger.

He was my son, not hers. I went to him, took his hand and tried to drag him outside.

"Don't fight!" he wailed. "Why do you fight?"

"I stay where I am and I will fight," Juliette directed at me, calmly.

I was going to say "So will I," but I didn't want to upset Roger any more, so out we went. We stopped by the Dairy Queen so I could ply Roger with Blizzards and tell him how important it was to keep adult business just among the adults involved.

That adult business would probably stop. Well, good riddance. She'd start swelling up anyway. Now I had to figure out which threat to make good on, as well as how to frame Flannigan for executing those murderous ants.

I was too tired from the long day to do much after dinner, except to make a stiff drink and to check email in my home office. Nothing from Fitzroy, surprise, surprise, but there was one from Miss Clarrissa and one, the earth will shake, from Flannigan.

"Red.

"So I see you be trying to bang my daughter. Well, she and I have sent an army of zombies your way. Be on your guard, Red, and don't approach us again until you have defeated the zombies. You dare reply to this, as soon as you do, you will feel a sharp pain in your left leg. Goodbye."

Yeah.

"Dear Royce:

"The New Orleans deal has gone through. Would you mind doing me the courtesy of stopping by my office tomorrow so I can discuss the payment. I am not sure to whom I should make it."

That would be an interesting conversation. I replied to Flannigan that I would stop by around ten. Then I replied to Miss Clarrissa: "Bend over, bitch, and just take it."

I finished my drink, and got up to go to bed when a sharp pain shot through my left leg and I fell to the floor. Now I was sure the ants roamed the earth as undead zombies.

22

The next day I stopped by the office to give a motivational speech to the agents on teamwork and fully expected Detective Payne to interrupt before I set off to see Flannigan. Actually, I would have welcomed a visit so I could plant the seeds in his detective mind against Flannigan, who, as I recalled, was already under Payne's detective radar. No such luck, so off to Flannigan I went.

He received me in his office, and had the same buffet setup as the last time. I sneaked a close look at it to make sure it wasn't crawling with ants. It was clean. I took some toast, sausage, and fruit. Flannigan asked me if I wanted champagne in my orange juice.

"Do we have something to celebrate with the champagne?" I asked.

"Quite possibly, O'Rourke," he said, like a Magic 8 Ball.

I took the champagne in the orange juice and sat across from him.

"Now Royce," he started, "as I mentioned in my email, I was not sure whom to pay, how to make out the check. Should I make it out to FitzRoyce, then have FitzRoyce put it back on the market?"

"No," I said. "FitzRoyce is no more. Let's keep this simple and direct. Just make it out to Royce O'Rourke Realty."

"As you wish," he said. "I'll write the check before you leave."

"Thank you," I said.

We ate for a bit. He asked about the family, about business, what I thought of the city council vote, yadda, yadda. Then he steered the conversation to the ants, of course.

"Ah, I am most disappointed in the Diamonds," he said.

"They are still no-shows?" I asked. I so wanted to use the word "zombies." And he was still carrying on as though he didn't know that I knew what he knew. OK. That was fair. I could play along, for that moment, to see where he would take it.

"I believe they are. All that work. All that investment. I was clearing the way for them to get into local government, you know. And worse, they have been ignoring their clients. They have lost sales. Shameful."

"Yes. I always knew those two were unreliable."

"I can see the Brotherhood will benefit from your excellent ability to judge character."

Really? And, SCORE◊

"I know you didn't want to involve the police," I said, pushing it. "But has the Brotherhood had any luck finding out why they left, what they were up to?"

"I'm afraid the police are looking for them. I was visited by Detective Payne, who asked the most intrusive questions."

"Really?"

"Of course I told the man that I, as their priest, could reveal few details of the inner spiritual trouble which plagued those girls."

Aha. Spiritual trouble? He was using code again.

"I'm sure he's the type of man the Brotherhood eats for lunch," I said.

"Yes, well, that's one way of putting it. I do wish, however, Royce, I do wish I knew what happened to them."

I was getting impatient with this game. Or else, well, they could be zombies and maybe he did think they were missing. I continued to play along.

"You think something happened," I asked, "as opposed to them just being irresponsible and jetting off to Disney World?"

"I am not sure I am yet inclined to think that way."

"Maybe those who got Fitzroy got the Diamonds," I pushed.

He looked at me, intently. Then said:

"Why Royce, you make it sound like a mafia situation."

"Not at all. I have been thinking. Thinking about the big picture. I can see now how Fitzroy must have turned out to be quite an embarrassment to the Brotherhood."

"So?"

"I'm just saying. Maybe, just maybe, the Brotherhood found it necessary to," I paused. He looked, not alarmed. He looked expectant.

"Yes?" he asked.

I just smiled, then said:

"Maybe the Brotherhood wanted them in for a specific purpose, then wanted them out, for a specific reason."

"Them? Do you mean Fitzroy or the Diamonds?"

"All three."

"That doesn't explain, even if it were true, where the Diamonds are now, does it? Tell me, Royce, Royce O'Rourke, where do you think they are?"

"Honestly?"

"Of course."

"I think zombies got them."

"Zombies?"

"Yep."

"Zombies."

He repeated it again, as if he had just learned the term. He looked really confused, a look I'd never seen on him before.

"Royce, I asked that question in all seriousness. I, I must say, whatever happened to the Diamonds, it, it must have been, I mean you certainly don't believe zombies took them away."

"Surely. Or they were transformed into zombies themselves."

"Zombies. That is a sin, Royce."

"Hail Mary."

"Now, Royce …."

"Let's leave it at this. The Diamonds must have, somehow, run into what is necessary, something necessary, and perhaps even easy. As to where they are now, as opposed to where they were when it was necessary, I can only guess and it's just as good a guess to say zombies took them as anything else."

That got him. His own circular deflection, it sure did. He paused, for a minute longer than necessary, then finally said:

"Yes, a mystery, to be sure."

He bussed the table, then filled two champagne flutes. He remained standing.

"Royce, stand please."

I did.

"Royce O'Rourke! It is my most esteemed honor to tell you, here and now, on the seventeenth of June, that I may announce to you, that I make this annunciation, to inform you that you, Royce O'Rourke, Realtor, have been accepted into and embraced by the Billion Dollar Brotherhood."

Whatever game he had been playing, I played it too. And I won. All my life had led up to that moment. To hear those words. The face of God turned its light on me. Jesus Christ invited me to join his apostles. Me. Royce O'Rourke. I was trembling. I was sweating. Take that you dead zombie ants. Take that dad. Your son, Royce, has ascended to the pinnacle in the Brotherhood of the movers and shapers, those who ruled over you, as you paced back and forth every day, in front of monkey cages. See me, mom. See your son, the one you saved, the one you taught, the one who left home and worked hard and missed your funeral to buy his first Montblanc, your only child, the one who sold and bought and moved and shaped, your baby boy, a big real man now. See me, Rocky, your husband, ascending to the highest levels of power and money. Oh, baby, how I will raise you up, up in society, clothe and house you in the finest, give you everything you want so those colored bottles will no longer rule you. See me, Randi, my smart daughter. See me Roger, my special son.

See Royce O'Rourke rule. See me, Miss Clarrissa. As you prophesied, so I am. I unite with you in an exotic, erotic, explosive epiphany into the hall of the gods of the round table of the knights of King Arthur, you Miss Clarrissa, my magical enchantress. Watch me, eeping ant zombies, writhing in the flames of hell, with the man before me soon to join you.

I was in tears. I had fallen to my knees. It was as if Miss Clarrissa and Princess Risa had taken out that voodoo doll and had held him in their warm black hands and caressed him, then held him up against the brilliant blue sky, releasing him into an ether of eternal access and privilege. Me, Royce O'Rourke, above all, master of all men, enforcer of all covenants. Covenants. Yes. No. What? Why? Why in my apotheosis of ascending glory did I see it? Staring at me. In flaming letters in Flannigan's eyes. In Princess Risa's smoldering stare. In the ants' eeping, hellish dance. Covenants. Coven. Ants. Oh no. Oh shit. A coven of ants reared their quivering antennae and charged at me. I wouldn't run from them. I would face them. I would take each one down with my bare hands, each eeping ant.

"Royce, are you all right?"

"Ants be gone."

"Royce!"

The face of Father Flannery O. Flannigan swam before me. Then a red rooster squawked. I almost threw up. I almost shit my pants. I was wet all over.

I felt a hand in mine, both of mine, raising me up, putting a flute in my hand. Shall I play it or drink it?

"Royce! Speak to me!"

I was standing again. Miss Clarrissa and Princess Risa had put away their voodoo toy.

"Father?"

"Royce, my son? My fellow member of the Billion Dollar Brotherhood. My brother."

"My brother," I said.

Then Father Flannery O. Flannigan, whom I would frame for the murder of those murderous red ants, kissed me on the forehead. Oh. If only. If only my own father had done that. If only that fucking prison guard had dropped his mask too .... No. I won't go there. I will stay here. Now. The reality. The truth. Flannigan. Champagne.

I took a long sip of it. Its exotic, erotic, explosive effervescence brought me to the top, the front of my consciousness. There, there before me was Father Flannery O. Flannigan, and that murderous crook had just given me the news I had long longed to hear. I was in. Finally. In the Billion Dollar Brotherhood. June 17. A day. A day that will live in eepfamy. No! Shit. An exclamation mark. And I've gone so long without one, and now here it comes to spoil my great moment, courtesy of a coven of ants. No. I won't let it. Not on a day that will live through all eternity.

"Royce, brother, please sit down," Flannigan said.

I complied.

"Just two things for now. One. Tell no one that you are now a member. Always keep that a secret. There has been far too much chatter about the Brotherhood, for which I blame Fitzroy. Loose lips sink ships, as they used to say. Do you understand?"

"Yes."

"Second. The initiation will be very soon. I will provide the exact instructions on where and when to go, what to be, and what not. You must be prepared at a moment's notice to drop everything and be inscribed. I will also arrange for an information package to be FedExed to you. I think it best to send this to your house instead of your office. We don't want anyone else to know about this. Do you understand?"

"Yes. Will my family get to go to the ceremony?"

"To part of it, yes. But don't dwell on that. The Brotherhood will take care of all the details."

"Yes. I just hope I'm in a good suit when the time comes."

"Ah," he said, moving to his desk. "That is one of the first lessons. One should always be, oh, how do they say, yes, combat ready in all regards. You almost are now and will later be an exemplar of the high standards of the Brotherhood and must show it in your dress, your bearing, your manners, at every moment of every day."

He had written out a check during all that.

"Here is the payment for the New Orleans transaction," he said, handing me the check. I took it with the nonchalant solemnity expected of a Brother.

"You should have no contact with me until the induction. Go with God, Royce, and no more talk of zombies!"

"Yes. But what about the sale of the haunted house? Don't I need that to qualify?"

"You are in, Royce. If the seller moves, I will contact you, alright?"

"Yes."

I was out of the office, into the street, in my car, driving, a new man. I wasn't sure where to go. Well, first things first. I went back to the office, gave Darleen the check to deposit, and sat in my office, at my desk, with excellent posture. Yes, definitely I must move the office downtown or maybe to a real hub city, once I was president of the Brotherhood and could move it too. That might be the real solution for Juliette as well, depending on how fast I could frame Flannigan.

I had a strong impulse, an urge really, to drive out to the ghost town, to scope it out for the bordello. No. That wasn't safe. Zombies might be lurking about. Then there's the old saw about not returning to the scene of an ant burial. Something else too. The mafia. Covens. Spooky.

Aha. I decided, as my first deed as a Brother, to pay Detective Payne a visit. That would be a nice change for both of us, and an unfortunate turn for Flannigan.

23

I had never been to the police station before. The place gave me the creeps, mainly because of the low life that hung out there, on both sides of the bars.

The first thing I saw was a dyke behind a Plexiglas counter. She looked me over, as if she had a right, and I felt offended. I cleansed myself by asking for Detective Payne. Cops. A step up from prison guards. Now don't get me wrong. They are important for keeping the riffraff out of gated communities. On the other hand, I've had to shoo away more than my share of cops from cruising blocks on which I was showing an open house. People like and want to live in a crime free area and have this idea that crime is like a bacterial infection, whereby a liberal introduction of the police is necessary to kick it out and clean it up. Then, they don't want to see cop cars cruising their block. In their world, the infection has been cured; more cops after the cure means a chronic disease or cancer.

Detective Payne appeared and escorted me to his "office," which was really just a desk in a closet. Jesus, the ants had a better setup in their strip mall.

"Nice to see you O'Rourke," he said, gesturing for me to sit down. Detectives. They think they are so smart with their people skills and body language. I knew what was up, so I waited for him to sit down first. That was the only way for a Brother to comport himself.

"Care to confess?" he asked.

"To what?" I protested innocently.

"Just a joke. What can I do for you?"

"I wanted to see how the investigation is going."

"We're making progress."

"Good. Anything you can tell me?"

"Why?"

"I am a concerned citizen."

"Have you heard from Crystal or Chrissy Diamond?"

"No. Have you?"

"No. We're getting a court order to get into their office on Speedway. They haven't been there."

"Have they been reported missing?"

"Missing? No."

"So it's a search warrant."

"Could be."

"What do you expect to find?"

"It's never good to approach something like that with preformed expectations."

"I suppose you'll take their files and computers like you did mine."

"There are standard procedures."

Ha. He would get the evidence to pin Fitzroy's murder on Flannigan and the ants, so I wanted to encourage him.

"For what it's worth, I think you are on the right track."

"You do?"

"Yes. I'm not convinced it was a drug hit. Fitzroy was mainly a user. He wasn't mixed up with the dealers."

"It's all connected."

"Perhaps."

"Why are you convinced it wasn't a drug hit? If not that, what do you think it was?"

"Zombies."

He stared at me. I can't say I blamed him.

"It's a code name," I said.

"For a gang?"

"A sort of gang, if three makes a gang."

"Three?"

"I'm not sure I should be telling you this. I mean, it's all circumstantial, but I saw the Diamond sisters and another man, late, very late, the night before Fitzroy was killed, hanging outside the office, across the street."

"No law against that, unless they were dealing drugs."

"There's more."

"Go on ...."

"I just met the man they were with. We had a business deal. He kept asking about them, the Diamonds. He seemed eager to know if any trace of them had been found. Those were his words: Trace, found. He seemed to be, and that's why I hesitate to tell you this, but he knows we've, uh, interacted, and it seemed to me he was pumping me for information on whether I know anything. And it wasn't like he was concerned about their welfare. It was more like had the police found their bodies yet."

"Bodies?"

"That's the impression I got. Like he expected them to be dead."

"What do you think?"

"I don't know. I'm concerned. I'm worried."

"That's not much to go on. Who is this man?"

"You know. You've talked to him. He's very big, very important."

"Flannigan?"

I nodded.

"I'll need a hell of a lot more than that. Hopefully, we'll find something in their office."

"There's something else."

"What?"

"A witness."

"A witness to what?"

"A witness who saw him carry two bulky blankets and hide them out in the desert."

"You?"

"No, my son."

Yes, I was improvising, brilliantly I might add, as would be expected of an initiate to the Brotherhood.

"Your son?"

"Yes. He told me. He saw him scatter stuff around. Saw him carry what looked like bodies."

"Where in the desert?"

"I'm not sure. I'll have to ask him," I said. I didn't want Payne to hightail it out there yet. I needed time to make sure he would find what I wanted him to find.

"Your son, how old is he?"

"He's twelve. But, he's special. That's why I hesitate."

He said nothing. I had made the whole thing up as I went along and I knew he was processing it all, checking to see if it made sense. He would find the ants' eepmail. It would make sense to him that Flannigan had a motive to silence the ants. I was only too happy to help Tucson's finest in this matter.

"I would like to talk to him."

"I'll arrange that."

He took out a card, wrote on it, then passed it to me.

"That's my cell. It's tough, with kids. It's almost impossible with special kids, if I understand you correctly. But he could give me something more definitive to go on. When did he see all this?"

"About two weeks ago," I said.

"OK. Call me as soon as I can see him, anytime."

"Will do," I said.

"O'Rourke, why didn't you come sooner?"

"I wasn't sure. It's not like me to go with something unless I'm sure, reasonably sure, and after that meeting with Flannigan, I was sure enough to pay you a visit."

"OK. Thanks."

I left him in his closet. That was enough to get him going. The big thing now was to talk to Roger and get him to corroborate what I said he said. Of course, there were no ant bodies to find, as they were really zombies, but maybe Detective Payne had Ghostbuster contacts. It would have helped too if I had something physical to link Flannigan to where I tried to dump the ants. No way was I going to lead Detective Payne or anyone else to that open house where the real, actual extermination job was done.

Speaking of which, I wondered if it had been sold, so I grabbed a quick late lunch and headed back to the office. I cornered the agent who was handling the listing. There had been some interest, but the asking price was too high. He also complained that someone stole the furniture coverings from the open house. I told him to pressure the owners to lower the price. I didn't tell him this, but I would also call the mortgage broker and ask them to step up foreclosure threats. The quicker that house was occupied, the better.

Once I got into my office, Darleen popped in.

"Oh, Royce, your wife called. She said not to pick up Roger today. She said he wasn't feeling well and is already home."

Well, that was good. Anything to keep me from Juliette. I finished some paperwork and headed home.

As I drove up to the house, I saw something that filled me with disgust. All manner of clothes, and books, and other debris was scattered about the yard. In my well-irrigated front yard, lowering my property values. My stuff. Oh shit.

I pulled into the driveway and walked in the front door to be greeted with a pile of CDs thrown at me. I hoped to god the neighbors hadn't seen the mess in the yard.

Or heard Rocky's banshee screaming:

"You bastard! You lying bastard! Get out! Get the hell out of here and take your crap with you!"

She was raging, almost foaming at the mouth. I spied Roger peeking around the corner, terrified. I was only able to utter "What the ..." before she dug in again.

"Liar! That's all you do. All you've ever done – lie! She was here, in my house, your whore – she brought Roger home this morning – oh, he is not sick. – He was fucking freaking out. And she told me all about it. You fucking liar! You – you – oh god! – you devil! So she blackmailed you? That's not what she said. She never took those pictures. Oh, how dumb and blind I was! To believe you! She confessed it all. How she fell for you, oh not just you, but you and him, Roger. Sick! Perverted! Oh! She said she learned enough from Roger to be convincing as she pretended to be me calling your office, to find out where you'd be. Oh, brilliant! It took her that long to get fucking pregnant. You left that out, you liar. She has your baby, your defective sperm. Well, guess what! Guess what, Royce O'Rourke, it's not her fault it took so long to get pregnant – No, it wasn't her – it was YOU! It is you, you weak, impotent, loud, obnoxious loser!"

She had to stop for a breath. I was frozen. I didn't want to hear more, well, I did want to hear more, but I didn't want Roger to hear more and be more terrified, but maybe it would be good to terrorize him, all the easier it would be for me to get him to frame Flannigan.

"And it's a pity, really, because I could like that woman, pity her, at least, for setting her sights on you. Pity her for her sick deluded desire for her own version of Roger, and the joke's on her! – Oh, how could I be so stupid!? Why did I listen to you? Why did I trust you? She was IN the pictures, you liar! She was in them, so how could she have taken them without you knowing? Someone else took them! And, oh god – when I told her what you said about her blackmailing you – as if she would do that? Oh god Royce, you think you can sweep her under the rug in Phoenix, fucking Phoenix, and you threatened her! And you threatened to have her deported? And you threatened to take her child and dump it on us, on me? You piece of cheap – you small, stupid man. And you fucked her, after, after, after! After you swore to me it was over. After you said she tricked you and used you and blackmailed you. Lies. Lies. Lies. All lies. That's all you know. All you can do! Lie! You, Royce O'Rourke, the big man, strutting around town like you are some hot cool stuff. You know they all laugh at you? Don't you? You know Father Flannigan thinks you are a joke! Don't you? Do you know why he puts up with you? Do you know why he tolerates your incompetence? Your insignificance? He has to. Because of me. Me! And Roger. His son, not yours. So your French whore will get Randi, not Roger. Serves her right! Serves you right. Now get out! Get out! Get out! Get out! Don't ever talk to me again. To hell with you Royce O'Rourke, Red O'Rooster! Get out now!"

She was throwing her colored bottles at me by then, missing mostly. The booze was running down the walls like thin blood. I didn't know what to say. There was so much in there to take in. How would it look at my induction if my wife and children weren't there? And I needed Roger.

"Rocky," I said. "Stop. OK, it's true. But look baby, I got in. Today. In. Flannigan told me. Today. I'm in the Billion Dollar Brotherhood."

"Ha!" She was actually laughing now. "You are so in, up your ass Royce! You still don't get it. You are so clueless. Just go. Go out there and be the big man. In Tucson. And leave me the hell alone."

"Didn't take you long," I said.

"What?"

Her shortest sentence ever. Now if we could just do something about those exclamation points.

"It didn't take you long to get me to sign away every dime, to you, before you called it in, did it?"

"Oh, you bastard. That's 'cause I know you, Royce. I know you better than you know yourself. You are their puppet. Just like fucking Fitzroy, but he was smarter."

"Give me Roger," I said.

"What?"

"You've never cared about him."

"Bullshit. Liar! Anyway, he's not yours."

"We didn't cover that with the lawyer. You keep Randi, I take Roger."

"No!"

"Just for awhile. I don't trust you around him now."

"You? Don't trust me? Oh, that's rich, Royce! Get the hell out!"

"Roger," I called. "Come to daddy."

"OUT!" she screamed.

"Roger," I yelled.

"I'm calling the cops! Get out Royce. To hell with you. He's mine, not yours. He's mine and Flannery's."

What the fuck? I let that hang in my mind. I couldn't pause to process that, at least not that part of it.

"Then you defaulted," I said. "You cheated too. That agreement is null and void now."

"Tell that to my lawyer."

"Mine will be calling yours and eating him for lunch. My lawyer will be in the Billion Dollar Brotherhood. Where will yours be?"

I looked for Roger. No sign. Rocky looked like the devil incarnate. I wouldn't have been surprised if she had waved her hand and cast forth two zombie ants to escort me out.

As to the stuff in the yard? I wanted to leave it, I did. But something in me, something deep in my soul, called out, cut through all of Rocky's sturm und drang, and admonished me not to break the covenants and not to threaten the property values, so I picked up everything and tossed it in my car. Just as I started the engine, Randi walked up, smirking at me.

"You know, dad, there's an iPhone app that walks you through how to win a divorce."

"Get in," I said.

"OK!"

Rocky came running out, yelling for Randi, something about child abduction. Well, she did say Randi was mine. I pulled out and drove down the street, stopping at a Circle K next to the strip mall on the arterial.

"How much of that did you hear?" I asked.

"Enough to get all the juicy bits. I downloaded this voice recording app on my iPhone and recorded it. Do you want to hear?"

"No."

"I'll sell it to you. Your lawyer might be able to use it."

"Cut it out Randi."

"So mom did it with Father Flannigan and it's his defective genes that made Roger?"

"Who knows what of all that is true."

"I buy it."

"OK. Give me a billion dollars."

"So we are now officially a dysfunctional family?"

"No," I said. "Look. I need your help. You have to get Roger for me."

"Why don't you just pull him out of school?"

"I doubt he'll be going back."

"His teacher? Your mistress? I wonder if I'm Flannigan's daughter too? I always thought I was the result of immaculate conception."

"You look too much like me."

"So how much for Roger?"

"What?"

"How much will you pay me to get Roger for you?"

"You are definitely my daughter."

"So you want me to get you Roger so you can steal him?"

"Just a little bit. A few hours. As soon as possible."

"I think I can swing that."

"Name your price."

"Hmm. Well, I love the iPhone. I don't need clothes. I'm not old enough to drive. Let's say five thousand in cash, and you take custody of me."

"What? Me?"

"Yes."

"I figured you'd prefer to stay with your mother."

"Think again. I think you'll be the more interesting experience."

"You just think I'll let you get away with murder. Anyway, who said anything about a divorce? We are Catholic."

"You don't think she won't go running to daddy Flannigan and ask for an annulment?"

"That will be hard."

"He'll go for it. He'll tell some lies and pull some strings," she said.

"Yeah, he probably will."

Randi seemed to have gotten a good grasp of Flannigan, at least his less charitable side, during her catechism.

"The irony of it all is so juicy," she said. "You always preferred Roger, and it turns out he's not even your son. And I, the daughter, the faithful daughter, who you have spurned, wants to stay with you."

"Randi," I started, but she cut in, like her mother, and before I could correct her grammar.

"Oh, and your mistress wants her own Roger and will now have to abort the one she's got and go try to seduce Flannigan. It's just too rich!"

"Enough. Look, the only reason I gave Roger so much attention is because your mother always seemed ashamed of him."

"So she should, her bastard spawn."

"Stop it, Randi."

"What do you need Roger for?"

"Business."

"What kind – oh, there goes mom's car down Sabino Canyon!"

"Probably chasing me. Hey, was Roger in the car? I could go back and get him."

"Not even she would leave him alone by himself."

"She might have dropped him off at the Pruitt's," I said.

"Doubtful. He was in the back seat anyway."

"OK."

"What do you need Roger for?"

"I need him to, to tell a story."

"A story? What kind?"

"Never mind."

"By story, do you mean you want him to lie for you?"

"None of your business."

"Who's he going to tell this story to?"

"Someone."

"Dad. You want me to get him for you? Then tell me why I'm doing this."

"I need him to corroborate something I told someone."

"Was he there? Is it your mistress?"

"No, and no."

"So you want to feed him some lies to regurgitate?"

"It's for the greater good."

"And you think you can trick him into being your mouthpiece? Dad. Roger's changed. Maybe you haven't noticed. Maybe it's because he goes into baby mode with you, but he does know right from wrong and any decent cross-examination will make him fess up."

I thought about that. It was a huge risk.

"You may be right," I said.

"So there is a chance he'll be cross-examined. Who is it? Flannigan?"

"No."

"Who?!"

"The cops," I said, getting irritated with her.

"The cops! Great! This just gets better and better. Look dad, let me do it."

"What?"

"Let me tell your story."

"And make you into a liar?"

"I already am."

"Randi."

"I lied just now about seeing Roger in the car."

"So he's back at the house? Let's go."

"No. I just lied about lying."

"Randi."

"I can do it."

"But if you do it, then there's no deal because there's no getting Roger."

"You need one or the other of us, so the deal is still on. And you'll get more for your money with me. You'll get greater value. A win-win."

I thought about it, as much as I could, given I couldn't believe I was having this conversation with my daughter.

The main thought was what would a knight of the Brotherhood do? Yes.

"Randi, do you like Father Flannigan?"

"No, especially not now."

"OK. Meet me in my office on Friday, after school."

"You'll have the cash?"

"Yes."

"Deal. Oh, and I go with you. We are both winners, dad."

"Yeah."

I pulled out of the Circle K and drove back to the house. Rocky was standing in the front yard, with more of my stuff.

I turned to Randi. "You said ...."

"I'm a good liar dad," she said, and bounced out of the car.

In a strange kind of way, I was proud of her.

I ignored Rocky's scene and tantrum and drove off. I went to the Sheraton and booked a room. Me. Royce O'Rourke. In a hotel. In my own home town. How unBrotherlike.

24

I spent a restless night wondering if a man facing divorce could still get into the Brotherhood. Then I worried over the timing of when to send Randi to implicate Flannigan. I thought I should wait until I was inducted. But how long would that be? How long would Detective Payne wait? And what of the ant carcasses? Zombies. No. Yes? Did Flannigan take them? But who rapped on my window? Did that really happen? Too much shit. I tossed and turned and thought of Miss Clarrissa and jerked off and fell asleep.

I woke up early and headed to the office. Once there, I emailed Miss Clarrissa, asking for an audience with her. She must have been up, or had her own zombie slaves, as I got an immediate reply:

"Do you Red? Have you won against my zombie army? Then explain in twenty-five pages why you are worthy of such an honor and include five references and full financials, as well as a psych evaluation."

Bitch.

It was odd. Just as everything I ever dreamed of was coming true, all the women in my life were failing me, having a go at me, ignoring me, extorting money from me, or flushing me away.

Then I remembered that yellow fanny pack in the trunk of my car. That did it. I had to act.

I drove to Flannigan's office. Score. His Lexus was there. I put the fanny pack in my briefcase and went to the door.

The door was still locked. I banged and banged on it until he came.

"O'Rourke!" he said, after opening the door. "I told you no contact until –"

"But it's urgent, Father. It's not business. It's not about the Brotherhood. It's spiritual. It's personal. My family. I need you."

"I was about to go to the parish. Can you follow me there?"

"Can't we talk here?"

"I'm nearly late for a marriage counseling session. Follow me."

Well, the church was as good a place as any. I followed him there, then inside.

"Royce. Please light a candle for Fitzroy, then wait in a pew and pray. I'll be with you as soon as I can, my son."

He was in full priest mode. Quite the consummate actor, Flannigan.

I didn't light a candle and I didn't pray. God was with me anyway. It was too early for choir practice, quilting, guilting, or any other dull activity for losers. That was perfect for my purposes. I scoped out the sanctuary and the altar. I knew there was a storage closet behind the altar. Fortunately, it didn't have a lock on it. And wouldn't you know, there was a monstrance on the shelf. It looked rather cheap and modern, like something out of Miss Clarrissa's shop. I was sure it wasn't the main one the church used. Oh, if only I could glue the fanny pack to the Eucharist in the center. Given world enough and time, I would have constructed my own monstrance, and would have made the Eucharist hollow and big enough to hold not just the fanny pack, but also Roger, Flannigan's bastard son. Oh, how my monstrance would gleam with the colors of Rocky's bottles and the sparkles of Miss Clarrissa's tchotchkes.

As I did not have world enough and time, because I was not yet in the Brotherhood, I slipped the fanny pack behind the monstrance, and covered it with some veils that were behind it.

I shut the closet and snooped around. Everything was too formal for what I needed. I mean, Flannigan would hardly assassinate the ants in his priestly regalia.

I took a chance and went to his car. He had been in such a hurry, running at least one red light, which must be a fringe dispensation for the those in the Brotherhood.

Damn. He did lock the Lexus. I thought it would have been a good time to have Fitzroy around. He would have know how to jimmy the lock.

I went back in, just as two dweebs came out, obviously the intended couple. Had it been any other time, had I not needed to appear distraught, I would have approached them about a house. Newlyweds are a realtor's wet dream.

Flannigan appeared and led me into his church office, very nice in an ecclesiastical way, but not screaming wealth like his business office.

"Tell me Royce, what is wrong?"

"Father, I, I'm, it's Rocky. She's gone nuts. She threw me out of the house."

"Why did she do that?"

"She's under some delusion I'm having an affair."

"Are you?"

"No."

"Royce. Don't lie. Are you?"

"No."

"Royce, I take it much more seriously, and so does god, if you are lying. An affair is a weakness of the flesh. A lie is a defect of the soul."

"I wouldn't call it an affair," I said.

"What would you call it?"

"A moment of weakness."

"A moment?" he asked, emphasizing the article.

"I apologized. I said I would never do it again. Now she's trying to break up our family."

"Perhaps I should speak with you both. I'm sure we can avert disaster."

"She first had me go to the lawyer to draft a post-nuptial agreement giving her everything. No sooner is that done, then I come home and find her tossing my belongings in the front yard like we're in some white trash neighborhood."

"Did you sign the agreement?"

He had a point. No. Neither of us had. Either he was extremely prescient, or he got the dirt from my lawyer. Either way, it just reminded me he would be a formidable adversary.

I told him neither of us had signed it yet.

"Well there you have it Royce. As soon as certain other matters are taken care of, quite soon I should think, I will talk to both of you separately, then together as a couple. In the meantime, give her some time to cool off."

"Thank you, Father," I said. Then I paused. I was so tempted. And I needed to buy more time.

"Father," I said.

"Yes?"

"There's something else."

"What else, Royce?"

"It's difficult. Can I take confession now?"

"That's very irregular."

"I need it. What I have to say is so much worse."

He looked at me deeply, intently.

"Royce, are you sure you want to do this?"

"Yes."

"Well, I suppose it is for the best. And it is confidential. Please wait here for ten minutes then meet me at the confessional."

Score. He left. I wasn't sure, then, what he thought I wanted to confess, the bastard, but it gave me the window I needed. I waited a bit then went through his desk. I used a Kleenex to pick up a pen, which must have his fingerprints on it. It was a Pelikan, his Montblanc and Visconti probably too ostentatious for his priest role. I also found a used collar which most certainly would have DNA from his sweat. I put them both in my briefcase, then thought for a bit.

I decided to go for it, since he had dropped that hint about "quite soon." I went to the confessional and recited the "Forgive me father, for I have sinned" line.

"What is this sin?" he asked.

"It's Rocky. I hope she was joking, but she wasn't in the mood to joke. She told me, she yelled at me that Roger is not my son."

He remained silent.

I went in for the kill.

"Father, she said he was your son. She said you are his father, not me."

He was still silent, then after a bit said:

"Of course I am his spiritual father. I'm sure that's what she meant."

"No. She was quite clear. She said you are his biological father."

More silence, then, an edge to his voice:

"Royce, this is supposed to be your confession, not mine."

Fair enough.

"Father, I confess to having sex with three women who are not my wife this month."

"Say six Hail Marys. We will discuss the other matter after a certain event. Is that agreeable to you?"

"Yes, Father," I said.

"Good. Be prepared soon. Very soon. Goodbye my brother."

He said that last bit in a deep prophetic voice, consummate actor again. Well, the church is all theater, isn't it? And Flannigan was the Barrymore, Olivier, and Redgrave all rolled into one. Well, he should be quite entertaining defending himself in court.

I beat it out of there in a better place of mind. Rocky had nothing on me. Without that post-nuptial agreement, signed, she had no power and would have to take me back. I would even pretend to be Roger's father. So all was back on track and very soon I would ascend the heights.

I had to move fast. I drove out to the haunted house. I avoided the house itself, as there was no evidence there. I walked to the out buildings and dropped the Pelikan near where I left part of the bicycles. The parts were still there, so that part was real. Apparently, zombies don't ride bicycles. I stuck the collar in a prickly pear cactus, a nice touch, and it wouldn't blow away. Poor Flannigan. He was now the Fool in King Lear.

You see, just then, with my learned reference to Shakespeare and by my use of Latinate polysyllabic words, and my earnest eschewing of exclamation points and dashes, and my elegant use of alliteration and assonance, that, unlike Fitzroy, I was a cultured, educated man, one who could write and think in compound-complex sentences, and also a man who was attractive to all kinds of women, and also a man who was a mover and a shaper, and a winner, and as a result of all the above, I, Royce O'Rourke, was a natural for the Billion Dollar Brotherhood, soon to be its shining new president.

When I got to the office, the agent responsible for that ant-eradicated house off Redington Road told me the owners freaked and would accept the highest of the low-ball bids. Good. I told him to move on it and to stop worrying about his furniture covers. He kept complaining about how expensive they were and how little his commission would be. I could tell then he'd never last in my agency once I was officially installed in the Brotherhood.

All was now set. The evidence to pin Fitzroy's killing on Flannigan was in the ants' eepmails. The evidence to pin the ants' disappearance on Flannigan was awaiting Detective Payne in the desert. And the next day, my own Randi would lead him right to it, clearing her father's way to the best of the Brotherhood.

I spent almost all day Friday planning the details for Randi's story. I kept hoping Flannigan would not call and summon me to the initiation before my trap could be activated. It was not likely. After all, I hadn't received my Brotherhood information package. Damn. He said he was going to send it to the house, which meant I had to go by there later to get it.

Randi stopped by after school, annoying all the agents with some light saber application on her iPhone.

"The force is with me!" she declared, coming into my office.

I told Darleen no interruptions, shut the door, and told Randi what to say.

"I get it. I was out at the haunted house late on a Sunday afternoon two weeks ago with a guy who shall remain nameless, but who I'll say was a cute Mexican boy old enough to drive. By the way, did you know mom did it once with the pool boys? Both of them? At the same time? You might be able to use that."

"Just stick to the facts," I said.

"Facts? That's ill. So anyway he doesn't speak good English, so there's no point corroborating the story with him, but dad, you've gotta think the cops here have Spanish-speaking staff."

"Just continue."

"We see a big sedan pull up. Probably a Lexus. We see a tall corpulent man get out, open the trunk, and take out what looks like a body. He takes that into the house, then carries it back out ten minutes later and puts it in the trunk."

"Good."

"Except. How come he doesn't see us? Wouldn't he see our car?"

"The house is on an elevation. Your boy drove behind it and you two were walking about."

"Making out?"

"Absolutely not. You are underage and you know it."

"OK. So we're walking about discussing global warming and third world hunger and see him with the body. I mean if we saw that, wouldn't we have reported it?"

"That's why I wanted Roger."

"Didn't you tell him it was Roger? What is he, our chaperon?"

"He's just there too."

"OK. Whatever."

"You didn't see a body. You saw him carry a bulky object wrapped in a blanket, that, on later reflection, you think could have been a body."

"OK. But how about I say we parked behind the house, went inside to explore, heard a noise, went to check it out, and saw him struggling with a bulky blanket?"

"OK."

"Then we slyly and stealthily followed him out, saw him put the bulk back in the trunk, then watched as he took two bicycles out and, sweating like a pig, carried them way out to the out buildings. While he was doing that, we snuck up to the car, checked the trunk he left open and saw two bodies. And we were afraid to tell anyone because we recognized the sweaty pig as the ever important Father Flannery O. Flannigan and were afraid to tell anyone because he is our priest, our spiritual light, a leader in the community, so there's no way he could be up to no good, and we just figured he was doing some ritual blessing of the bodies before they were buried."

"Excellent." And she had some excellent alliteration also.

"Then we ran back to the house and watched until he came back without the bicycles, shut the trunk, crossed himself, then drove away."

"And what was he wearing?"

"His priestly garb, which adds weight to us thinking what he was doing was some last rite we didn't know about."

"Brilliant. You are my daughter."

"A chip off the old block."

"Good. Now when you looked at the bodies, what did you see?"

"Just the feet of one ... wearing?"

"Cheap sandals," I said.

"Got it."

"You're sure you can do this?"

"Absolutely. I won't even ask why you want me to."

"Why?"

"Because I have my own reasons for hating that pig priest."

"Roger?"

"No. He's a hypocrite and I hate him."

"Fair enough," I agreed.

I called Detective Payne's cell phone and told him I was ready. He quite kindly offered to come by the office. Randi and I went over the story one more time, and finished just as he arrived.

I introduced Randi. He was surprised that it was she, not Roger. I made up that when I talked to Roger he said Randi was there too, but didn't initially want me to know, because of the guy she was with. He seemed to buy that and appreciated Randi's cooperation.

"Aren't you going to record me?" she asked him.

"No. Not now."

"Do I need to swear an oath?"

"No, but I'm sure you'll tell the truth."

"Indubitably. Should dad leave the room?"

She was getting too full of herself already.

"No," Detective Payne said. "He can stay."

"She's OK without me," I risked.

"How old are you?" he asked Randi.

"Fifteen."

"Your dad has to stay. I can't legally interview you without a parent being present."

"Cool," she said.

She then repeated the story as we had rehearsed it, but adding some rather convincing emotion here and there, almost crying when she got to the part about seeing the sandals on the feet.

I watched Payne, mostly. He didn't betray one way or the other whether he believed her.

"So it was you, your brother, and this other boy," he said after she had finished. "What's his name?"

"I can't tell you," she said.

"Why not? Just his name."

"His family are illegals. If I gave you his name, first off, they'd never talk to you. Second, you'd have to report them. I won't have that on my conscience, even if you break out the rubber hoses and electrodes."

"We'll skip that for now," he said. "And you are sure it was Father Flannigan?"

"Absolutely. He is my priest. I'd recognize him anywhere."

"When you saw the bodies in the trunk, did you recognize them?"

"All we saw were the feet of one, so no."

"Wearing sandals?"

"Yes."

"Recognize the brand?"

"Cheap crap from Wal-Mart."

"You are a smart, intelligent young lady. Why didn't you report seeing one, possibly two dead bodies?"

"Like did you hear me say we saw it was Father Flannery O. Flannigan? Do you know who he is? How important he is? That means two things. One, he is not to be questioned or challenged. I mean in addition to all that, he's our priest, and for us to question him in what we were safe to assume was a strange last rite, well, that's not cool. Two, if we had questioned him, if we assumed then, on the spot, that he was up to no good, he could have killed us too, or worse, as our priest, if we told later, I mean he could consign our souls to hell. So, like, what do you think we should have done?"

Wow. She sure told him. A teenage girl. To a middle-aged cop. Well, she was an O'Rourke.

"Fair enough," Detective Payne said. "And you are sure it was Flannigan."

"Father Flannigan, yes. He's hard to miss, what with being in his priestly garb and all. And for what it's worth, officer, I'm not convinced he was up to no good. After all, he is a priest."

He just smiled and thanked us, saying he would follow up and warning he might want a formal statement from Randi at a later date. He didn't say it, but I assumed that meant under oath. That meant perjury. Yeah, well given Randi's performance and avariciousness, I doubted a trifle like perjury would phase her. Plus, she was still a minor.

As he left, she ran up to him, almost in tears.

"Oh, please, officer, please don't tell him I told you all this!"

"What happened here today stays here," he said, and left, hopefully to go bug Flannigan and to arrange a search party for the grounds of the haunted house.

Randi turned and beamed at me.

"How'd I do?"

"Your Oscar is on the way."

"You can do better than that!"

"Hepburn, Redgrave, and Streep put together couldn't have done better."

"Huh?"

She put her palm out.

"Oh."

The office had cleared out. I went to the safe and got five thousand dollars. The safe, and petty cash, was Fitzroy's idea, one he had clung to in an era of electronic bank transfers. Cash, he thought, spoke a more persuasive dialect. How true.

I went back to my office, counted it in front of Randi, to teach her to trust no one and to avoid the embarrassment of her asking me to count it out in front of her. I put it in a manila envelope, similar to the one the ants used to send those cheap pictures to Rocky, and sealed it.

"I'd prefer we keep this here for now. Tomorrow we'll open an investment account for you."

"Not necessary. I'm skipping school tomorrow and going to the mall."

"Don't spend it all in one place."

"Can I stay with you tonight? Are you in a hotel or camping here?"

"No. I'm driving you home. I want to talk to your mother."

"Living dangerously? I'll spy and record it all on my iPhone."

"No you will not."

It occurred to me there that she had probably recorded her performance for Detective Payne. I thought she'd make an excellent candidate for the Brotherhood one day.

25

We drove home. Before I walked her in, I warned Randi not to let her mother know about the money I gave her.

"Like I didn't just demonstrate how hip and clued in I am," she said, rolling her eyes.

Rocky wasn't in the living room, so I checked a pile of mail she had obviously been keeping for me. There was the FedEx package from the Brotherhood. I took that and ignored the rest.

"What the hell are you doing here?" Rocky's voice came at me.

"Just here to get my mail."

"Well get it and go."

"Really?"

"Really what?"

"That post-nuptial agreement, I don't remember signing it. In fact, I didn't, did you?"

"I signed it today."

"Well I did not, babe. All you've got now is what a judge may give you, what little he may give you in alimony because I'll be damned if I pay child support for your and Flannigan's bastard."

"There's still Randi. And that agreement –"

"Sorry mom," Randi cut in. "I'm going with dad."

Rocky looked stunned. For a split second. But her mouth ruled her and took over.

"What has he been saying to you?" she spat at Randi. "Don't believe him. He's a born liar and will cheat you like he did me."

"Seems you are both equal on that score mom," Randi very, very bravely said.

Rocky made to slap her. Randi dodged it, screaming "Child abuse!" as she ran over to me.

"The agreement's no good Rocks, even if I had signed it. You've admitted to cheating on me way before I cheated on you. God, you make me out to be the liar. Shit. I wouldn't be surprised if you were humping the pool boys, the exterminator, the garbage collection guys, the mailman, and Randi's school principal."

She turned a shade of red, deep crimson, just like one of her red bottles.

She was speechless.

"Look Rocks, we both lose, all of us, if we split. Look at this," I said, brandishing the package from Flannigan. "I'm in. It's official. The induction is right around the corner. We come to an agreement between us, and live high on the hog and happily, more or less, ever after. Or, you just try to get Flannigan to grant a divorce which divulges his own moral turpitude, and you lose. Big time."

She was still speechless.

"It makes sense, mom. He makes sense."

"Shut up," she said to Randi.

Then she looked funny at me.

"I should have known better than to use your fancy new lawyer. I should have known."

"I don't want to force you into this, Rocky. But if you look at it objectively, if we stay together as a family, we all win. We divorce, you stand to lose a great deal. It's just simple business."

"I don't know."

"All I ask is one thing. You think about it. Sleep on it. Then, when the Billion Dollar Brotherhood contacts you, asks you to play a role in my inauguration, you show up. If you do, then we're all of us set for life. If not, well you take your chances babe against me with the Brotherhood at my back."

With that brilliant ultimatum, I headed for the door.

"Royce!"

Ah.

"Yeah?" I turned and said.

"But, the lies. The lies. They have to – I, I can't deal with the lies."

"Oh really?" I said. I went to the mantle and pointed. "What about the red lies, the blue lies, the green lies, the yellow lies? What about the Roger lies and the Flannigan lies? The world, the real world, the one that counts, the one for brave people, shit, it's built on lies, which is another word for dreams."

She looked strangely solemn, not yet thwarted, but close.

I left it at that, and went back to the Sheraton. OK, yeah, well, I went by the RE/MAX office. She was long gone, so I took that ant folder out of the car, the one with the cheap pictures of me and Juliette, and I jerked off behind the office and let it spray all over the ant folder. I could have been arrested as a sex deviant, except Detective

Payne must have been too busy organizing a search party after seeing Flannigan sweat like the pig he was. Priest. Pigs. A coven of ants. My voodoo priestess shaman. There was art in there somewhere. Some twisted sick art, sanctified by my splurge. Shit. I needed a drink. Good thing the Sheraton had a bar.

After the bar I took a shower. I kind of liked it there in the hotel, all mine. I lay naked in bed. Rocky always wanted me to sleep at least in my underwear, even after we had enjoyed our scheduled sex. I started looking over the package Flannigan had FedExed to the house. Help god, there were so many rules and regulations, rightly so, to keep the riffraff out. But, Jesus, get this:

	The Billion Dollar Brotherhood Levels of Brothership		
Level	Currency	Rank	Mineral
7	Penny	Private	Pyrite
6	Nickel	Navigator	Niter
5	Dime	Defender	Dolomite
4	Quarter	Qualifier	Quartz
3	Half Dollar	Director	Diamond
2	Greenback	General	Gold
1	Officers of the Obsidian Order		
0	Emerald Emeritus		

The depressing thing was what it took for me to qualify constituted Level Seven, Penny Private. No fucking way would I be that. And to get all the way up to Officers of the

Obsidian Order, I guessed it took Flannigan decades to do that.

And he must have had his black obsidian heart set on being an Emerald Emeritus for the rest of his life.

I could just see Fitzroy retching over this stupid hierarchy. And the ants. How their antennae must have quivered in eager anticipation of cheating and breaking covenants all the way up to Quarter Qualifiers, as if they could have ever ascended that high.

I didn't bother reading the pages and pages of requirements and duties for each level. I would, in a single bound, leap to the top. I had to. Miss Clarrissa predicted it, made it real, just as she made zombies real.

There followed a long color section highlighting all the good works of the Brotherhood, funding children's hospitals, building parks, promoting green building trends, etc. Boring.

I flipped through to the membership list. Then I got pissed off. You could only see the members in your own level, rank, and mineral. Like the Penny Privates were too low and full of leprosy to see the Nickel Navigators. As Randi would say, "Whatever." The only thing above one's level one could see was the president, Flannery O. Flannigan. Lame.

In my own level (it shamed me just to read it) was a one page list with lots of Esqs, names of Arab princes, some MPs from the UK, some US congressmen, a few university chancellors, and some retired two-star generals. No cops, no prison guards, no women. No wonder they wanted the ants. Except they weren't women. They were insects.

There were some annual report-level financials, which meant they said very little about the real financial workings of the organization. The rest was so boring, I fell asleep.

Some time during the night my cell phone rang. Repeatedly. I answered it. It was Flannigan.

"It's time, O'Rourke. Where are you?"

"The Sheraton."

"Get dressed. In a suit and tie. You will be picked up outside the entrance in thirty minutes."

He hung up.

Shit.

Score◊ Double Score◊ Triple Score◊

I rushed into the bathroom, pissed, took a shit, then a quick shower. I was rock hard. I didn't dare touch it. I dried off, brushed my teeth, put on deodorant, avoided my cologne, then got dressed. Thank god Rocky had thrown my best suit in the yard. I made a pot of coffee, had time for a quick sip, then rushed to the lobby and outside into the night.

The air was cool. The stars were shining down on me, smiling at my ascendance. A black Hummer limo pulled up. A door in the back opened. It had to be for me.

I got in. Yes. There was Flannigan.

"Put this on and remain silent," he ordered.

He handed me a purple silk blindfold. I started to put it on. He pushed me forward and tied it in back for me, tight.

I concentrated. The limo turned right on Grant, which meant we were going west. It turned left, then went in a circle. Another circle. Circle. Circle. Circle. It went one way, then another, then another.

"You forced our hand, Royce," Flannigan spoke, with low gravity. "Silly what you did, you'll see. But the Brotherhood can be assembled at the drop of a pin, as you will soon find out."

I smelled something chemical, like a cross between Randi's fingernail polish remover and a nice stiff gin and tonic with a hibiscus flower in it and I felt very warm and fuzzy with Flannery O. Flannigan and then I was sitting still in a hard chair, with a slight headache.

I was still blindfolded and I couldn't move. I tried, only to find I was tied to the chair, my wrists tied to the arms of the chair, my ankles to the legs of the chair, and my torso bound to the back of the chair. I didn't like this. At least I wasn't gagged.

My throat was parched. I tried to call out, emitting only a hoarse eep. Did I say that? An eep? I swallowed hard, then again and again. After that I was able to call out a loud Hello. There was only a slight echo to it, so I knew I wasn't in the great hall of the Brotherhood. Maybe this was a staging area.

I struggled against the ropes, realizing I was naked. Completely naked. Maybe there was going to be a baptism of sorts. That would be right up Flannigan's alley. But why did he want me to wear my best suit? I called again. I called Flannigan by name.

"Father Flannigan. Father Flannigan."

Nothing.

I felt a draft of chilly air. I hadn't realized I had been sweating. Oh, it felt so good blowing on my wet skin. That must have gone on for ten minutes or so. I really couldn't tell.

Then it stopped. I could sense someone behind me, untying the blindfold. It fell between my legs. Before me stood a red figure. As my eyes adjusted, I recognized it as Father Flannery O. Flannigan, President of the Billion Dollar Brotherhood. He was all in red and gold and black robes, with a tall cylindrical red hat. It looked like church vestments, but not. It must be, I thought, official Brotherhood regalia.

"Royce O'Rourke, Realtor!" he proclaimed in a loud stentorian voice. "You are now before the Billion Dollar Brotherhood. Prepare to prostrate yourself to the goals and mission of the Brotherhood."

Oh god. It was happening. It was coming true.

Then he leaned in close, and whispered to me:

"You really needn't have thought you could take me down."

He withdrew into rows and rows of what must have been a hundred men in copper colored robes, calling to them: "Let the Penny Privates provide the punch!"

Two of the copper robed men rushed toward me. One was carrying something I couldn't make out. I started to wonder what Flannigan meant, if he was royally pissed by Detective Payne, or if he thought he could deflect his crime on me after Randi's ace testimony, or if he had caught wind of my wanting his prime position in the Brotherhood, or if, well, I couldn't think anymore because one of the Penny Privates grabbed my head and thrust it back while the other shoved what felt like a gas mask over my face. Then the grubby hands of one of them pushed his fingers through an opening in the mouth and shoved a tube almost to the back of my throat.

I started to gag. They tied the mask tight around my head. I steadied myself, focusing on breathing through my nose. This was getting intense. It reminded me of a fraternity initiation, not that I, Royce O'Rourke, was ever in a loser fraternity. This was the real fraternity, the ultimate Brotherhood.

That thought calmed me down and I stopped gagging. Then a liquid came through the tube, down my throat. It largely bypassed my tongue, but I could tell it was some alcoholic beverage. Maybe beer. Yeah.

I couldn't swallow it. I felt it go down my throat into my stomach. Maybe it was the secret ambrosia of the Brotherhood. I so wanted to taste it.

It stopped. They pulled out the tube, loosened the mask, and pulled it off my head. The row of Penny Privates retreated, slow marching backward, receding as my vision blurred and I got dizzy.

I was shivering, shaking, almost convulsing. Then, a silver light filled the room and what must have been twenty men in dull silver-gray robes appeared: The Nickel Navigators. They untied me, threw a long silver cape over me, and hustled me out of the room.

They each held a silver candle. One stayed in front, two stayed on either side of me, holding my arms, and the rest held back a bit. I think they were chanting something, Latin, or Greek, something I couldn't make out. They led me from one room to another, making hardly a sound other than their low chanting. Each room was bare. No furniture at all. Hard, creaky wooden floors. Everything lit by candles and Chinese lanterns of all different colors, like Rocky's bottles.

Our train went up one staircase, then down another. Then they led me to an outside veranda, into the night, under the stars.

I knew this place.

It was the haunted house. My bordello.

Then where was the Billion Dollar Brotherhood headquarters? Would that come later? Or had they already anointed me as their new high leader and figured I would want the headquarters here?

They had flanked me, ten on each side, and were all pointing to a telescope between them, at the edge of the veranda. I looked into it. There, before my eye, was the Ant Nebula, just as Roger had drawn for me, dancing and twinkling at me.

The Nickel Navigators led me back inside, down to the ground floor and into a room lit with hundreds of candles in various colors. They passed me off to ten Dime Defenders who wore silver and black robes. Two of them pulled the cape off of me, and another drew a curtain revealing what looked like a large round wading pool in the center of the room. The water glowed a deep cobalt blue. Two held my arms while another produced a silver vial and poured a black liquid into the pool. He turned to me and gestured for me to get in the pool, which had turned bright sky blue.

I stepped up to it, and stumbled a bit, whereupon the two behind me lifted me up and dropped me in.

It was deep. I had thought it was just a wading pool, but it went way over my head. I sunk to the bottom, which was surprisingly warm. I opened my eyes and the water had turned red. I floated to the top, as if I were floating up Miss Clarrissa's birth canal, as Princess Risa had done, all the way to the oxygenated world beyond. When my head surfaced, the water turned cold and cobalt again. The Dime Defenders had gone. I tried to pull myself out of the pool, but couldn't. It was like being in quicksand or liquid concrete. I started to panic, almost to the point of despair, when four red robed figures emerged before my eyes. Two of them pulled me out.

I noticed their robes were studded with crystals so they must have been Quarter Qualifiers. I waited for them to give me a robe. Instead, two of them reached up and pulled two golden chains from the ceiling, manacled my wrists to them, then pulled me up by my arms, so that I was hanging at least three feet above the floor.

They each extracted some kind of high intensity penlight from their robes and shined the light all over me, turning me about. They seemed to be inspecting me. Ouch. They stuck a probe up my ass. They lowered me to just a few inches above the floor and stuck another probe in my mouth. They stuck some cold metal thing in each ear and up each nostril. I did not like this at all and resolved to ban this part of the process when I became president.

They removed all the probes and withdrew behind a black curtain. After some time, I'm not sure how long, they came back out and stood still before me.

"Royce O'Rourke, you pass inspection," said one to me in a monotone. Then an impudent other one dared to say:

"We deem you Red O'Rooster."

I wanted to scream out a protest. I tried, but I was strangely mute, unable to turn a thought into speech.

Two of the Quarter Qualifiers released me from the chains. The other two produced my suit and ordered me to get dressed, which I gladly did. Then, the four of them marched me out of that room, tackled me, and thrust me into a cage in the next room. It was something you'd keep a dog in.

The Quarter Qualifiers arranged themselves two in front and two in back, raised the cage from poles on the bottom, and slow marched me forward. On and on we went, then down and down and down in a dizzying circle on a metallic spiral staircase I never knew was in that haunted house.

I was tired and in pain. I was not happy. I hated this initiation and vowed to punish all those who took part in it. I tried to remember every face of every Penny Private, Nickel Navigator, Dime Defender, and Quarter Qualifier I saw. Only every one of their faces melted and melded into the face of Flannery O. Flannigan. Flannigan. Maybe he was was on his way to Mexico, or waiting just long enough to transfer power to me. Surely this whole ceremony was extraordinary: The cost, the preparations, the rehearsal, the rentals, the participation of so many. Surely this was not done to inaugurate just any rank and file Penny Private. It was too much.

We finally reached a metal door, where they stopped and released me from the cage. One of the Quarter Qualifiers produced a brass key and opened the door. The other three marched me in. To my destiny.

26

I was brutally disappointed. All this buildup, all these expectations, and my grand coronation hall turned out to be a rather shabby, antlike affair, in a lurid purple and green glow.

It was a wood paneled room, no bigger than a Rotary ballroom. There was a gallery in the back, filled with Penny Privates. We marched through the gallery to a table up front that they bade me sit at. How tacky. A Half Dollar Director sat down next to me. And the Obsidian Order sat off to the side in their own box seats. There was another table across from me. It made my blood run cold. For sitting at that table, with their own Half Dollar Director, were the ant zombies, and, my blood froze and shattered my arteries, the Fitzroy zombie.

So he did send those emails. Shit.

Then, a man appeared, a very effeminate man, one I hadn't seen before.

He was green from head to toe, a sparkling mossy green. His skin, all over, was covered with this green makeup. His hair was dyed green. He wore a crisp moss green uniform, very trim and precise, with green gloves and green boots. He had to be the sole Greenback General. Yes. He was. His eyelids were painted gold, as were his fingernails and it looked like real gold. And all the medals and chains and buttons on his uniform were, had to be, solid gold.

He walked to a podium in front and faced the Brotherhood.

"All rise and be silent," he said, or I should say 'she said' for I then recognized the Golden Greenback General as Princess Risa. "Let there be order. I announce the grand Miss Clarrissa, Voodoo Priestess Shaman and Emerald Emeritus, and Father Flannery O. Flannigan, Officer of the Obsidian Order and President of the Billion Dollar Brotherhood."

What? Miss Clarrissa. Emerald Emeritus?

She and Flannigan entered from a door on a stage at the front. They both sat down and faced the assembly. Then Princess Risa instructed all to be seated. Flannigan got up and addressed the Brotherhood.

"We have two items before us," he said. "One is Royce O'Rourke. We shall deal with him now."

Deal with me? How dare he. The fat pig hypocrite ought to be in jail instead of demeaning me here. And what was the second order? Making me president when they were done with the first order.

"We call forth the witnesses," the Golden Greenback Princess Risa cried. "Approach the podium!"

I turned around to look. My heart lept for joy at the wondrous sight: My family, Rocky, Randi, and Roger, came down the aisle in their finest clothes. They were directed to three open chairs in a gallery opposite the Obsidian Order.

"We call the first witness, Veronica O'Rourke," Princess Risa ordered. "Please approach the podium and state your case."

Rocky slowly got up, looked blankly at me, then back at the assembled Brothers, and approached the podium. With no further prompting, she began.

"My husband, that man, Royce O'Rourke, has been unfaithful to me. He has lied to me. He hates women and uses them like houses to buy and sell. He also breaks his promises. I demand he sign this document, as he arranged, and promised, and failed to do."

That was remarkably short and sober for Rocky. She opened her purse and took out a sheet of paper. I noticed Randi glaring at her.

One of the Half Dollar Directors took the page and looked at it. Then he said:

"We have reviewed the entire document and find it to be in order. This is the execution page. All it lacks is the signature of Royce O'Rourke."

"Let it be signed!" the crowd of Brothers said all at once.

The other Half Dollar Director produced a clipboard, attached the paper to it, and handed it to me. He then took out of a pocket in his robe a black Montblanc Meisterstück, uncapped it, and offered it to me.

What the fuck? My family was supposed to be here to witness my coronation, not to settle old scores with me. This was my great moment, not hers, and I didn't want to spoil it by signing that agreement. However, I had no choice, really. The Brotherhood insisted on it. Maybe it was important to clean up all old affairs before being admitted. Maybe it was for the greater good of the Brotherhood, so I signed my name in the blank space left for it.

The other Half Dollar Director took it from me and dismissed Rocky, who was tearing up and trying to avoid looking at me. Randi, on the other hand, was boring through me with an urgent look. She propped her iPhone discretely in her lap and displayed to me a little message scrolling across it like one of those electronic marquee signs. It said, in red chasing letters "THIS IS ALL SO BOGUS!!!"

Princess Risa called Roger to the podium. He, good boy, not mine, that he was, refused to go. She called him again. This time, Rocky tried to pull him out of his seat, to which he responded by screaming bloody murder.

The Brotherhood sat stone silent, as if nothing were going on. Roger's screaming seemed to go on forever. Finally, Rocky was able to get him up to the podium, standing by him.

"Roger O'Rourke. State your case!" Princess Risa prompted.

Roger started crying again. He punctuated that by pointing at me, jabbing in my direction. I hated this. It was one thing to put me through hell night. It was quite another to subject a child like Roger to it.

After it went on far too long, Princess Risa made a strange signal to the back. Almost immediately, two Penny Privates brought a Styrofoam cooler to the podium. Honestly, I thought, given all the expense so far, the Brotherhood ought to be able to spring for a nicer cooler.

The Half Dollar Director sitting with the ants rose and faced me.

"The complaint has been reported. The complaint is that you stole his blueberry Popsicle. You will now repay that debt by bestowing on the boy these blueberry Popsicles."

The Penny Privates carried the cheap antlike cooler to my table. The Half Dollar Directors gestured to me, so I stood up, opened the cooler and took out one yellow fanny pack of blueberry Popsicles. Jesus. That whole big Styrofoam cooler and just one pack among a ton of ice. And why was it in an ant fanny pack?

I extended it to Roger, who bounded over, grabbed the fanny pack, said "Thanks, Dad!" and returned to his seat, tearing into the pack to get his blueberry goodness. OK. That was nice, if a bit strange of them. I guess. It seemed like so much over so little.

Then they called Randi. She darted up as if she'd been dying for this moment and strode over to the podium. She didn't even wait for the Princess Risa to prompt her.

"I just want it on record that this is totally bogus. It's beyond ill. It's an epic fail."

Well, she was off to a good start, her misuse of the verb "fail" for the noun "failure" notwithstanding.

"I am here under protest," she continued.

"State your case!" the two Half Dollar Directors intoned.

"What do you think I'm doing, butt wipes?" she retorted.

I was ambivalent about this. I wanted to stop her, but didn't think that was my place, yet.

"I have the evidence here, here on my iPhone. A recording. Whether Father Flannigan is a murderer or not —"

"Be silent!" the Half Dollar Directors shouted.

"I will be heard," Randi said, clutching the podium with one hand and brandishing her iPhone with the other.

"Flannigan is worse than a killer. He's a hypocrite. A fat pig hypocrite skimming a sinful profit off the backs of the poor. Sure, my dad's a liar. And a cheat. Big deal," she said. "Who in here hasn't lied or cheated or stolen? Who would rather not admit it? All of you."

"The witness will step down," the Half Dollar Directors said in a low ominous tone.

"I am not finished yet. Sure, we all lie. We all cheat. We've some of us done even worse. But the real evil, the real cancer here, is the fat pig who struts down the street, up to his pulpit, where he oinks and exhorts us all to be honest and good while he turns his other butt cheek against his vow of poverty and rapes the poor and innocent –"

"Be silent!" the entire room chanted.

"Remove the witness!" Princess Risa cried.

"No!" Randi screamed. "You can't, you won't take my father, you vultures! Dad! Come with me. Come with me! I'll save you."

The four Quarter Qualifiers had surrounded her.

"Get your filthy hands off me," she spat at them.

I stood.

"Come with me dad!"

"That is not possible," the Half Dollar Directors aimed at me.

Randi was on the verge of hysteria. It really was unseemly. I couldn't understand why I was even listening to her radical rant. Surely it was an indictment not just of Flannigan, but also of the entire Brotherhood. It was the height of disrespect. Yet, I remember, one of the few things I can still clearly call forth in every detail, every move-ment, every sound, every color, every emotion, I can still feel a tight chord of desperate sincerity in not just Randi's whole demeanor, but in every atom and molecule stringing about me in that moment. It was enough to make me pause for I don't know how long, but it couldn't have been more than a split second, to pause just long enough to feel the sincerity of it. I will spend the rest of my days wondering where going with Randi might have led.

Of course, then and there, she was nothing, her pull too insignificant to pose any threat to the Brotherhood. They closed in on her, and as they were pulling her out, Randi screamed "Filthy pigs! Venal hypocrites! Pedophiles! Dad! Save yourself!"

She was gone. So were Rocky and Roger.

That Golden Greenback General, Princess Risa, called for order to be restored. Then she announced:

"The assembly will now hear the victims' statements. I call Crystal and Chrissy Diamond!"

The ant zombies did as Princess Risa commanded. But they were not zombies. They were fully insect. Crystal and Chrissy Ant. And they stood before me laughing and eeping and mocking and pointing and burping, and spitting drizzles of ant poison from their insect mandibles. Then, they dared to dance about my table, circling me, laughing and eeping and dancing about me.

There was no music. Just the clicking of their twelve hairy ant legs and their incessant eeping.

Then the ants stopped dancing, reverted to zombie form and started to spit furiously at me. (I'm cogent and me enough now not to split that spit infinitive.) They spat their vile, slimy poison at me. It stung. Each spit of ant spew stung. It felt like I was being flagellated. Like I was Christ himself, their new king, being lashed and beaten and stung prior to my final crucifixion and subsequent resurrection as god of the Brotherhood.

They finally stopped spitting and stood erect.

"You murdered me, Red O'Rooster," Chrissy wailed.

"You raped and strangled me," Crystal Zombie eeped.

"And you refused to love me," Chrissy butt in. "That is the worst of what you did to me."

Crystal glared at her zombie sister.

I could say nothing.

They returned to their table with Fitzroy and their Half Dollar Director.

"Royce O'Rourke," Flannigan said to me. "We have heard enough. Stand and face the Obsidian Order."

My Half Dollar Director took me by the elbow and helped me to stand.

"Royce O'Rourke. You are guilty of the murder of Chrissy Diamond, the rape and murder of Crystal Diamond, and the murder of Roy Fitzroy. Have you anything to say before the Obsidian Order passes judgment on you?"

What the fuck? Talk about a kangaroo court. Maybe it was another detail to deal with, another encumbrance that had to be ceremoniously absolved.

However. I was sick and tired of all this bullshit, as I'm sure you can imagine, having to read this insanity, so I let him have it.

"Me? Guilty? Bullshit. You know you put the hit out on Fitzroy and you know you ordered the ants to kill him and they did and you know you then killed them and hid their bodies here before that voodoo shaman bitch turned them into zombies."

"What is all this about ants and zombies?" Flannigan said. "We are talking about three human lives here. Three creatures of god."

"Randi was right. You are a big fat hypocrite. You know you put the hit out on Fitzroy. The ant emails prove it."

"Be silent O'Rourke," Flannigan said.

"I will not be silent. You are a hypocrite and you killed Fitzroy and the ants. And as to zombies, what do you call the three undead monsters sitting there across from me, sniggering at me?"

He looked at Miss Clarrissa. They whispered to each other. Then she said:

"Put a sock in it Red. You are wasting our time. Don't make me tell the assembly how I was here one night setting this place up, and heard a disturbance downstairs. How I saw you carry two bulky objects in expensive furniture throws down to the basement, how after you left I discovered the dead bodies of Chrissy and Crystal Diamond. How I saw you spread the pieces of their bicycles in among the out buildings. You don't want me to go there Red."

What the fuck? I suppose she drug her self-important ass to my house to rap on my window.

"No," I said. "No. You won't pin Fitzroy's death on me. I had nothing to do with that. It was Flannigan, and those filthy ants. I have proof."

"Let it go, Royce," Flannigan said.

"I will not," I replied to that hypocrite. "You know who you are and what you did. You are a hypocrite and a liar and a blight on the community. You demean the Brotherhood."

I saw my chance. I turned to the assembly and announced:

"I call for the immediate removal of Flannery O. Flannigan from the Billion Dollar Brotherhood. He is unworthy of us. He pollutes us. Cast him out."

That was met with stony zombie silence. In fact, the whole of the assembly looked so much alike, I realized that they were all zombies.

"Red," Miss Clarrissa called.

I turned to the mistress of the zombies.

"Quit while you're ahead, Red. Flannigan found that fanny pack you planted. Give it up and face the consequences like a man."

Fucking bitch. I was more a man than she's ever had. Her daughter, Risa, was more a man. More than Flannigan, who had a big smirk on his pudgy face.

I stared at her.

"What, when, will I finally be initiated?" I demanded. "When will I be in? When will I be the president?"

"You are close, Royce. Just cooperate and all will be well," Flannigan said, patronizingly smug.

What a load of shit. I really wished Randi were there with me. I sat down. What more could I do?

"We sentence Royce O'Rourke to a life term in the Billion Dollar Brotherhood," Flannigan said.

"Hear, hear," the zombie gallery chanted.

I guessed that was it. What a bizarre way to let me in. I cast a glance at the zombie ants and sneered at them. Insect ants. Bitches. Ha. I was in. Me, Royce O'Rourke, had made it. They had not, as if they ever could. They just stared blankly, soullessly ahead. Crumbs of rotting flesh were falling off of Fitzroy. I thought, in the strange purple light, I saw steam coming off of him.

"And now for our second order of business," Flannigan said.

I sat up straight. Here it came.

"It is now time to swear in our new president. Before I do so, I just want to say how rewarding this year has been for me. I have met so many wonderful souls ...."

Zombies, I thought.

" ... and I have seen the Brotherhood grow in power and influence. I have enjoyed leading ...."

Blah, blah, blah. He would do all he could to hog the limelight like a pig and bask in his own self-important glory. Randi was right. He was a pig. I tuned out his oinks and squeals until he got to his "disappointments" some three hours later.

"I am sad that the Diamonds, who were so promising, did not live to become Quarter Qualifiers. We must not be daunted, however. It is a changed world out there. We face increased exposure, increased regulation, potential prosecution, political correctness run amok. It saddens me that an encroaching socialism that has already choked Europe threatens the States. We must fight, but we must fight smartly, strategically. Let Wall Street take the heat while we appear to be the friend. In this respect Chrissy and Crystal would have been important tactical assets."

I wanted to vomit. They were right there before him, eeping silently, decomposing in a fetid filth on the floor with Fitzroy. Flannigan could have taken them in. Why not? They would have fit in perfectly with the zombies in the gallery. They were steaming now too, in the purple and green light.

" ... And in emulating the Asian markets we would do well to remember the States, the Western world, the New York Stock Exchange, the Chicago Mercantile Exchange, the London Stock Exchange drive our nearest concerns. So, while mourning the passing of the Diamonds, I am heartened, indeed, overwhelmed, that a new light is before us."

Me.

"An innovator. An iconoclast."

Me.

"This light has graciously agreed to shine on us, to put a new face on the Billion Dollar Brotherhood, to position us uniquely to face twenty-first century challenges. It thrills me, as I move to the exalted ranks of the Emerald Emeritus, to welcome, to appoint our new leader and president, Mrs. Risa Sclar."

What the fuck? OK. Time for honesty. I just stopped and read all this up to this point. I didn't see it coming then and I didn't see it coming just now. Did you? I should hope so, being an evolutionary improvement over me. Yes, I said it, but only to you, only for you.

As to me, I saw something else then. It was so clean and clear. Devoid of deceptive color. The Brotherhood, no, the brotherhood was fucked. Had always been fucked. It was shattered. It had turned from Flannigan's squealing pigs to Miss Clarrissa's steaming zombies.

I tracked back on myself. I repudiated it all. I decided to be really honest, childlike honest, Roger-like honest, and see it for the filth it was.

I stood. I stood as bitch Princess Risa accepted her regalia. I was about to shout the truth, when, oh shit, some insidious honesty made me look to the right and see the sad, plaintive, sorrowful faces of Crystal Diamond and Chrissy Diamond glance at me, a tear running down each of their cheeks. I killed them. I had hated them. Why? Because of some failing, some fault in them? Or was it a fault in myself?

It didn't really matter. I was a greater friend to them than the fucking brotherhood because even in killing them I cared for them as individuals instead of the greedy, filthy, globally approved way of the brotherhood. It, the brother-hood, more specifically that hypocrite Flannigan and his whore Clarrissa, saw the Diamonds as chits, tokens, Holly-wood window dressing. I, me, Royce O'Rourke, thought of them always as real people. As real threats. I gave them more due, more respect, more legitimization (is that a word?) than the brotherhood ever could. I, Royce O'Rourke USED them, obsessed over them, hated them, loathed them, yes, I say it now, wanted them, in a more sincere, more honest, more real way. And that's why they looked at me, then, in zombie form. That's why they noted me, marked me, appealed to me. And for them, I would destroy the evil that surrounded us all.

Even if it cost me everything – the bordello, the New Orleans deal, my family, my life – I would, under the gleaming glory of the Ant Nebula, which, in its bright lustrous red splendor, broke through the haunted house, down, down to the basement we were in, under its light I would defend and save the ants.

I lept up on top of the table as Princess Risa was finishing her acceptance speech. She broke off, looked at me, and bossed:

"Red, get down and go take your place among the Penny Privates, where you'll spend the rest of your days digging for pyrite – fool's gold!"

Miss Clarrissa cackled at me.

"Fuck you, bitch," I said. "Fuck all of you."

"There will be order!" Princess Risa called.

"There is no order here. It's all disorder and deception," I said to the entire hall. "I'm taking you all down and saving the Diamonds from your poison."

"Order!" Princess Risa called.

"Take O'Rourke by force and imprison him with the Penny Privates. Bind and gag him too," Clarrissa ordered.

The ten Dime Defenders rose and gathered around my table. Some of them started to grab at my legs; some started to climb up on the table.

I wished I had the sword of Excalibur then, as I kicked and swatted at them. Or the Roomba to sweep and suck them up. They were zombies, after all, and easy to disintegrate, yet there were more and more as the brotherhood of zombies pressed on me.

I heard both Flannigan and Clarrissa laugh obscenely, and was almost overcome by the zombie brotherhood. Then, I heard a feral howl from above and saw a black and white mass streak through the hole the Ant Nebula had made in the ceiling. It was Zombie, the Roomba riding cat, with Randi's iPhone tied to its back.

The iPhone was opened to the light saber application Randi had used when she came to my office to frame Flannigan. I held the cat up in the air, extracted the saber, and swung it in a three hundred sixty degree arc.

Oh, how the zombies fell, moaning. I took down one ring of them, then another, and another, until I had cleared enough of them to see the Diamonds.

"Crystal! Chrissy! Come. I'll save you," I said, using exclamation points.

"No!" Miss Clarrissa cried.

I flung Zombie the cat at the devil Clarrissa, right at her, and he clawed deep into her face, holding on for dear life.

She screamed and wailed in pain, trying futilely to get Zombie off of her face. Flannigan just stared at her.

With them thus distracted, I lept off the table, cutting down zombie brothers on the way with my light saber.

I tried to make my way to Crystal and Chrissy, fearing the zombies would go after them, knowing they were my goal, my target.

Aha, there was Princess Risa. I grabbed her and held the light saber to the throat of the president of the Billion Dollar Brotherhood.

The zombies fell back.

There was the prize, the Diamonds, still sitting, staring straight ahead.

I maneuvered Princess Risa to the table and called again to the Diamonds.

"Chrissy. Crystal. Come with me. I'll save you."

They refused even to look at me.

I let go of Princess Risa and extended my hand to them.

"Come. Now! Before it's too late!"

Nothing.

I moved in closer, to grab them, but then Fitzroy turned, embraced them both, and the three dissolved into dust.

Damn.

The zombies snapped back and closed in. I cut a path through them to the back of the gallery, to the metal door. I tried to open it, but it was locked. Zombies started to pile and press on me.

I used the iPhone light saber to cut the door open, fell through it, and spun around to slice down the zombies behind me.

I made a dash for the spiral staircase and ran around and up, finally reaching the maze of narrow passages, sprinting through them until I reached a brightly lit purple door. I crashed through the door and collapsed on the floor.

27

It might have been day, or night. I wasn't sure, but there was light. Beautiful colored lamps like Rocky's bottles, but softer. And there were boas, fluffy boas of fanciful colors.

I thought for a minute it was my bordello, all equipped, all provisioned, making me lots and lots of money. That was only a minute because the rows and lines of objects I saw were not sex toys. No. They were voodoo dolls, tarot cards, magic spell potions, plastic pentagrams, shrunken skulls, spooky candles, and beads, beads, beads, and incense. Lots of incense, some of it recently lit.

After all the insane drama below, it seemed an oasis of quiet calming color. I sat for awhile among the feather boas, voodoo dolls, and shrunken skulls, all crap from China.

It was completely quiet. The zombies had had time to follow me there, but didn't. Maybe zombies couldn't climb spiral staircases.

Go back to be imprisoned with the Penny Privates and spend the rest of my life digging for fool's gold. What nerve. Maybe that was OK for Flannigan, and Fitzroy, and Crystal and Chrissy Diamond. It was decidedly not OK for me, Royce O'Rourke. But what was OK for me now?

I had signed everything away to Rocky. Juliette was now a big, pregnant expense. Roger was not my son. And Randi, protégée that she was, would one day eat me for lunch if it served her purposes.

And what of my dream, being in the Billion Dollar Brotherhood? Penny Private. OK. I admit it. I cried. In the artificial rainbow glare of Miss Clarrissa's voodoo shop, I bawled for a dream that was in reality a nightmare. Big fucking deal. Why cry then? Why? Was I crying forfeiting my family? Was I crying for killing the Diamonds? For Fitzroy? For the loss of the brotherhood? The brotherhood. I still wanted it. I still wanted to play and win and rule in it. It occurred to me then that maybe all that below wasn't the Brotherhood. Maybe it was a bizarre, hideous nightmare concocted by Miss Clarrissa to avenge herself on me. Maybe the real Brotherhood was still out there, awaiting me.

I heard a door open.

"Well, if it isn't Red O'Rooster."

It was Miss Clarrissa. She looked beautiful in the colored lights, and her face bore no scars from Zombie the cat.

"Don't call me that," I said.

"You presume still to tell me what to do? Some boys never learn."

She sat down beside me.

"So you fucked up big time, Red, just as I predicted."

"But I got in."

"Yes."

"Just like you foretold."

"I foretold that?"

"You did, you bitch, but you lied about the best part. You took it away from me and gave it to your own daughter."

"I did?"

"And you are taking over my bordello idea. I see you've already set up your voodoo shop here. Where do you get off?"

"Red. Who do you think I am?"

"You are Miss Clarrissa, Voodoo Priestess Shaman."

"Yes, DBA Miss Clarrissa, Voodoo Priestess Shaman. Do you know what that is?"

"You."

"Yes, me. A multi-billion dollar international business."

"Huh?"

"Oh Red, don't be dense."

"But ...."

"You are a rooster, not a goat. I am the brains behind the biggest voodoo business on the planet. And I also own and control more high value prime real estate, commercial and residential, than you can shake a hundred zombies at. I am also Monstrance Holdings, Red."

"I thought Flannigan ..."

"One of my agents. You are right about him, Red, at least your bright little daughter is."

This didn't compute. She was Monstrance Holdings? She bought all those New Orleans mortgages and she owned my bordello? Bitch. Cheating ant bitch.

"I don't understand," I said, tired of her already.

"You caught my interest, Red, way back in New Orleans."

"I know that."

"No you don't. Fitzroy was a tool, a true Penny Private. You, on the other hand, well, let's just say the cards allowed me to see some uses for you that others, like Flannigan, did not."

"Bullshit. You spat on me. Twice."

"Spit spat," she intoned, as if casting a curse on me. "Get up Royce O'Rourke. I want to show you something."

I got up, and we left her illegal shop in my bordello, passing out of the maze of rooms in the labyrinth basement. As we drew closer to the front basement, I gagged and vomited. There was a putrid stench, ungodly, straight from hell.

The room illuminated. I saw two expensive furniture throws, unrolled, and two stinking, rotting ant corpses atop each.

"Ain't pretty, is it, Red," Miss Clarrissa said.

"Did you conjure this up?" I asked.

"Hon, even I ain't got the power to conjure that ungodly scene. Flannigan's folly. Silly girls and foolish man! Follow me out of here. I can't stand the smell."

I gladly bypassed that ghastly pile of insect rot and followed her up to the large kitchen, which hadn't seen a meal for a century, or more.

She lit a cigarette and passed it to me. I declined.

"You're going to need it."

I still refused. I wanted to kill the bitch. And Flannigan. What did I have to lose?

"Just what the fuck is going on? Penny Private? Bullshit. Your days of fucking with me are over."

"Calm down, Red."

"Don't call me Red," I said, advancing on her with my hands approaching her throat.

"Back off O'Rourke. Calm down and listen to me. Your whole future is at stake, hanging by a little silken thread, which is about to snap."

"You've got two minutes," I said, backing down.

"I take all the time I need O'Rourke. OK? Now that I've got what I want, we'll deal with what you want. Yes, I did send you emails from Fitzroy. I found your secret little email account in your wallet and I knew his address."

"Why?"

"I was checking you out. Fitzroy and Flannigan told me you wanted in so I put you to my test. I looked at the cards and in your palm. You passed and you gave me the last laugh on Flannigan."

"How was spitting on me a test?"

"Spit spat."

"Stop that. How was chasing me and Fitzroy out of our housing development a test?"

"You mean my development, my ninth ward gold mine."'

"Yours?"

"Oh, I like teasing it out of you Red. You'll make such an excellent zombie."

"You are full of shit."

"Why would I let you know back then that I, and Princess Risa, were running that game? Would you have played with us? No. You were all prepared to believe that I would let the great Princess Risa, my daughter, live in the ninth ward. You thought Flannigan was the game master. Well, now you know better, and now you, my boy, need a dose of reality. You are damned lucky even to get in. And you only got in because Fitzroy got greedy and careless, like Flannigan. Men!

"Did you read who is in the Penny Privates? Do you have an Ivy League degree? Have you worked in top management at Goldman Sachs? Morgan Stanley? Chase Manhattan? Do you own a country sitting on top of oil fields? Do you even know how the World Bank and the International Monetary Fund work?

"Are you now, or have you ever been willing to run for high political office or accept a cabinet appointment? Do you travel in such circles that you are ever likely to be?"

"No," I admitted. "Not yet anyway. Do you?"

"Do I? Of course. Just because I'm a black woman who has a voodoo empire business you think I'm no better than you? Than Flannigan? I am in the Emerald Emeritus. I graduated top of my class at Yale, baby. I have shaped and sent many a man and woman to Congress. I sit on boards and think tanks that set policy. What policy have you set, O'Rourke?"

"I don't believe you," I said. "Do you expect me to believe that the whole world economy can by influenced by a lying cunt like you who used palm reading and tarot cards to predict what I planned and did myself?"

"Those predictions came true, Red. All mine do. And how do my methods differ from the voodoo of Wall Street or the irrational fear that drives change in the world?"

"They are based on science, for one thing," I pointed out.

She laughed.

"Oh, they all think that, don't they. Tell me Red, can you or even a real economist predict an outcome with certainty? Are their methods any more common sense or understandable than mine? Spend about ten years studying economic theory and history, then come to me and say the power of those wizards is any better than mine."

"But the markets –"

"Are driven by my tarot cards."

"No."

"Ever heard the term 'voodoo economics?'"

"That was –"

"A joke. My joke on the public at large. A very funny joke that I played and profited from."

"That was twenty-five, thirty years ago. You're not that old."

"I am a voodoo priestess shaman. I am ageless. My powers cross the centuries."

"But that's magic. It's not real."

"Ask your pope what's real, O'Rourke," she said, laughing again at me.

"And you want me to learn voodoo?"

"I want you to do as I say."

"So those people from Yale and the World Bank, they take orders from you?"

"Indirectly, some do. Others take direct orders, once they are ready, once they can be deployed."

"And you want to deploy me. How?"

"You're not ready, O'Rourke."

"I can learn," I said.

"Yes, you can learn and you will. You see, I'd like nothing more than to remove Flannigan. The thing is, now that Princess Risa is president I have almost total control of the Brotherhood, except for Flannigan, who is a careless, sloppy threat to us all, dabbling in Tucson politics with those pasty white Diamonds, all to enrich his own operation while ignoring the larger mission of the Brotherhood. I know he ordered the hit on Fitzroy, but that will be harder to prove. If I can pin the Diamonds' death on him, much more convincingly than you did, well then, so much the better. That was not in the plan, but it's why I was right about you. Princess Risa told me about your idea to blame Flannigan for your deeds, and I can take it and make value out of it. And that's what you need to know, O'Rourke. I see value in you that others do not. The cards showed me. Really, the choice is yours. I can remove the blame, if not the guilt, and take down Flannigan. That saves you. If you cooperate. If you suppress that dangerous ego and do as you're told and have some damned patience. The choice is yours O'Rourke, Royce O'Rourke."

"How so?"

She sighed and produced two of her tarot cards.

"There are two cards this time. This one leads you back to the basement, where we remove those tacky furniture covers and place something far more incriminating – against Flannigan. You follow that destiny and you go with me. You are a Penny Private but you are my Penny Private and you learn the ropes from Princess Risa and maybe, just maybe, one day, you'll be a Quarter Qualifier I send out to do our business, to plant in national politics or international business. Accomplish our mission. Our mission, not yours."

"What's the other card," I asked, for I didn't expect it would be the presidency of the Billion Dollar Brotherhood.

"The other card? That's the 'you take your chances' card. Keep in mind your wife only got you to sign that agreement. She hasn't divorced you yet. Oh, how your pretty little special red family will help us. That cute son of yours. Did you know Flannigan took him here that day, to lure you here. That was my idea!"

The bitch. Worse than an ant she was.

"You mean Flannigan took his own son up there that day? He's not mine."

"Oh this is too rich!" she cackled. "Royce O'Rourke, realtor, adulterer, and cuckold," she wailed, waving the second card before me.

"So the other card is not the Brotherhood," I pressed.

"No. Not the Billion Dollar Brotherhood. I predict, an official prophesy, you may not like what's on that card."

"Why?"

"Oh Re– O'Rourke. You will only find yourself on it. You. Royce O'Rourke. Alone. Disgraced in the world. No Fitzroy. No Flannigan. No Diamonds. No me. And probably no family. I'm giving you an easy choice."

"I don't have to go back all the way. I don't have to deal with those zombies again?"

Oh my god.... It hit me.

"Shit!!!" I cried. "You mean to turn me into a zombie, don't you!!"

She cackled. "Oh Red, that was the beer talking. I oughta thrash Princess Risa for putting that idea into your weak mind."

"What? What do you mean? All those zombies downstairs. The ant zombies who left their graves and roamed the desert. The ones I tried to save but who refused me to go straight to hell with Fitzroy."

"My boy, I found them after you dumped them on my property. I had them buried proper. Now, I had them dug up after I got back here and put them out to incriminate Flannigan, or you."

Nothing made sense. All that initiation. All those sick, smelly, drooling zombies. They were as real as I was – am – was. Oh, I know I'm using exclamation points and dashes now, but I'm running out of time.

"What's it gonna be Red? Card number one or card number two? Just remember, there may be an executioner on card number two!"

She was almost giggling over that last bit. What a bitch. As if I, Royce O'Rourke, would follow her and become Princess Risa's lackey for the rest of my life. And I had already mentally prepared myself to turn my back on the Billion Dollar Mafia. I was so much better than that.

"You know what?" I said to her.

"What?" she mocked.

"I'm on to your game. I bet you aren't really even in the Brotherhood. I bet this, all this drama, was just your way of getting back at me."

"Think a lot of yourself, don't you Red."

"STOP CALLING ME RED! Even if you were in the Brotherhood, even if you did cheat me out of the presidency, I'm not going to stand in line behind Princess Fuckface and all those zombies. I'll create my own brotherhood. I'll create a pure, noble, honorable brotherhood, real movers and shapers, and above all else, a brotherhood that respects and enforces covenants, not covens of ants."

"I take it you choose card number two?"

"No. I choose card number three, cunt."

"Idiot always. I guess my prophesy has come true after all."

I spat in her face and walked out of the old kitchen, through the decrepit living room of my bordello, which was designed decidedly not on an open floor plan, and out the creaky front door.

It only occurred to me that I had no conveyance out of there when I saw the black sedan, with Detective Payne standing next to it. There were also two Pima County sheriff cars with flashing lights.

Payne took out a set of handcuffs and walked toward me.

"You have the right to remain silent, O'Rourke. Anything you say –"

Shit. Fuck. This was real.

I ran the length of the porch, lept over the railing, and sprinted into the desert, toward the out buildings. The Ant Nebula lit my way and a cool slight breeze carried me on toward the rising sun. I ran and I ran, where I wasn't sure, but to anything, anything other than that.

It was like zombies were chasing me all over again. Except they weren't zombies. They were real cops with uniforms and guns and Tasers.

I got as far as the first cluster of out buildings. I saw the reflection of a bicycle mirror, then felt a sharp pain in my back, a pain that instantaneously spread throughout my body and slammed me to the ground next to a mesquite tree where I saw Flannigan's old collar pinned to a prickly pear.

I knew what had happened. That bitch Clarrissa had stuck a silver pin in my voodoo doll.

Then they were all on top of me, zombie cops, raping me and binding me. Shit. Oh shit. Nothing the Brotherhood or Miss Clarrissa could do was more definitively humiliating and self negating as that.

28

OK. There are two things I have to get off my chest at this point. One is something that took me a long time to come to grips with. It was only after a stint in the hole and a long spiritual discussion with Flannigan that I could and can now address it.

Here I am, Royce O'Rourke, a convict, doing hard time in the same exact prison my father used to work in. I'm in the Big House, the biggest house I've ever lived in. There are those who would see obvious, delicious, and just irony in this. Not me. Irony is for effete, over educated, coven-ant-breaking, liberal losers. My situation, the first few months at least, is a black mark on the powers that guide the universe. A man like me wasted in such a way must throw off the cosmic balance.

When they brought me here in leg irons and handcuffs, chained in a train of the scum of the earth, it hit me, really hit me, what it all meant. I collapsed during intake, when I, Royce O'Rourke, was treated like cattle, processed like cheese. I almost tried to kill myself. I say almost because suicide is for losers. Yes, a big part of me felt like a loser. But I was saved by that thing in the pit of my stomach and rallied later on.

The second thing to get off my chest is what happened between that night at the haunted house and my unfortu-nate new situation. To be honest, it's all a big fuzzy purple dark shadow. Even now, I can't, in my mind, separate and distinguish between the events of that night and a sordid series of events that must have included enduring interrogations, being denied bail, having hairs and fluids taken from my person, being intrusively poked and questioned, conferring with my lawyer, zombieing out in holding cells, copping a plea, standing before the judge, then, that final squishing stamping out of my identity, individuality, and humanity, the transformation, the brutal assault, turning me, Royce O'Rourke, into an insect, an ant: That bus ride to Douglas, my ant hill for the, oh shit it's still so hard to say, the rest of my life.

Yes, all that and all of that night is a melange of zombies and darkest voodoo sleeping sickness. For I was sick, a long time, one, two, three months? I don't know.

I do know, as I said earlier, that I copped a plea. I had to. So did Flannigan. They had him for conspiracy to commit murder, murder for hire, murder, and murder for profit. He told me all this later. He told me that whore, Miss Clarrissa, pulled enough strings to keep the Billion Dollar Brotherhood out of it. She had managed to make Monstrance Holdings appear to be Flannigan's game alone, and poor Flannigan found when raiding it for his defense fund that Miss Clarrissa had siphoned off almost every fucking penny. Bitch.

They had me on two counts of murder, aggravated murder, rape, and, get this, improper disposal of a body, two counts. What a load of shit.

The upshot of all those aggravated charges was that the dork district attorney threatened us with the death penalty. Oh, Flannigan had much less to worry about. The whole thing caused a great scandal, to be sure, but no one could bear to see a priest executed, especially for stomping out a lowlife like Fitzroy. Me, oh me, Royce O'Rourke, they would have formed a mob, stormed the Tucson jail, had me drawn and quartered in front of the Pima County

Courthouse, and hung me from a pole atop Mount Lemmon.

With lethal injection facing me, I paused. Could it be worse than Miss Clarrissa's voodoo beer? I decided not to gamble and got life in prison with no chance of parole. Flannigan got twenty-five years to life. Oh, I know he'll sweet talk some parole board later, but that's Flannigan. He acts as if he'll get released any day so he can take out Miss Clarrissa, who, it turned out, had a direct line to Detective Payne.

I will not go into any detail about my moronic criminal attorney who pleaded with me to take an insanity defense. As if. Me? Royce O'Rourke? In the loony bin? Never.

Neither will I go into any detail about where they put me those first few months. Suffice it to say that I learn fast and learned to stop talking to all the staff about zombies, voodoo, and ants. Though, I put it to you, how could I be found guilty of two counts of murder when the supposed victims, for all I knew, got a monthly hall pass out of hell to walk the desert in their soulless zombie form to collect their allowance as the entertainment at Miss Clarrissa's Haunted House and Voodoo Emporium, right where my bordello was supposed to be? I'm just saying. I'll also say that I heard Miss Clarrissa is actually using the double murder tie-in to increase the ghoulishness quotient of the place and drive up business.

Once I got out into the general population, where every crud convict called me Red, I found out Flannigan was sent to Douglas too. He looked even more corpulent and venal in orange. It was Flannigan, of all people, the putz, who joked that Roger missed his chance to visit me and feel at home when I was in the "special" ward. No loss; the kid is not my son.

Rocky never bothers to come visit me. She just sent her lawyer with divorce papers. Whatever.

Randi does visit regularly. She thinks it's cool to visit the state prison and has even brought some of her hot girl-friends. That said, things don't look good for her. With me locked up in here like an ant, Randi is at Rocky's mercy, and Rocky apparently has not forgiven her for siding with me. The scariest thing, oh, I lose sleep over it, is that Randi has a huge crush on Detective Payne, who at least was clever enough to find the ant emails to seal his case against Flannigan. She's stalking him. I think she has a daddy complex and it really breaks my heart that I'm not there for her. Well, at least Father Flannigan isn't either.

Oh, and surprises of surprises, the RE/MAX chick came to see me. Clever girl. She picked up not only my business, but also all of Flannigan's and the Diamonds'. I'll bet anything Miss Clarrissa has an eye on her.

So much for all that. Lest you think my life is all in the shitter, I must tell you one more thing.

Once the guards learned there was a new game in town things actually got pretty good. The guards. Ha. Loser scum who indeed are below the prisoners in terms of intel-ligence, creativity, and basic humanity. I mean who the hell grows up wanting to be a prison guard? No one. So those who end up in that job do so because they failed in another. Worse than losers, I tell you. Failures. People who couldn't get work collecting garbage. And not just a few of them are sick sadists, who are weak followers getting bossed around until the state gives them a uniform and some authority and then they turn into that sheriff in Phoenix, but worse. Knowing that as I did, I found it was no problem putting those putz pigs in their place.

It was my idea. All mine. I had to get Flannigan to go for it because he had some special clout just being a famous disgraced priest who was not a pedophile but an honest-to-god real upstanding murderer. That gave him great cachet among the cons and the guards.

I was inspired by the gangs. It became real clear that we would be safer in a gang, but the two of us, well, we didn't really fit the profile of the Arizona Aryan Brotherhood or the Mexican Mafia. Then the idea hit me, came to me in a flash of brilliance. Why not start our own gang, our own brotherhood? And the special brilliance of my plan was that we wouldn't take just anyone. Oh no. We would recruit the best and brightest, the bravest and strongest, the smartest and streetwisest from the other gangs. That wasn't necessarily the leadership. And you know what? It worked.

Flannigan got a cushy assignment as the prison priest, even scoring his own temple. He still has connections on the outside and can bribe enough guards to get anything he wants. With such offerings, we soon achieved unprecedented power and influence, and in short time picked off the best from the Aryan Brotherhood, the New and Old Mexican Mafia, the Border Brothers, the Grandels, the Mau Mau, the Warrior Society, and the Surenos. We limited membership to thirty and I established a special tattoo, gang colors, and even a distinctive set of art and icons. I wrote the bylaws and devised a simple rank structure. Me and Flannigan are the Castles. The next level is the Mansions, then the Ranches, then the Trailer Parks. I came up with a motto and a pledge, as well as an elaborate baptismal initiation rite. I'd tell you the motto and the pledge, but they are super secret.

We also have a secret handshake. I wanted it to include spitting into each other's hand, then shaking on it, but sharing spit in prison is not a wise thing to do, as Flannigan pointed out.

I established covenants for our members' cells. I have strict rules on cleanliness, order and arrangement of personal effects, proper display of art, position and allowable volume of TV and radio, and standards of dress and decorum while occupying the cell. It all enforces and encourages discipline, cooperation, and cohesiveness. And, the resulting behavior gives the impression to prison authorities that our "gang" is a positive thing.

And what power we have behind that facade. We are the prime and only effective mover of narcotics; we regulate all forms of gambling, taking a cut of all winnings; we approve and arrange assaults and even eliminations. We enforce a dues and tax system because all the other gangs depend on our fealty. It's been a year now, and I must tell you this is the best run state prison ever. And it's all thanks to our gang, which I named the Best of Blood Brotherhood.

So that prophesy from Miss Clarrissa was right after all, as I am the President, the Castle Owner, and the Covenant Keeper of the Best of Blood Brotherhood. And that woman visited me not long ago, to gloat over her Haunted House and Voodoo Emporium off of I-10, which features an Indian burial ground, ghost, and two honest-to-god zombies, who haven't, at least not yet, ranged their way to Arizona 80 and hovered down to Douglas to terrorize me here.

Well, I told her how successful I have been and that I am practically running this prison.

"If you are, Red, why are you still in it?"

"Ever illogical, Clarrissa," I said. "How can I run it if I'm not in it?"

"True enough, for you. Oh Red! Oh Royce O'Rourke, you know, you make me really sad."

"Why?"

"I could have so used you. In Congress. On a committee. You would have made the perfect political plant."

"I could have been President of the United States," I said.

She looked at me, then pulled something out of her purse. We were visiting in my lounge, no guards present. Such is the power of the Best of Blood Brotherhood. She handed me the voodoo doll she made of me.

"I have no more use of it. Or of you. What a pity. You had a choice, and you got the goat instead of the golden parachute."

"I'm comfy."

"That's your problem, Red. It's not that you're too stupid. That's an advantage for my purposes. It's that you are too comfortable, too easy. Ah well, there are others."

"None like me."

"Oh baby, they are all like you," she said.

"No," I countered. "There's only one Royce O'Rourke and that's me."

She looked funny at me, like she had just taken a swig of her own strange beer.

"Give that back to me, Red," she demanded, taking the voodoo doll. "I may yet find some use for it."

"Yeah," I said. "Whenever I have a pain, I'll think of you."

Then there was the visit from Juliette, a day after Clarrissa. She brought you, my son. My real son. My only son.

You are beautiful. A bright, smart, strong baby who will one day be a leader of men. I cried when I saw you. I loved you then, I love you now, and I will love you always.

After she left, after she broke my heart and told me she was moving back to France with you, and would probably never come back, I cried even more. I was despondent. I feared I would go back to that special ward.

It was Flannigan who made me feel better, guided my soul, and advised me on what to do.

So I've spent the last two weeks doing nothing, nothing but writing this memoir of my life story for you. At least this way you can know me. And while I can't get Internet access or even a good big unabridged dictionary, Flannigan did arrange for me to get a Meisterstück to write this! Oops.

Juliette is due tomorrow. She will pick this up then fly it to France with you.

I don't know what more to say, except eschew exclamation points and excessive assonance and alliteration, and damn dashes. Vanquish voodoo. Avoid ants. And alcoholics. Don't become all French and liberal and faggy. Just do better than I did, like I did. Read this when you are eighteen (that's what I'll put on the outside of the manila envelope) and then come see me. I'll still be here. Me. Royce O'Rourke, President of the Best of Blood Brotherhood.

Colophon

Royce O'Rourke – Realtor! was written with a Pelikan M805 (medium nib) on Omni assignment books. A Visconti Wall Street LE (1.3 stub) was used to edit the text which was prepared in OpenOffice using OpenSuse Linux. No Microsoft or Montblanc products were actually used in the commission of this work.

A Note from Miss Clarrissa

Well, well, Royce O'Rourke thinks he can slip this to his French whore without me, Miss Clarrissa, most high voodoo priestess shaman, intercepting his missive of lies.

Think again, Red.

Oh, I will do with this as you wish, but not before attaching appropriate acknowledgments to those who are not ants:

To Bill and Lavon, for support, financial and otherwise, To Colin and his iPhone for making the cover image, To Mark, Amanda, and Jen who read and helped, But most of all to Lori, who perused, proofed, and proselytized as no other,

I deem you all members of the Emerald Emeritus.